What Lies Beyond

The Liminal Fates Duet:
What Lies Between
What Lies Beyond

THE LIMINAL FATES DUET

WHAT LIES BEYOND

BY: C.N. PETTIT & T.D. FINDLEY

CONTENT NOTICE

THIS BOOK CONTAINS **GRAPHIC VIOLENCE** AND **SEXUAL CONTENT**. IT IS NOT INTENDED FOR ANYONE UNDER THE AGE OF LEGAL ADULTHOOD. ALL CHARACTERS DEPICTED HEREIN ARE ADULTS. THIS BOOK IS NOT TO BE USED AS A RESOURCE FOR SEXUAL EDUCATION OR AS AN INFORMATIONAL GUIDE TO SEX OR BDSM. **THE ACTIVITIES AND SCENES ARE NOT MEANT TO DEPICT REALISTIC EXPECTATIONS OF BDSM OR FETISH-RELATED ACTIVITIES... BUT YOU CAN ALWAYS DREAM.**

Trigger Warnings

Welcome back to the **Trigger Warning** page, you *filthy* little freaks. It has become quite clear that you are like us and enjoy the thought of being railed by an angel or a demon. Please disregard this page and carry on with your disgusting little fantasy.

What Lies Beyond may contain triggers for some.

Trigger Warnings include but are not limited to: sexual content, knife play, consent/non-consent, graphic violence, explicit language, multiple partners, breath play, fantasy mind control, blood play, and bondage.

Playlist

A curated list of songs from the authors to help immerse yourself in the scene. Asterisks (***) are placed next to the coinciding scene

Chapter 1: Wasteland By: Royal & the Serpent

Chapter 3: The Death of Peace of Mind By: Bad Omens

Chapter 8: The Kill By: Nate Vickers

Chapter 12: Neon Grave By: Dayseeker

Chapter 16: Medicine By: SLYBAND

Chapter 19: Rescue By: Lauren Daigle

Chapter 23: Alter By: Saint Vice

Chapter 30: God Is a Weapon By: Falling in Reverse

Chapter 39: Feeding the Gods By: Wind Walkers

Chapter 43: Kool-Aid By: Bring Me The Horizon

Chapter 49: Angel with a Shotgun By: The Cab

The Liminal Fates Duet

What Lies Beyond

Dedications:

To my mother, thank you for being my toughest critic and my loudest cheerleader. All of your ideas and time have not gone unnoticed. I would not be here without your words of encouragement. -C.N. Pettit

To not hiding the dark parts of ourselves that make us who we are. Without us, the world would be a very boring place -T.D. Findley

Guide to What Lies Beyond:

Arcane: factions of magic

Fire- Ruling God: Vulcan. Faction color: Red. Control/manipulation of fire
Water- Ruling God: Neptune. Faction color: Blue. Control/manipulation of water
Earth- Ruling God: Gaia. Faction color: Green. Control/manipulation of Earth
Air- Ruling God: Shu. Faction color: White. control/manipulation of air
Necromancy- Ruling God: Cato. Faction color: Purple. Ability to control the dead, resurrection, summon spirits, and commune with the afterlife
Healing- Ruling God: Apollo. Faction color: Yellow. Ability to heal injuries, illnesses, and mental issues
Time- Ruling God: Cronos. Faction colors: Silver. Control/manipulation of time, see past occurrences, and prophesize the future
Chaos- Ruling God: Loki. Faction color: Black. Ability to manipulate a being's mind and create illusions

Definitions

Hellion-/hel-yen/ demon-like being

Elysian-/uh-lis-ee-an/ angelic being

Nephilim-/nef-i-lim/ Mixed blood being of either Hellion/mortal or angel/mortal.

Chimera-/ky-mer-uh/ A mixed blood being of an animal and a mortal. For example, Wixen- fox/mortal hybrid, Lynx- cat/mortal hybrid, deerArchons- reptile/mortal, satyr- deer/mortal hybrid

Elemental Sprite- small fairy-like beings with earth, air, fire, and water magic

Windemere-/wind-uh-meer/ World of the living. Capital: Swindon

Elysia-/uh-lis-ee-uh/Celestial land

Helheim-/hell-hyme/Underworld

What Lies Beyond

Chapter 1

Edin

***

"Fuck," I hiss. I crack my eyes open, but pain detonates behind them, blurring the world into a nauseating smear of shadow and stone. My head throbs in time with my pulse. With shaking fingers, I reach back, my hand tangling in matted hair slick with dried blood at the nape of my neck. "What in all of Helheim happened?" Jerking myself up, the room spins violently, then something tightens around my throat. A strangled yelp tears through my lips as I am wrenched backward, slammed flat against the floor. Air vanishes from my lungs. I claw at my neck, panic flooding my veins, until my fingers scrape cold metal.

A collar.

"No," I choke, fumbling behind my head until my nails catch on the lock embedded at the base of my skull. "No, no, no!" My throat constricts as reality crashes down on me in a single, crushing wave.

Osiris. My stomach twists. *Endricks.*

The memory strikes without mercy, steel flashing, poison blooming, his body collapsing as the veil sealed shut around him. My heart splinters, fractures echoing through my chest as tears spill freely. I curl inward on the stone, numbness creeping through my limbs, paralyzed by the look in his eyes as Helheim swallowed him whole.

I am the cause of this.

Water drips onto my forehead, pulling me from the spiral. Blinking, I squint through the dimness. A single barred window high along the far wall bleeds in weak, overcast light. The silence is oppressive, broken only by the steady drip of water, a slow, deliberate rhythm that sinks deep into my bones. Cold presses into my back, uneven and damp, as though the dungeon itself was sculpted to deny comfort. Shifting, the chains softly rattle, old iron, heavy, and tight enough to remind me they exist, yet loose enough to let time stretch endlessly.

Carefully sitting up, I scrunch my nose from the overpowering stench; the wet stones reek of mildew. The dungeon is vast, but it feels close. The ceiling disappears into shadow, where faint shapes hint at arches half-swallowed by darkness. Shadows seem to pool there, thick and watchful. The air tastes wrong, almost metallic, stale, threaded with the scent of damp stone and something long forgotten. Every breath feels borrowed. Somewhere nearby, water drips in a slow, deliberate rhythm, each sound echoing like a countdown that I do not remember starting.

Searching the wall for anything to free myself, I notice the intricate runes that have been carved into the walls. Not fresh, but ancient, worn smooth by time and repetition. They glow faintly, reacting not to movement but to awareness. My heart skips, panic stirring within me, and they brighten. Forcing myself still, I watch as they dim, as though disappointed.

Blowing out a slow, deep breath, I shift again, and the chains creak softly. The sound carries far, swallowed and returned by the chamber in a way that makes it clear: nothing here goes unheard. Iron rings are set into the stone at different heights, some empty, some not. Yet there is no movement from the shadowed figures. My throat tightens, and I pull my gaze to the ground to avoid looking too closely.

This place was not built for haste. It was built for waiting, for breaking resolve slowly, for letting the mind wander where the body cannot. More shivers run down my spine as nightmarish thoughts rush in. The dungeon does not rush you. It does not threaten. It simply exists, patient and certain, confident that time will do its work.

My eyes fall on the chains hanging across the wall that look similar to the one around my neck. A blood-stained wooden table sits in the middle, covered with an array of what I can only assume to be torture devices. Large rusted blades attached to perfectly carved handles sit in disarray, cluttered with iron clamps stained a deep shade of burgundy. My stomach turns with thoughts of what hellish things have been done in this dreadful place.

Reaching for the collar again, a fresh surge of panic rolls in. *Where is Blythe?* "Hello?" I yell, my voice cracking against the stone. "Hello? Blythe? Nyx!" Met with only the sound of my pounding heart, I grip the collar. "Osiris, you prick, show yourself!" Wild rage boils within me. Slamming my eyes shut, I draw deep, pulling my magic up through my arms. Purple mist coils around my wrists as electricity crawls beneath my skin. Gritting my teeth, I force my power into the chains. The metal shrieks, and my collar trembles violently as my magic weaves downward. A luminous braid of plum-colored energy snakes into the bolts embedded in the floor. For a heartbeat, it works. Then the glow dulls. Cracks spider through the light, the color draining into gray. Agony explodes at the base of my skull. Gasping, I claw at the collar as pain lances down my spine. The metal tightens viciously, feeding on my power, turning it against me. *Enchanted.* "Fuck you, Osiris," I rasp.

The room tilts, and my vision tunnels. The collar cinches tighter, stealing what little air I have left. My nails split. Blood slicks my neck as I pry uselessly at the metal. Black dots flood my vision, and the ringing in my ears swells. Gasping for air, I fall back onto the stone, darkness completely shrouding my sight.

Chapter 2

Edin

A noise from above jolts me awake. I blink hard, pushing myself upright, dread snapping through me as the sound registers, footsteps. "Osiris!" I shout, dragging myself across the stone. "You fucking coward! Face me, you piece of shit!" The footsteps grow louder, hammering directly overhead. Dust rains down from the floorboards, drifting through the dim air. "Osiris!" I scream, my voice cracking with fury.

A door creaks open, the sound echoing off the stone walls. I lunge forward, ignoring the vicious bite of metal at my throat, bracing myself. Heavy boots descend a set of hidden stairs across the room. Each step lands like a drumbeat in my chest. I swallow hard and steady my breathing. "Osiris!" Sparks snap from my fingertips as electricity crawls up my arms, fueled by anger. The boots hit the stone floor, then silence falls over the room.

"Edin?"

The voice slices through me. The figure steps into view, and familiarity sends a shiver racing down my spine. I stumble back toward the wall, words abandoning me entirely.

"Edin!"

He moves faster than my eyes can follow. One blink and suddenly, bright blue eyes are inches from mine. "Endricks," I whisper. Tears burn as they well over my lids. With a trembling hand, I reach up, brushing my fingers over his cheek. "No… this can not be. I will not cast judgment on your soul."

"Edin," he says firmly, cupping my face. "It is me." He takes my hand and presses it to his chest. A heartbeat, strong and steady. "All of me."

A sob breaks free as he presses his lips to my forehead. Brushing my cheek, he leans past me, inspecting the chains, following them down to where they disappear into the stone floor. I grab his shoulder and pull him back. "I do not understand," I say hoarsely, locking eyes with him. "Osiris stabbed you with poison. I watched the veil to Helheim close around you."

He tilts my chin up and snorts. "Such little faith. It will take more than a pathetic Elysian with a god complex to take me out of this realm."

Despite everything, my eyes nearly roll out of my head. *He is definitely back to full health.*

"What happened after the veil closed?" I ask. "How long was I out? How long have I been down here?"

"Not long. A day, maybe." He drags a hand through his hair, glancing toward the window. "I was taken straight to the infirmary. King Adonis," his eye twitches, "was not pleased. It took some persuasion to have him reopen the veil to Purgatory."

"I thought only I could open it."

"The ruler of each realm can open the gateway," he explains. "Only you can decide where souls reside."

My stomach sinks. "That is why Osiris needed me as his partner… to use me…." I grimace. "Speaking of Osiris. Where is the bastard?"

Endricks chuckles darkly. "Where he belongs, in Helheim prison. Not before I beat him within an inch of his worthless life. He will not see daylight again."

"May he rot in Helheim," I mutter. Then my chest tightens. "And Blythe?"

"She is upstairs," he says quickly. "I found her unconscious on the catwalk in the Room of Revelation. She woke up while I was carrying her and bit me. Vicious little fox." He huffs. "Sera is tending to her." He glances at his hand, where red and blue welts bloom across his skin. "Now, please, let me tend to you."

I nod as relief washes over me.

"Stay still," he says, gripping the chain. "I will take you to her as soon as we get you out of here and your wounds taken care of."

I squeeze my eyes shut as the collar pinches tighter. "They are enchanted," I gasp.

He smirks, raising an eyebrow. "No need for magic." He grips the chain with both hands and braces a foot against the stone wall.

Metal bites into my neck as the wall behind me begins to crack. I lean back, eyes locked on him, tracking the flex of muscle and veins along his arms. The collar cinches brutally, stealing my air, and spots form across my vision. The stones give way, violently crashing down all around me. Chains and rock slam to the floor, and I pitch forward, but Endricks catches me, strong arms wrapping around me before I can hit the stone again. I suck in a ragged breath as the shackles fall away. Tears spill freely as I look up at him.

"You are safe, Belladonna," he murmurs, brushing a stray strand of silver hair behind my pointed ear. "Let us get you taken care of."

CHAPTER 3

EDIN

Hot tears spill down my cheeks as the weight of the chains leaving my body finally sinks in. Relief washes over me in a trembling wave, and my knees buckle as I collapse into Endricks's arms. My breaths come uneven and shallow, my chest fluttering as though it has not yet learned that the danger has passed.

"Shhh, Edin," he murmurs, holding me closer. "You are safe now. I am here." His voice is steady, anchoring. He presses a soft kiss to my forehead and draws in a slow breath, his eyes closing as if he is memorizing this moment, me, alive and in his arms.

He bends and lifts me with careful ease, as though I am something precious. Warmth spreads through me at once, loosening the tight ache coiled deep in my body. I relax against him, resting my cheek over his heart. His smoky scent fills my lungs, familiar and calming, and for the first time in what feels like forever, I let my eyes close without fear.

We climb the staircase slowly. Each step carries us farther from the dungeon, farther from the cold and the dark. Endricks moves with quiet purpose, unhurried, as though there is nowhere else he would rather be. I lift a hand to his face, brushing my thumb along his jaw. The faint rasp of his stubble grazes my skin, grounding me. He looks down at me, his blue eyes bright even in the dim stairwell, steady and full of something achingly gentle.

When he pushes through the heavy doors, light pours over us. I squint against it, warmth kissing my skin. The smell of fresh bread drifts through the hall, and somewhere nearby, Blythe laughs, clear and carefree. The sound makes my chest ache in the best way. Joy wells up, slow and overwhelming, and tears slide down my cheeks.

"Do not cry, Belladonna," Endricks says softly, drawing me closer. "No one will harm you again." Then he calls out calmly, "Sera, please let Blythe know we will return shortly. I need to tend to Edin's wounds."

"Of course, Lord Endricks," Sera answers warmly. "I've prepared healing salves in the upper quarters."

Moments later, he nudges open the double doors to the chambers. A grand wooden bed dominates the room, dressed in a feather-soft duvet and thick pillows that seem to beckon. Weariness settles deep into my bones. Endricks lowers me gently to my feet, but I sway, unsteady. I trail my fingers along the wall, needing the reassurance of something solid.

In the mirror, I barely recognize myself with dark shadows beneath my eyes, tear-streaked cheeks, and tangled, dull hair. I lift a hand, tracing the evidence of what I survived.

Endricks steps behind me, wrapping his arms around my waist. His touch is warm and sure as he turns me away from the glass.

"Come," he whispers. "Sit. Let me take care of you."

He guides me to the bed before stepping away briefly. Water runs, quiet and steady. When he returns, he carries a basin and folded towels. He kneels before me, his movements unhurried. The cloth is cool as he gently cleans the dried blood from my neck, his thumb brushing soothing circles into my skin afterward.

***

I watch him, my fingers sliding along his arm, feeling the strength there, not frightening now, only comforting. When our eyes meet, there is no rush in his gaze, only warmth and patience.

I lean forward and press my forehead to his, breathing him in. "Thank you," I whisper.

He smiles softly and presses a lingering kiss to my lips, slow, tender, full of promise, but asking nothing more than what I am ready to give. Heat coils low in my core, needy, sharp, and undeniable. I tug him closer.

"I want you, Endricks," I whisper, teeth catching his lower lip in a breathless promise.

The kiss quickly explodes into something feverish, and the throbbing in my skull dissipates as need builds inside me. He pulls my top down my shoulders, popping the buttons off the front, exposing my breasts. Turning me around, he pushes me face down onto the mattress and pulls my clothes down roughly. I watch in the mirror as he slides his belt off and frees his already hard cock from his pants.

Positioning himself at my entrance, I feel the pressure and then the delicious stretch as he pushes into me hard. Pain radiates through my brain with the force of his thrusts, but I grind down on his length just as hard, wanting, *needing* all of him inside me. I *need* to hear the slap of his thighs against my ass. I *need* to make myself forget the events that led us to that god-awful prison. He pulls out slowly and slams into me harder, erasing the memories with every pump of his hips. Our bodies connect again, and I feel the tightness coil within me, almost to the breaking point. Endricks pulls out with a smirk and bends down. I can not help but let out a whine of irritation with his absence. When he comes back up, he is holding his belt.

Before I can fully register what is happening, his hands are at my throat, fastening the leather there, firm, possessive. The pressure draws a sharp breath from my lungs. I meet his gaze in the mirror, my reflection wide-eyed, silently pleading. He looks down at me, head tilting slightly, one brow lifting as a wicked smile curves his mouth, equal parts warning and promise.

His grip tightens, grounding me, pulling me back against him. Heat coils low in my body as he moves, deliberate and unrelenting. The tension builds with every thrust, winding tighter as the collar draws snug against my skin. My pulse roars in my ears. The room narrows. Dark flecks dance at the edges of my vision, the mirror blurring as sensation overwhelms thought, leaving me suspended on the brink, aching, breathless, and undone.

My muscles contract, squeezing down on his cock, and the dots turn into white, hot fireworks as an orgasm crashes over me. Fighting for air, tears prick my eyes while I ride out the waves of pleasure.

I look back up at the mirror, tears streaking my cheeks, and freeze. My reflection trembles in the glass, but it is not just mine I see. The fog of panic and confusion clears, and I finally notice him, Endricks, but not entirely.

Feathered wings unfold from his back, dark and shimmering, and a single red curl falls over his forehead. His presence fills the room like a storm held in human form, and my chest tightens as realization spreads through me. Dread coils low in my stomach, crawling upward in icy tendrils that grip my throat.

"Endricks," I stammer, my voice barely more than a whisper, questioning the reality in front of me. My instinct screams to pull away, to put distance between us, but his presence is magnetically overwhelming. His arm circles my waist, retraining me, and I feel the power radiating off him, impossible and undeniable.

"Look again, Little Hellion," he murmurs, a smirk tugging at his lips, his eyes bright and intense. There is a heat in his gaze, a challenge, and something deep inside me trembles at the realization that the man I know does not stand before me. Instinct kicks in, and I attempt to push off the bed, but his arm wraps tighter around my waist, and he pulls me in harder as his body jerks, reaching orgasm. My heartbeat races, caught between confusion and terror, as I stare into the mirror, forced to watch.

He yanks on the belt, snapping my head back, but the belt is gone. In its place hangs the heavy metal collar from the dungeon, cold and unforgiving against my throat. My disbelief is a living thing as my gaze follows the chain link by link until I find the hand holding it.

Osiris.

His knuckles are wrapped tight around the chain, thick muscles in his arms flexing as he gives it another sharp tug. He smirks down at me, satisfied, victorious. His breath is hot against my cheek as he leans in. "You really thought you could get away from me that easily?"

Reality crashes down on me, shattering.

The damp stench of mold and dirt floods my lungs. Stone replaces warmth. Shadows shift at the edges of my vision, bodies stirring in the corners of the dungeon. I turn my head sharply, flip over, and freeze. The man from the village of Purgatory stares back at me. The one I gave lavender to. More faces emerge behind him. Watching. Waiting. Flashes of the empty village slam into me: the silence, the missing doors, the absence that screamed. My villagers. All of them… gone.

The cold floor bites into my back beneath Osiris's weight, knocking the breath from my chest. Panic tightens until my lungs burn. His scent, salt, teakwood, sweat, hits me all at once, thick and suffocating, and my stomach turns.

"You disgusting bastard," I snarl, fighting for leverage, for air, for space.

At last, he shifts away, and I drag in a ragged breath, my chest heaving as the pressure lifts.

"Oh, Edin," he says softly, almost fondly. He brushes my damp hair from my face as though we share a secret. "You made it so effortless." His fingers hook beneath my chin, forcing my gaze up to his gleaming smile. "You wanted *him* to save you so badly. You built the fantasy yourself, every detail. I simply stepped inside and let it grow." His eyes darken with satisfaction. "All I needed was a scent. Memories are *such* fragile things. So easy to bend."

Cold realization sinks its claws into me.

None of it was real, and I never left this hellhole.

Betrayal and disgust churn in my gut, twisting my empty stomach until I feel sick. I claw at the stone, trying to crawl away, nails scraping uselessly against the floor.

"You are a fucking monster," I choke.

Osiris's mouth curls into a smug smile. "As I recall, Edin," he says mildly, "You never stopped me."

The words land like a blow. My stomach lurches as the implication sinks in, revulsion flooding my throat. I turn my head and retch, bile splattering across the stone.

His expression darkens instantly. "Disgusting slut," he snarls, stepping closer. "You really believe a title and a prophecy make you untouchable now?" His lips twist cruelly. "Your mate is gone, and when I take my throne, every realm will bow."

I glare at him through tears. "I will never kneel to you."

The impact comes without warning. Pain flashes white as my head snaps to the side, my vision blurring. I gasp, struggling to focus as his hand closes around the collar at my throat, jerking me forward.

"You will," he growls low and close. "Before I am finished, you will *beg* for mercy."

"I will never beg for anything from you, prick!" I snap.

Osiris rears back, slapping me hard. My vision blurs, and I rapidly blink, attempting to right myself. Grabbing my collar, he jerks me forward, grinding out, "By the time I am done with you, Little Hellion, you *will* beg. You will beg for death because dying will be a welcome reprieve from what I have in store for you."

The chains tighten, biting into already-raw skin. Hope drains out of me in a hollow rush, leaving only numbness. My head falls back, my gaze drifting past him, and then I see her. In the adjacent cell lies a familiar shape, small and still. Fox ears. Curved hips. Chains glint faintly in the dim light.

"Blythe," I rasp, my voice barely a sound. "Blythe, please." Silence answers me. Panic claws up my spine, stealing my breath. "Blythe," I try again, louder this time, my heart pounding so hard it drowns out everything else.

Osiris chuckles. "Perhaps your little fox is not as resilient as you."

"Is she alive?" I sob, tears spilling freely, streaking my face and pooling on the floor. The thought of losing her, again, splinters something inside me.

How did it come to this? My best friend. My mate. Everything I was... stripped away. Imprisoned in my own castle. Reduced to this.

I blink through tears, forcing myself to look again. Her chest rises. Falls. Shallow, but real. Relief hits me so hard it almost hurts. She is alive. Rage follows close behind. I twist, kicking weakly at Osiris, but the collar tightens further, slicing into my skin. Warm blood trickles down my neck, mixing with my tears.

I bare my teeth at him, voice raw but burning. “What do you want from me?”

Chapter 4

Osiris

"Do you not see?" I fling my arms wide, releasing the chain at last. Edin collapses forward, dragging in a ragged, desperate breath, and I savor it, the sound of relief earned only because I allow it.

"I am already well on my way," I tell her calmly. "And let me assure you, I have been very patient." I draw in a deep breath, letting the moment. "This is my hour, Edin. We have tolerated half-breeds and diluted bloodlines for far too long. I waited a century for my efforts to bear fruit, and now," I smile. "Now everything is finally falling into place."

She turns her face away from me, jaw tight, eyes blazing with revulsion. "You will never take the throne," she screams. "You are insane!"

"Do not look away from me," I snap. The chain jerks taut again, sharp and unforgiving. She coughs, choking as I force her attention back where it belongs. "Look at you," I sneer. "A squandered vessel of power. Arcane wasted. A goddess title sullied by weakness." I lean closer. "I am almost impressed by how long I managed to pretend to care for you."

Her eyes burn with hatred.

"Oh, Little Hellion," I continue smoothly, "You devoured every word I gave you. Every carefully placed confession. Not that it was difficult, you were always so eager to believe." I brush a knuckle along her cheek. She recoils, and I grin. "What is wrong, Belladonna? Have you stopped loving me?"

"Do not call me that," she spits.

I laugh softly. "Ah. Reserved for Endricks, I assume?" I tilt my head. "But he is not here, is he? No, he is gone. *Dead.*" I watch the words land. "Tragic. It seems everyone who might have cared about your fate has disappeared."

Her voice cracks, but she forces it steady. "Why, Osiris? What do you gain from this? What have you done with my villagers?"

"You truly still do not understand?" I shake my head. "Then allow me to be perfectly clear." I crouch before her, delighting in the way fear begins to eclipse her fury.

"I will take the throne. All of them. Every realm. Exactly as I was always meant to."

The moment of realization is exquisite, her face crumpling as the truth finally takes root.

"You do not deserve to rule," she snarls. "You will destroy everything."

My smile tightens. "I was exiled from my home and condemned to rot in Helheim Prison for daring to claim my destiny. I was born to rule, Edin. And nothing, *no one*, will stand in my way, least of all you."

She scoffs weakly. "You are not royal. You have no claim."

"Ah," I say pleasantly. "But I do have the prophecy, *your* prophecy."

I straighten, pacing slowly. "During my time in that pit, I overheard Endricks's precious seer ramble about fate, about a goddess bound to him. That was when I understood what was required." I glance back at her. "All I needed was access. Proximity. Trust." I smile at the memory. "And fortune favored me. A woman in the neighboring cell, Fallon. Clever. Devoted. She understood sacrifice." My voice softens, almost reverent. "She took a punishment meant for me, and had her wings torn from her body. She played her part flawlessly. I ensured the guards saw only what I wanted them to see, a pathetic Elysian man receiving punishment."

Edin recoils, horror etched across her face.

"And that pitiful story I fed you?" I chuckle. "The grieving child. The tragic parents. You looked at me like I was something worth saving." I shake my head in amusement. "My parents were fools who chose righteousness over survival. Their deaths were… unfortunate, but unnecessary sentimentality has no place in power."

Footsteps echo behind me.

I do not turn. I drop to one knee as slender hands slide along my arms, tilting my chin upward. Fallon leans over me, her dark hair spilling forward, her presence commanding without a word.

"My love," I murmur, breathing her in. She smiles and presses a kiss to my jaw.

I glance back at Edin just in time to see recognition dawn. The color drains from her face as the final piece clicks into place. She folds inward, burying her face in her hands.

"Yes," I tell her softly. "It was all real, just never for you." I rise, wrapping an arm around Fallon's waist. "Give up, Little Hellion," I say gently. "Hope no longer serves you."

Chapter 5

Edin

"Disgusting halfbreed," Fallon spits, her mouth twisting with contempt.

"Fallon, My Love," Osiris murmurs smoothly, placing a hand on her back. Then his gaze snaps to me, dark and merciless. "Do not address such… vermin."

The chain jerks violently, pain detonating behind my eyes. I gasp as he looms over me, his wings unfurling wide enough to swallow the light. Shadows crawl across the stone as he backs me into the corner, every instinct in me screaming to flee. The fear is animalistic, bone-deep, worse than the ache pulsing through my skull.

I am trapped. Caged.

Osiris guides Fallon toward the stairs, his hand possessive at her lower back. I listen to their footsteps fade, each echo a nail sealing us into silence.

"Blythe," I choke. My gaze finds her sprawled across the stone floor, limbs twisted unnaturally, her body frighteningly still. A dark stain glints beneath her head in the dim light.

"No," I whisper. "Please. Blythe, wake up. Please."

My heart stutters. *Did her ear just twitch?*

"Blythe," I rasp, voice breaking. "Talk to me. Say something. Anything!" Time stretches thin as I hold my breath, watching, waiting. If she dies here, because of me…

She groans.

Relief slams into me so hard I almost sob. Blythe rolls onto her back, her face pinched with pain, breaths shallow and uneven. She turns her head toward me, eyes glassy with tears.

"Edin," she croaks, dragging her hands over her face. "Shit… Where are we?" She pushes herself up slowly, wincing, rubbing her temple. Her ears twitch at the clatter of chains, and she freezes, staring at the shackles on her wrists. "What in all of Helheim?" She jerks at the chains frantically and hisses as they bite into her skin. Tears begin to fall down her face.

"Blythe! Listen to me. Breathe!"

She cries out, clawing at the metal.

"Blythe, stop! Are you okay?"

She tosses the chains to the ground with a huff. "I'm just peachy, over here in my cushy *cell*, sipping winter wine," She rasps out.

Well, at least she still has a sense of humor.

I sag against the wall, breath finally coming. "Blythe," I say softly. "Breathe. Please."

She exhales sharply. “I’m fine,” she mutters hoarsely. “Just sore. And annoyed.”

Of course she is.

“Are you hurt?” I ask.

“I’ve had worse mornings,” she says, attempting a weak shrug. “I’ll live.”

“Gods,” I whisper. “I am so sorry. This is my fault.”

She snorts faintly. “Please. I’ve dated psychos before. Osiris just happens to be… ambitious.”

The dungeon door creaks open, and my blood runs cold. Heavy footsteps descend the stairs, and Osiris appears again, fury etched into every line of his face. He does not look at me; he goes straight for Blythe.

“No,” I gasp, scrambling forward. “Osiris, what are you doing? Leave her alone!”

The collar tightens, choking the words from my throat.

He ignores me. His hand closes around Blythe's throat, lifting her off the ground. She kicks, choking, eyes wide with terror.

"Stop!" I scream. "Please, do not do this!"

I throw my magic at him, desperation ripping it free, but it snaps back violently, searing my arms. The collar hums, swallowing my power whole. My violet mist dies into a dull gray haze. Osiris snarls and hurls Blythe against the wall. She hits hard, crumpling to the floor in a broken heap.

"Stop!" I drag myself forward, chains screaming as they pull taut. Pain tears through my neck as the collar constricts.

Osiris spins towards me, eyes blazing. "I have heard enough from you."

His power slams into me, and the chains yank me backward until the shackles pin me flat against the wall. I claw at the collar, gasping.

"Blythe," I sob.

The room spins. My strength bleeds away, leaving me trembling and useless. Tears stream unchecked as I stretch my hand toward her, fingers falling short by inches.

"Blythe," I whisper, watching her chest stutter as she struggles for breath. I hold mine too, praying to the gods who have already abandoned me.

Blythe is going to die in this hellhole, and there is not a damn thing I can do about it.

Chapter 6

Endricks

Days prior…

My eyes shoot open as pain runs across my chest, and the sound of cracking sweeps through my head as I gasp, every breath scraping raw. The ringing in my ears fades, my vision clearing just enough to register a black and gold boot planted firmly against my sternum. I follow the laces of the boot up to a face, which just so happens to belong to the piece of shit I was so honorably gifted as my sperm donor. “Hello, Father,” I say, the smirk coming easily, even as blood spills from the corners of my mouth.

He looks down at me like I am something he scraped off his heel. “Such a fucking disappointment you are, Endricks,” King Adonis spits, as he swings his boot into the side of my ribcage, sending me across the room. Picture frames rattle as I slam into the wall, landing on my face. "Get him out of my sight," King Adonis orders.

"Back to my old room, I suppose," I chuckle between coughs. My mouth tastes metallic, and blood drips from my nose. He slowly walks over to me and squats down, jerking me up by the collar.

"You are a pathetic excuse of an heir," he grinds out.

"The feeling is mutual," I choke, sputtering blood onto the stone floor.

"You had *one* task."

"I will not let you near her, even if it kills me."

"*That* can be arranged," he smirks, dropping me back down.

Lifting my head, I watch as he stomps out. The door slams shut behind him, the sound like a final verdict. My father's minions crowd around, snatching at my body. I press my hands to the stone floor, and a trail of fire crawls up behind them. The flame catches the cuff of a soldier's jacket, setting him alight. A knee presses down into my back, and pain radiates through my entire spine, traveling all the way to my toes. Heavy chains clatter across the floor. Frantically, I rear my head back, making contact with another soldier's face and knocking him off me. My heartbeat pounds in my ears, either from the gaping hole still in my chest, the beating from father, or the poison now vigorously pumping through my veins.

I am running out of time.

Throwing my arms forward, I latch onto two separate ankles, forcing what little power I have left in me through them. Ice begins to form at their feet and crawls up their legs. Within seconds, they stand there, frozen solid, and I jerk them forward. The two guards topple backwards, shattering across the floor. Something hard slams into the back of my head. My vision doubles, and the room begins to spin. Soldiers start to pile on top of my back, crushing my ribcage.

The sound of metal chains scraping across the floor blares in my ears, then suddenly fades off. Black spots form in my view, and my head lolls forward. Shackles snap tightly around my wrists and ankles. I flail, snatching at anything I can in an attempt to burn this entire chamber to the ground. Flames light on my fingertips, but power runs back into my palms, scorching them in the process. *Of course, the chains are enchanted. Typical Father, always on the defensive.* Darkness seeps into the corners of my vision, and my eyelids grow heavy. The doors crash open, and white flashes through the chaos of the room. The soldiers' gaze turns as I fight to stay conscious.

"Enough!" A familiar voice yells.

Time suddenly slows down, and I watch through spotted vision as an entirely new brawl breaks out. I squint, watching as the soldiers seem to move in slow motion. "Verenia, give him air! He is drowning in his own blood!" I hear faintly. The darkness takes over, and the sound of tortured screams and metal on metal fades off into the distance, replaced by shrill ringing.

“Endricks!” the voice shouts.

“Valker?” I mumble, as the silence consumes me.

Chapter 7

Valker

"He is still the Prince of Helheim!" I shout as I swing my sword. "And you will treat him with respect, no matter his charges!" My blade bites cleanly through a soldier's neck. I look up as the severed head hits the floor with a thud and watch the remaining minions' gazes drag, slow and horrified, from it back to me. They move as though trapped in quicksand, my time magic thickening the air. I cut through them swiftly, methodically, denying every soul the chance to beg. Across the chamber, another set of doors blast open, torn from their hinges as armored guards pour in. I meet their stunned stares and offer a wink. I glance back, relief washing over me as Verenia drops to her knees at Endricks's body. She looks over her shoulder, giving me a nod.

Rolling my shoulders back, I settle into position and ready myself to meet them head-on. I reach into my jacket pocket and pull out my stopwatch, letting it dangle in front of the guards. I lift an eyebrow and click the side twice. Silver mist sweeps across the stones. Silence crashes down as time locks in place, everything frozen but Verenia's harsh breathing as she works. I smirk and draw my sword, dragging the blade along the stones as I stroll toward the immobilized crowd. I lift the tip to a guard's throat, teasing the moment.

"Eenie, meenie, minie…" I spin on my heels. "Moe."

I drive the blade forward, and the world erupts. A hand clamps around my neck from behind, slamming me to the floor. Stone cracks against my skull, and pain blooms as my eyebrow splits open.

"Valker!" Verenia screams.

I twist, trying to reorient myself, but a boot crashes into my back, grinding me down as a blade's edge kisses the back of my neck. A deep laugh rolls through the chamber, hollow and cruel, turning my stomach.

"Foolish creature," the commander drawls. "Never underestimate the Helheim Militia. We *always* come prepared." He flicks his armor, metal gleaming as if on cue.

"Let him go," Verenia demands, forcing herself upright.

"Ah, yes, Miss Verenia," the commander chuckles. "It seems your twin has landed you in quite a predicament."

"This is your final warning," she growls. White fog coils around her ankles, rising, thick with promise.

The guards break into laughter. I steel myself, knowing my sister's rage all too well. A cold, biting wind sweeps through the chamber. Verenia lifts both hands, and the air answers. The gale strengthens, her long white hair snapping wildly, tangling around her antlers. The soldiers stagger, widening their stances to hold their ground. Pressure builds, thick and crushing, as the wind rotates into a spiraling vortex. I slip a hand beneath my shirt and clutch my necklace. Our mother enchanted the gems to shield us from one another's magic in battle. From Verenia's ear, a matching green stone sways, catching the light as the storm swells.

Metal-soled boots scrape across the floor, and the soldiers grunt as they are dragged inch by inch towards the center. Verenia flashes me a wink, her plan snapping cleanly into place. I slip free of the guard's grip and stride into the heart of the storm. The wind coils tighter, collapsing into a roaring cyclone that drags every soul toward its center. I crack my neck and swipe the blood from my brow. From the sheaths beneath my vest, I draw my daggers, weighing them like toys.

What a perfect time for target practice.

The soldiers howl as they fight against the pull of the cyclone, their boots skidding, and their armor screaming. I lock onto the commander and offer him one last smirk before I throw. He screams, a wet, guttural sound, as the blade buries itself deep in his cheek. Clawing at his face, he drops to his knees, still sliding toward the cyclone's core.

"Damn, I missed," I laugh, shrugging sarcastically. "Round two."

"Quit messing around, Valker," Verenia huffs, rolling her eyes.

"Fine," I grunt, slinging my second dagger straight into his jugular.

A smile creeps across my face as I glance at the remaining soldiers, watching them cling to anything solid to keep from being sucked in. Metal armor shrieks against rough stone as they beg for mercy. *Mindless pricks, they deserve every second of this. The kingdom has never given Endricks the respect he's owed.* A choking sound cuts through my thoughts, and the storm collapses.

"Verenia?" I spin, dread slamming into my gut. I blink rapidly, unsure of what I'm witnessing. She is frozen on her knees, and a dark puddle of water spreads beneath her, shadowed deep blue, so deep it is nearly black. She gasps, coughing up water. I hit the floor beside her, lifting her head. "Verenia!" Her eyes are bloodshot. Water streams from her nose as the puddle surges upward, coiling around her throat and hoisting her into the air.

"Fuck! No, no, no."

I grab for her ankles, hands shaking, but my touch only tightens the spell. I watch in horror as she claws at the collar of water, fingers slipping straight through it as if it is not there at all. My gaze snaps to Endricks, still, unmoving on the floor. I rip my sword free and whip around, scanning the chamber, pulse roaring in my ears.

A low voice echoes through the mist, "I commend you for your efforts, Valker, but I have seen enough."

"Show yourself," I growl.

"Your loyalty to this bastard is… impressive."

"Release her!" I shout, my eyes locked on her as her lips darken to a shade of purple.

"Bow to me."

"I will never."

"So be it."

Verenia thrashes in midair, gagging for a single breath. Blood slips from her nose as the blue shadow behind her swells, towering over me. I snap my gaze around, hunting the source of the magic, but movement catches my eye. The soldiers are hauling themselves up, one by one, readjusting their armor and settling into battle stances.

"I am being gracious, Valker," the voice murmurs. "Will you watch your sister die like this, drowning from the inside?"

Verenia's eyes roll back into her head, and her body slackens, her head lolling forward.

"Verenia!"

"This is your final chance, Valker."

My gaze snaps between her and Endricks, then to the soldiers closing in. My heart hammers, sweat stinging my eyes.

"Fuck," I hiss, dragging my hands through my hair, fist knotting tight. "Release her!" I drop to my knees, thrusting my wrists into the air.

"Wise of you, *Deer*."

The chamber darkens to a deep navy. Behind me, the soldiers sink to their knees as one, heads bowed. "My Lord," they intone in unison.

King Adonis steps from the mist, and the spell breaks. Verenia crashes to the floor, coughing violently, water spilling from her lips as she drags in air.

"Verenia," I whisper, starting toward her.

"I think not, Valker," King Adonis booms. "Remain where you kneel, your sister's life depends on it."

Every bone in my body screams to be at her side, but for her safety, I comply. I clench my jaw as soldiers swarm around me. My stomach turns, looking over at Endricks, begging him to move even an inch. I drag my eyes away, unable to contain myself. Verenia's eyes crack open, and my heart lunges in my chest. Metal bites down, and shackles snap closed around my ankles and wrists.

"Valker!" Verenia yelps, jerking up from the floor.

"It's okay," I nod, half smiling.

"No, Valker, I can not allow this!" she cries, and the white mist begins to form again.

"Verenia, enough!" I grind out through bared teeth and lock eyes with King Adonis, "Stand down." King Adonis lays a hand on her shoulder, sending me into a spiral.

"Escort Valker and my pathetic excuse of a son down to Greybar." King Adonis instructs the lieutenant. "And clean up this mess," he says, nodding to the commander's body.

I smirk at the soldiers as they pick the corpse up, then spin back around to Verenia and Adonis. "No harm is to come to my sister."

King Adonis laughs, "That is the least of your worries. I would never allow myself to stoop so low as to consort with such… scum."

I look to Verenia, “I will find you. Stay strong, stay safe.”

Verenia nods back, tears welling in her eyes.

Adonis jerks her by the arm, laughing, “I would not hold out for your brother, Verenia.”

“Valker!” Verenia screams as we are dragged in opposite directions.

“I will find you, Verenia!” I yell, watching the doors slam shut.

“I have heard just about enough out of you,” the lieutenant says, slamming the hilt of his sword into my temple.

White-hot pain explodes across my face, and my vision fractures into a constellation of dots. The world tilts violently as they drag me out the door. Shackles bite into my wrists as two Hellions haul me upright and throw me into the back of a wagon like trash. I hit the wooden floorboards hard, the impact knocking what little air I have left from my lungs. “Well, fuck,” I rasp, dragging my bound hands up toward my head. My eyes struggle to focus just as they haul Endricks over the side of the wagon. He hits the ground with a sickening thud, coughing violently as blood spills from his mouth. "Endricks," I breathe, my vision doubling. There are two of him, and both look half-dead.

"You idiot," he croaks.

Despite everything, a laugh claws its way out of my chest. "Always a prick," I rasp, "Even when I come to your rescue."

He turns his head just enough to look at me, one eye already swelling shut. "And how," he wheezes, "did that turn out for you?"

I swallow, the edges of my vision darkening. "You are," I mumble, words slurring as the world fades, "such a smartass."

His mouth twitches, barely, but it's there, and somehow, that hurts worse than the shackles.

The wagon jolts forward. The sudden movement sends a fresh wave of nausea rolling through me, and my stomach twists as iron wheels grind over stone. I curl onto my side, the chains around my wrists clanking loudly with the motion. Every sound feels too sharp, like it's scraping directly against my skull.

Gasping, I jolt, fingers scrabbling for my dagger that is no longer there. Tree limbs knot overhead, casting warped shadows in the mist that seem to reach out for us. *Focus.* I squeeze my eyes shut, then open them again. *Big mistake.* The world fractures, doubling, tripling, the edges of everything smearing into one another like wet ink. My stomach lurches, time stretching thin and slippery.

How long have we been traveling?

Lantern light swings overhead, casting long, monstrous shadows across the interior of the wagon. I can't tell how many soldiers are riding with us, only that there are too many. My head throbs in time with the wagon's rhythm, as blood slowly trickles down my temple. Straining to look across from me, Endricks lies sprawled against the side rail, his chest rising unevenly. Each breath seems to cost him something. The iron collar around his neck glows faintly, pulsing in time with his heartbeat. *Magic suppression. Of course it is. Bastards learned fast.*

I swallow hard and drag myself a few inches closer, the chains scraping wood. "Hey," I whisper, though my voice comes out hoarse. "Don't die. I'm already having a shit day."

One of his eyes cracks open. "You always know," he murmurs, "how to sweet-talk a man."

Relief loosens something tight in my chest, just a fraction. Then the wagon sways as it turns sharply, lifting a wheel from the ground. My shoulder slams into the wall, and stars burst behind my eyes. I bite back a groan, tasting copper again. The smell of iron, oil, and damp stone fills the air, familiar, in a way I don't like.

"Welcome to Greybar, you pieces of shit!" a guard yells out.

My stomach drops, and the wagon slows. The iron wheels screech, echoing too loudly, and the sound carries downward. My ears pop as the air grows colder, heavier. The light dims as stone swallows us whole. A gate groans open. The wagon passes beneath it, and I feel it settle in my bones. *This is a place meant to break people.*

Shouts echo in the distance. Chains rattle, and muffled screams begin to fill the air. My fingers curl into fists around the shackles. "Endricks," I murmur, panic bleeding through despite my best efforts. "Whatever happens in there,"

"I know," he interrupts softly. "You run. First chance you get."

I shake my head, even though it makes the world spin again. "Not happening."

He turns his head just enough to look at me. There's something dark and steady in his gaze now, something resolved. "Valker," he says, using my name as if it mattered. "If you stay, you will die. Then what happens to Verenia?"

Before I can answer, the wagon jerks to a stop, and boots pound across the ground. The doors swing open, and cold torchlight floods in, blinding and merciless. Hands grab me, dragging me toward the edge. As they pull me from the wagon, I catch one last look at Endricks, bloodied and broken, yet still defiant.

"Prisoners out," a voice barks.

I don't know how we're getting out of this, but I know one thing for certain. If this prison is meant to break us, they picked the wrong bastards.

The cold hits me first, not the clean kind; this one seeps, crawls under skin, into bone, and settles where it knows it won't be chased out. My stomach twists the moment my boots touch the ground. The smell confirms it before my eyes do: damp stone. Old blood scrubbed poorly from its crumbling surface. Burnt iron and rotting beams line the walls. My pulse stutters, then spikes. *I know this place. Greybar isn't a myth you tell your spawn to be obedient. It's a memory.*

Hands shove me forward, my knees buckling as I stumble. The chains bite deeper into my wrists, familiar in a way that makes my chest tighten. Too familiar. The rhythm of my steps falls into something automatic, measuring distance, counting turns, noting exits I already know don't exist. The gate slams shut behind us, its sound travelling down every twisting hall. We're marched down the main corridor, boots striking stone in brutal unison. Torches line the walls at a precise interval. A guard barks an order, and we're dragged down a side passage. My heart drops into my stomach.

Not this way. Not processing. Processing means collars. Collars mean numbers instead of names. Numbers mean pain, measured carefully, repeated until it stops feeling new.

A door looms ahead, thick and iron-banded, with a sigil carved deeply into its surface. My vision tunnels. I remember screaming in that room. I remember learning how long a man can hang from chains before his shoulders give out and then eventually dislocate. The door creaks open. The sound alone makes my knees threaten to buckle. The guard shoves us forward. I stumble, catching myself just before I fall. Gritting my teeth, I steady myself. A guard yanks me to the left, tearing us apart. I twist back just in time to see Endricks being dragged the opposite direction, his jaw set, his eyes locked on mine. The door slams between us. The echo rings through my skull, old and cruel, and I close my eyes.

"Valker!" Endricks shouts.

I survived this place once. Gods help them now because I'm not the same man anymore.

CHAPTER 8

EDIN

My eyes crack open to dull sunlight seeping through a small hole in the wall. The smell of dirt, sweat, and dried blood floods my senses. It is a sharp reminder of where I am, and it sends a jolt of anxiety through me. Every inch of my body feels as though I have been thrown down an embankment, battered by stone after stone. I would kill for a single smear of my mother's healing salve.

I must have slipped into unconsciousness from sheer exhaustion. With a groan, I push myself upright against the filthy wall of the cell. Pain screams through my joints as the collar grinds against my skin. It steals my breath, igniting another flare of panic.

Blythe is still asleep on the mildewed floor in a cell across from mine. I watch her chest rise and fall, clinging to the rhythm like a lifeline.

It is the smallest comfort, but right now, it is everything.

I have to get us out of here.

The thought beats in time with my pulse. I reach for my magic again, forcing it to answer, but the effort is fruitless. *Pathetic.* I knew it would fail even before I tried. The enchantments woven into this place are too strong, pressing down and smothering every spark.

Hunger claws at me. Exhaustion drags heavily through my limbs. With every shallow breath, I can feel myself slipping, growing weaker by the minute, and fear coils tight in my chest at the thought of what that might mean for both of us.

Heavy footsteps drift down the corridor, echoing off the stone walls and growing louder the closer they get. My pulse instantly picks up, thudding hard in my ears. "Fuck," I murmur as polished boots slip into view.

Osiris follows them a heartbeat later, unhurried, like he has all the time in the world. *I know I have none.* My stomach twists as his smile blooms, warm and utterly wrong. The kind he used to give me when he wanted something.

How did I ever fall for this?

"Good morning, Little Hellion," he says lightly, as if we are sharing a private joke. "I do hope you managed to get some rest." His gaze flicks over me, lingering, assessing me. "You look… tired."

"What do you want?" I snap, forcing the words past clenched teeth.

He chuckles softly and tilts his head, all feigned concern. "Straight to business. I always admired that about you." He steps closer, crouching so we are eye to eye, his voice dropping to something intimate. "But you and I both know this does not have to be unpleasant." He leans in, close enough that I can feel his breath brush my ear. "It is time for you to earn your stay here."

Cold dread coils tight in my chest. "I am not staying," I bite out. "You are my *captor*. I am being held against my will."

A flash of rage fractures his handsome features. In the next breath, his hand is on my jaw, fingers brutally digging into my face as he hauls me to my feet. The collar bites deep, grinding into the tender skin of my throat. Pain explodes white-hot. I gasp and choke, as my wounds tear open again. Warm blood trickles down my chest, slick and slow, soaking into the fabric of my bustier.

Osiris laughs, loud and unrestrained. There is no humor in his eyes, only something sharp and ugly and glittering. *Hate. Disgust.*

"Held against your will?" he scoffs. "Whatever do you mean?" His grip tightens, just enough to remind me how easily he could end everything. "You have been given *every* luxury," he gestures broadly to the barren, filthy cell around us, his grin stretching wider. Too wide. "All your needs are met. Shelter. Protection." His gaze flicks lazily toward Blythe, "I even brought you a friend, so you would not be lonely."

My vision swims as I struggle for air. "Wha…," I choke, fingers scraping uselessly at the collar. "What… can *I* do?"

His voice drops, turning syrupy sweet, intimate enough to make my skin crawl. "Nothing difficult," he murmurs. "Just open the veil to Elysia… so I may take my *rightful* place on the throne."

The words curdle in my stomach. Rage burns hot and fast, crawling up my throat as I stare at the monster wearing the face of a man I once *thought* I loved. "I would rather rot in this cell for all eternity than help you take Elysia, you *disgusting* pig," I snarl, the words tearing out of me as I spit them in his face.

If I could just break the enchantment on this damned chain, I think wildly, *I would have the earth swallow you whole.*

"Oh," Osiris murmurs. He smiles down at me, wide and toothy, a grin that turns my stomach. Then he shoves me aside like I weigh nothing.

I slam into the stone floor, the impact knocking the air from my lungs. Pain shoots through my skull, sharp and blinding, and my headache fractures into something unbearable. For a moment, I cannot move, cannot see, and cannot even breathe properly. The agony pulses through my head, all-consuming, as seconds stretch into something endless.

Sound returns first, with boots retreating slowly, deliberately. My vision swims back into focus just in time to see him pause. Osiris turns, meeting my gaze across the cell. A sickening grin carves itself into his face. He *winks*, and then he turns toward Blythe's cell.

My heart seizes so violently, I am certain my chest will collapse in on itself. Cold dread floods me, drowning out the pain.

Fuck.

"No, Osiris, leave her alone," I try to say, but pain shoots behind my eyes, and the words collapse into a raw croak.

He does not even look at me. Osiris reaches for a large knife resting on the blood-stained table, lifting it with idle curiosity, as though choosing a dessert.

"I have always wondered," he muses lightly, stepping over Blythe's prone form. He studies her like an object, head tilted. "Does a fox's ear grant cunningness the way a rabbit's foot grants luck?" A soft chuckle slips out.

"Do. Not. Touch. Her," I snarl, rage burning through the pain. "You bastard."

He sighs, bored. "An eye for an eye, Edin," he says, almost gently, and then he winks.

He grabs Blythe, hauling her toward the blade. Her scream rips through the corridor first. Then her eyes fly open, wild with pain and terror, and she fights. Blythe snaps her head back, connecting with his face, and twists violently, teeth sinking deep into his hand.

"You fucking *bitch*," Osiris roars, jerking away and slamming the knife back against her throat.

"No!" I scream, thrashing uselessly against my chains.

Blythe turns her head toward me, bloodied but defiant. "Edin, don't let him open the veil," she gasps. "It will end *everything*. I'd rather die than kneel to this *prick*."

Osiris's jaw tightens. "I have had quite enough of you."

He strikes her with the hilt of the knife, and she crumples, her body going slack as her eyes roll back.

Silence crashes down.

Osiris looks at his wounded hand with mild irritation as blood drips between his fingers. He tears a strip from Blythe's skirt, wrapping it around the cut with practiced ease. Then his gaze lifts, slowly, until it locks onto mine.

Whatever twinkle I see in his eyes makes my stomach drop straight through the floor.

"Oh, Edin," Osiris murmurs, his gaze lingering on Blythe as if she were something he owned. "I never noticed it before, but your friend is absolutely… *gorgeous*." He purrs the word so low it barely registers as sound, and bile burns up my throat.

"Do not touch her," I say hoarsely. "She can not open the veil for you."

He smiles, slow and knowing. "No, she can not." He crouches and rolls Blythe onto her back with careless ease. She stirs, letting out a soft whimper, but does not wake. My chains rattle as I strain forward, helpless.

Osiris's hand trails over her as if she were nothing more than a bargaining chip. A possession. He cups her breast, running a thumb over her nipple. "But *you* can," he says softly.

My chest caves in. “Osiris, please. She has no connection to this. This is between you and me.”

His eyes flick to mine, bright with satisfaction. “Exactly, yet you refuse to help me, Edin,” Osiris says with a pout that might almost be comical if it were not so calculated. “And that disappoints me.” His gaze drifts back to Blythe, slow and deliberate. Possessive. “So now I have a new toy.”

“Do not,” I snarl. “She has nothing to do with this.”

He laughs softly. “Everything has to do with *this*, Edin.”

Osiris drags a finger along Blythe’s side, not lingering, just enough to make the threat unmistakable. “I have been grinding against skin and bones for the last few months. This one has hips and tits to spare. She would be a good time,

I am certain of it." His hand travels down to her hip, his nails digging into her skin. "She is softer than you," he muses. "More… *receptive*. I wonder what she dreams about."

My blood turns to ice.

"Do I step into her mind?" he continues lightly. "Rewrite a few memories? Convince her I am someone she trusts?" He glances back at me, eyes glittering. "Or do I simply let her wake up in a nightmare she will never escape? Either way, *Little Hellion*, you get a wonderful show."

"Get your hands off her!" I scream, chains rattling violently. "Blythe would never choose you!"

Osiris's smile sharpens. "Choice is such a fragile thing."

"Get your grimy hands off her, you fucking *bastard*!"

He leans closer to her, lowering his voice to a murmur meant only for me, then runs his tongue up her cheek. "You would be amazed at how easily people bend when you show them exactly what they want to see." He lifts her top and peers down at her breasts with a wide smile. "It is my favorite pastime. Women are so open about what they want if you just take the time to listen. Give a woman an ounce of attention, and she will pour her heart out to you."

My chains rattle frantically as I pull my hands up, grabbing at my hair. "Stop," I grind.

His eyes flick to me, smug and triumphant. "Are you ready to open the veil… or should I keep proving my point?" Whatever mask he was wearing falls away. No smile. No pretense. "Open the veil for me, Edin."

My voice shakes, but I force the words out. "I will not take part in the destruction of the Elysian realm."

The change is instantaneous. Osiris moves faster than thought, his hand closing around Blythe's throat as he slams her back against the stone wall of her cell. Her eyes fly open, wide and bloodshot, a broken sound tearing from her as she claws for air.

"No!" I scream. Tears spilling freely, panic ripping through me so violently I can barely stay upright.

He glances at me over his shoulder, almost amused. "You did this," he says calmly. "This is *your* fault."

Blythe's gaze finds mine. Terror floods her eyes, raw, pleading, and something inside me shatters. Her lips move, trying to form a scream, but only a pitiful gasp escapes. Her hands scrabble uselessly at his arms as her heels strike the wall in desperate bursts.

The room tilts. I feel detached from my own body, like I am watching this through shattered glass. My nails dig into the stone until they burn, until pain is the only thing anchoring me to reality. "Please," I sob. "Osiris, please. This is on me. *Punish me.*"

***

He does not even look back at Blythe as he tightens his grip. His attention is entirely on me now. She kicks, landing a few hits, but they are fruitless against his stature. He begins tugging at his belt, pulling it from his waist. "Then prove it," he says quietly. "Open the veil."

Blythe's eyes never leave mine. Tears streak down her dirt-smeared face as her strength begins to fail, and I know that if I do not break right now, she will.

"Edin!"

Blythe's hoarse scream rips through me, yanking me back into my body like a blade to the spine. Her eyes lock on mine, pleading, terrified, and whatever resolve I had left shatters completely.

"Osiris, *stop!*" I scream, my ruined throat barely able to carry the sound. "I will do it! I will do whatever you want, you sick bastard. Just leave her alone!"

He stills.

Slowly, deliberately, Osiris turns his head to look at me.

"I will open the veil," I sob, the words burning my tongue. "Just, please, leave Blythe alone."

The silence stretches. Then his mouth curves into a satisfied smile.

"Oh, Edin," he says softly. "It took you long enough."

His grip on Blythe tightens just enough to make her whimper. He tilts her face, squeezing her cheeks, then presses his lips to hers. His eyes never leave mine.

"See how easy that was?" He gleams.

I shake violently, hatred and shame choking me.

"Now," he continues calmly, "You will give me what I want." His fingers dig into her jaw, possessive and cruel. "Or she suffers."

Blythe's gaze flicks back to me, tears streaking down her face, and in that moment, the truth settles heavy and final in my chest.

I did not save her.

I just damned us all.

"Another time, Little Fox," Osiris murmurs, dropping Blythe back to the floor as if she is nothing more than an afterthought. Blythe wipes her mouth with the back of her hand and spits at his boots. Osiris arches a brow, amused. "I like the spunk," he says lightly. "I will remember that when I come back for whatever you have left."

Laughter seeps out of the darkness beyond the cell bars. My blood runs cold as Fallon steps into the dim light. She had been watching. Every second of it. His shadow smiles just as cruelly as he does.

His whore is just as sadistic as he is.

"There truly are no limits to what you'll do to get what you think you deserve," she sneers, her eyes nearly black in the gloom. "And I do *love* watching you work."

Blythe curls in on herself against the wall, arms wrapped tightly around her bare body. Tears drip silently from her chin, but she does not make a sound. Something in my chest splinters. I meet her gaze across the narrow space between our cells. *I am sorry.* I mouth the words, useless and too late. The look she gives me, hurt, fear, resignation, kills something inside me.

"Blythe!" I say as I strain toward her, needing a response, a flicker that she is still in there. Pain explodes through my hand as a boot slams down on it. A scream rips from my throat, sharp and uncontrolled. My vision blurs as I look up. Osiris looms over me, eyes cold. He jerks hard on my collar, hauling me up. Air vanishes from my lungs. I kick uselessly, then a lock clicks, and my knees slam into stone; black spots crowd my vision.

He drops me back to the ground. I collapse, dragging in a desperate, burning breath as oxygen floods my lungs. The relief barely registers before his grip clamps around my arm. I am dragged across the floor, out of the cell, my body scraping stone as Blythe's face disappears behind iron bars. The last thing I see before the corridor swallows me whole is her curled against the wall, silent… broken… *because of me.*

Stone scrapes my bare feet raw as Osiris drags me through the castle corridors. I stumble more than I walk, my body lagging behind the iron grip locked around my arm. Every torch we pass throws warped shadows across the walls, twisting, reaching, watching. I feel like prey being paraded through a den of monsters. My lungs still burn. The hand around my neck is a cruel reminder of how little of myself I still own.

"Move," Osiris snaps without looking back, yanking harder when I falter. My shoulder screams in protest, but I bite back my yelp. Pain is pointless now. Pain will not save Blythe. My thoughts spiral anyway, her curled against the wall, silent. The way she looked at me.

I broke her. I have broken everything.

Unjudged souls flatten themselves against the walls as we pass. None meet my eyes. A few look at me with something like pity. Most look afraid, not of me, but of him. The air changes as we step into the library. Damp. Old. Magic-sour. Each step forward feels like being lowered into a grave. The labyrinth entrance yawns open ahead of us, pulsing like a slow, waiting heartbeat, and it recognizes me the moment I cross the threshold. My knees nearly buckle.

Osiris moves through the labyrinth as if it were etched into his bones, his fingertips gliding along the ever-shifting stone as he drags me behind him. The walls breathe and crawl, rearranging themselves with quiet intent. Behind us, Fallon and a mob of villagers follow in a vacant procession, eyes dull, steps perfectly in sync, puppets on a string.

The floor ahead *opens*.

Stone peels away into a chasm, a gaping maw in the path. I know, *I know*, it is an illusion, another trick of the labyrinth, but instinct screams louder than reason. I wrench backward, heart lurching, nails scraping uselessly against stone as my body fights to save itself.

"Enough," Osiris snarls. He grabs my arm with both hands and *yanks* me forward.

The world drops out from under me. Weightlessness steals my breath, my stomach flipping violently as I squeeze my eyes shut. For one terrible, fleeting moment, relief washes over me.

At least this way, I do not doom an entire realm.

Then the ground slams back into existence beneath my feet, and Osiris is hauling me upright again, the illusion snapping away as if it had never been there. The doors loom ahead, massive and ancient, and he throws them open without hesitation. I barely register my surroundings as he half-drags, half-carries me across the catwalk.

Each step feels like a countdown.

Every instinct inside me screams to fight.

To run.

To turn back, *to save Blythe*. Run *where*? Do *what*?

I need space. Time. One breath away from him to think, just one.

He rips me back against him by the hair, then shoves me forward until my face is inches from the veil. The force nearly crushes my nose against its shimmering surface. The air hums, alive and wrong, vibrating straight through my skull.

"I can see your wheels turning, Little Hellion," Osiris murmurs into my ear, his voice low and pleased. "Do not." His grip tightens. "One wrong move, and I will send my friends to tear your little foxy friend to pieces," he pauses, "You would not want that, now would you?"

My heart pounds so hard it hurts. I shake my head, barely, desperately, but it is enough.

He loosens his hold, just slightly.

"Good," he growls. "Now open it."

There is no choice. The realization lands heavy and final, crushing the air from my lungs. Regret blooms instantly, hot and suffocating, but my arm still rises, traitorous and trembling. I press my hand to the veil. I think of Elysia, of its golden spires and airy streets, of laughter drifting through open skies, of people who have no idea what is about to break through their world, and the veil begins to respond.

I can already feel it...

Everything unraveling.

Chapter 9

Endricks

Loud metal bowls crash down against the stone floor, jarring me awake.

"Chow time, dogs!" the guard yells smugly.

My ears ring from the sound of metal on stone clanging through the cells, and I crack my eyes open. The guard smiles down at me, and I blankly stare back, reaching for the bowl of slop, chains rattling as they drag across the ground. I snatch up the bowl and sling it at the metal bars, minced meat and god knows what landing across his uniform. A smile creeps across my face, watching it drip down the side of his cheek. "Thought I might share," I say with a nod.

"You entitled, little bastard. I will have your ass for this," the guard growls, wiping the slop from his face. He wildly digs through his pocket, pulling out a set of keys. He thumbs through them, never taking his eyes off me. Jamming it into the lock, he turns the key and swings open the door; it flies into the metal bars, vibrating the entire cell.

I cannot help but chuckle at his tantrum.

He stomps across the room, still wiping minced meat from his uniform. Jerking me up by my collar, he slams me into the wall. "You are in my house now, you pathetic piece of shit. Your daddy left me in charge, and I choose when you take your last breath." He presses my face to the wall, growling, "Do you understand?"

"Oh, yes," I mumble, "How I await the sweet kiss of death."

He drops me, letting me slide down the gritty stone wall. "Arrogant asshole," he spits. Trudging out, he slams the cell door shut. "Welcome to Greybar," he smirks, as the bars of my cell shake.

Rolling to my back, I look up at the rusted metal ceiling. I take in a deep breath, pushing it out slowly. *Osiris's poison must be wearing off, ignorant bitch.* Sharp pain runs through my chest. *Is that a fractured rib from Adonis or the gaping hole in my sternum? It will buff out.* I pinch the bridge of my nose, rolling my eyes, as torturess screams begin to fill the corridors. *Begging will do you no good in Greybar. I have learned that lesson at least a thousand times down here.* I drag my eyes from the ceiling, taking in my view. The same familiar cell, every gash and dent still stands as a reminder of my childhood. My blood still stains the stone floor, almost taunting me. I walked this small cage day and night, broke every dish and cup handed to me, and took every gruesome torture session from within these four walls. I glance across the hall to the empty cell and my stomach drops, my breath hitching in my throat. I drop my head back, unable to look any longer, and memories unwillingly pour in.

Shaking, I hid under the covers, my body stiff against your arm. You held me so tight I thought my bones might break, but I would not dare say a word. The soldiers banged so hard on the bedchamber doors that our portraits fell from the walls, shattering across the onyx floors. You gently hushed me, kissing the top of my head. The wooden doors splintered under the pressure, and a slew of guards rushed in, destroying everything in sight. I kicked and bit every asshole that attempted to lay a hand on you...But I was small, and so disgustingly weak. Watching as they tore you from me, muzzling and beating you to the ground, will forever be etched into my mind.

Father's face appeared in the sea of monsters, and I fell to my knees begging him to save you. His face twisted with disgust, and he turned away, waving a hand towards a lieutenant. The lieutenant locked eyes with me and pushed through the crowd. My heart leaped, knowing we were being saved, then it all came crashing down. A bag was pulled over my head. Hands grabbed at me, tying my wrists behind my back. I screamed for you, begged with snot running down my face. Then silence fell over me.

I awoke to your cries, pleading for me to be spared. My eyes adjusted, and I took in my own personal Hell. A collar, locked tight around my neck, and metal bars surrounding me. You were shackled at the wrist and ankles in the cell across from me, beaten and bruised. You wore a smile through every lashing, and when they realized you would not break, they opted for emotional warfare. Your bright blue eyes slowly lost their spark with every tear that dripped down my face. I was chained to your cell door, forced to watch for five hundred years as they tortured you for my weakness, starved you for your kindness, and ultimately killed you for power. You were right out of my grasp, and now your voice will haunt me for eternity, Mother.

Chapter 10

Endricks

"Endricks?" Valker chokes out, pulling me from my nightmare.

"Valker," I whisper.

"You good?"

"Never better," I grind out, shaking off the remnants of my memories.

"I hope this girl is truly worth all of this."

"That *woman's name* is Edin," I say, my voice catching in my throat, "and she will always be worth it." I squeeze my eyes shut, taking a breath. "Even if she were not, the look on Adonis's face would be. Also, you may want to watch your tone. You might just be meeting her soon in the afterlife with the life choices *you* have been making."

"Life choices, as in saving your ass?"

"Oh yes, Valker, I am quite safe. Thank you. What exactly was your plan again?"

"Well... I didn't really have a plan. The news of your return spread like wildfire, and I just knew your ass was grass," Valker says with a laugh, then a cough.

"How are you holding up?"

"Eh, just a busted forehead, maybe a broken rib or two, possibly a concussion."

"It will buff out," we say in unison.

"Just like old times," Valker says with a wince. Dirt scuffles in the background as he pulls himself up to the small barred window that connects to my cell.

I glance over to the empty cell, then back. "Sure," I mumble, looking at him from the floor. I pull myself up, grunting through the pain shooting from my chest. "That is quite a shiner you have," I chuckle, looking over his disheveled face. Blue and purple hues surround his right eye, traveling up his forehead. Dried blood has stained his icy white hair a deep shade of red, and a small nick across his throat has begun to scab over.

"You don't look much better yourself," Valker smirks, pulling his matted hair from his face. "With a still bleeding hole in your chest, and blue veins streaking your face, I would mistake you for the undead."

"Minor details, Valker."

The halls fall unnaturally silent as the access gate groans open somewhere beyond the cells. The sound crawls through the corridors, heavy and deliberate. I lift an eyebrow toward Valker and take my place at the bars, already bracing. Boots strike stone. I know that cadence better than my own heartbeat. The torches dim, their flames sputtering as the air thickens. Shadows stretch along the walls, and an inky blue mist coils at my feet, cold and familiar. Whispers slither through the halls, soft, reverent, and afraid. My blood ignites, and my eye twitches. "Father," I say, the word a blade between my teeth.

"Endricks," Adonis replies, his form peeling out of the vapor as if the darkness itself were giving birth to him. He gestures lazily toward the cell. The bars hum in response. "Back where you belong, I see."

I bare my teeth in something close to a smile. "I am quite fond of what you have done with the place in my absence. Cozy. Really leans into the *tyrant* aesthetic."

He shoves his hand through the bars, clamping down on my neck. The world narrows, and air vanishes. He lifts me off the ground with infuriating ease, eyes burning like coal as he drags my face close to his. "You will rot here," he snarls. "You are nothing but a disgrace. A mistake I should have corrected long ago."

I gasp, vision darkening at the edges, but I refuse to look away. "Funny," I choke, a grin cutting through the pain. "The apple does not fall far from the tree, I suppose."

Adonis tightens his grip. Spots bloom across my vision, bright and furious, but I refuse to give him the satisfaction of looking away. The bars dig into my chest as he pins me there, the magic in the cell reacting to his presence, runes flaring, metal screaming softly under the strain.

"You think defiance is strength," he says calmly, almost conversational. That has always been the worst part. "But it's just noise. You were born to serve a purpose, Endricks. You failed it."

From the corner of my eye, I see Valker move. Just a fraction. A shift of weight. A mistake. A ripple of power snaps through the corridor like a warning growl. Adonis does not even look at him, but the ink-blue mist lashes out, slamming Valker back against his cell wall, and the chains rattle violently.

"Do not," Adonis says mildly, "interrupt a family discussion."

My blood burns hotter than the lack of air. "Touch him again," I rasp, forcing the words past crushed lungs, "and I will tear your kingdom down, stone by stone."

Adonis finally smiles. It is slow, cold, and proud. "There he is," he murmurs. "That fire. That arrogance. You always did confuse cruelty with conviction." He leans closer, his forehead nearly touching mine. I can smell the magic on him, ozone and ash and something rotten beneath it all. "She is not yours to protect," he continues softly, "And he," his gaze flicks briefly toward Valker, "is not yours to save."

My hands curl uselessly at my sides. The collar at my throat hums, suppressing every instinct to burn him alive where he stands. "You are afraid," I choke out. The grip on my collar tightens just enough to hurt.

"Of what?" he growls.

"Of what I become," I whisper, "without you."

For a heartbeat, the torches gutter violently. The whispers swell, frantic and excited, like the walls themselves are holding their breath. Adonis's expression hardens. He releases me abruptly. I drop to the floor, gasping, hands scratching against the stone as air tears back into my lungs. Blood splatters the floor between my knees.

Adonis straightens, smoothing his cuffs as if nothing of consequence had just happened. "Enjoy your stay," he says coolly. "Now, we shall remind you why this place exists." He turns, his form already dissolving back into shadow and mist.

As the torches flare back to life and the pressure lifts, I look up just in time to see him pause at the end of the corridor.

"Oh," he adds without turning. "Valker?"

Valker stiffens.

"You survived this prison once," Adonis says pleasantly. "That was mercy." The mist swallows him whole, and silence crashes down.

I drag myself upright, gripping the bars as my breathing steadies. My hands shake, not from fear, but anger. I glance toward Valker. He is pale, jaw tight, eyes locked on the space where my father stood.

"We're dead," he mutters.

I smile, slow and sharp, despite the blood on my teeth. "I will make sure you make it out of here alive. You have a sister to get back to."

"What about Edin?"

"She is better off without me, even if it is with that arrogant, possessive dog of an Elysian. She is out of my father's reach."

Before Valker can argue, every torch in the corridor extinguishes at once. Darkness crashes down. Cries for mercy erupt from the cells, frantic and overlapping, and voices crack as panic spreads through the halls. Boots thunder against stone, drawing closer, multiplied by the echoes until it sounds like an army is coming for us. Metal shrieks as bars are thrown open, the noise slicing through the chaos.

"It's showtime, boys!" a guard shouts, laughter sharp and eager.

I slide back down the wall, the last of my strength bleeding out of me. Thoughts of Edin surge forward, unbidden and relentless, filling every crack the fear tries to seep into, and I accept my fate. The cold creeps through my clothes, biting into skin already raw and bruised, but I let it. I cling to it. Pain is grounding; it is proof that I am still here, still breathing. Vanilla and clove linger in my memory. Gold eyes. A sharp tongue and a softer heart, one she never lets anyone see for long. Then my door slams open, rattling the chains on my wrist, and a sack is jerked over my head.

If this is how it ends, then I will meet it with her name on my lips.

Chapter 11

Edin

The blood of innocent people is on my hands.

Osiris, Fallon, and his *traitorous* group of souls dissolve into the veil, their forms unraveling like smoke. My stomach turns as bile rises in my throat, then whatever strength I have left abandons me. I hit the stone floor hard; exhaustion, shame, or both stealing the breath from my lungs. Before I can recover, Osiris's minions, *my villagers*, *my betrayers*, push off the walls and seize my wrists, dragging me upright.

I kick and strike blindly, wasting what little energy remains. My cheek slams into cold stone, and the sound of locks snapping shut echoes in my skull. Someone hauls me up and throws me over his shoulder like cargo.

"I do not understand!" I scream, pounding his back. "Why would you follow him? I have not even passed judgment on you yet!"

He laughs in a low, hollow sound. "We were condemned to Helheim long before Purgatory ever took us. Osiris promised Elysia," he adjusts his grip. "Freedom."

"He is a liar," I snarl. "A traitor. And you are nothing more than pawns."

No one answers. They exchange looks, annoyance flickering between them as we wind through the labyrinth. Every turn tightens the knot in my gut. When the final wall grinds open, and the staircase appears, dread crashes over me, followed swiftly by rage.

We march through the castle halls. I crane my neck, searching desperately for Sera, for anyone, but the halls fall eerily quiet. When we reach the dungeon, my thoughts splinter into frantic escape plans that never quite form. Every step down the stairs, a new plan comes to my mind, then falls through the cracks as we descend. They throw me down and fasten my restraints to the iron ring embedded in the wall. The door slams shut, and that sound is like permission to speak again.

"Blythe," I whisper.

She looks up. Tears streak her face, but when our eyes meet, something hardens inside her: resolve, sharp and unyielding, like she has read my mind. She grabs her collar and follows the chain to the wall, yanking violently at the links.

"Get these damned chains off me, Edin," she growls. "His ass is mine."

I draw on my magic. It rises sluggishly, pooling in my chest before spilling down my arms, burning as it reaches my fingertips. I brace myself and release it into the chains.

The iron screams. The links rattle and buck against my power. Cracks splinter across the metal, and for a moment, hope flares inside my chest. Then the mist shifts, purple turning to sickly gray, and the magic lashes back along the chain, slamming into my neck. Pain detonates through me. I collapse to my knees, gasping.

"The enchantment," I choke. "They are warded. Magic will not break them."

I watch in horror as the fractures seal, the metal smoothing as if it had never been touched. The air grows thick, heavy with fear and resolve tangled together. My hands shake. I curl them into fists, trying to anchor myself as panic claws upward. The need to move quickly overwhelms my thoughts, sending me into a spiral.

How long before Osiris reaches the Elysian army?

How many will die before anyone stops him?

Will he be stopped?

The ground shudders beneath us, pulling me from thought. I jerk my head up as the tremors deepen, violent enough to rattle my teeth, like something ancient is waking beneath the stone.

"Blythe," I say urgently, "I do not know what is happening, but we have to leave. Now."

No answer.

"Blythe!"

I spin around to find her kneeling, utterly still, eyes closed, with palms pressed flat to the floor. The stone beneath her hands fractures, glowing faintly as green mist pours from the cracks.

"Blythe!"

"Shh."

The floor splits open. Thick green vines erupt upward, writhing with purpose. I stagger back, pressing myself against the wall as they weave through her chains, threading impossibly tight between iron and skin. They coil beneath her collar, and her breath stutters. Veins stand out sharply on her forehead as the vines twist, forcing space where there is none. Her lips fade to blue.

"Stop!" I shout, fighting against my restraints. "This is not working! You are going to kill yourself!"

Her body trembles violently, but she does not release the spell.

"Blythe!"

A sharp metallic *ting* cuts through the air. Something flashes past my head. I duck instinctively as the chain bursts apart, link by link, each snap echoing like a gunshot. The destruction races upward, faster. The collar explodes open with a clang and crashes to the floor. Blythe collapses forward, dragging in a ragged breath, coughing hard as she braces herself on shaking arms.

"Oh gods," I breathe. "Blythe, are you alright?"

Her coughing breaks into laughter. Hoarse. Breathless. Alive.

"I thought you were going to suffocate," I snap, my own laughter tearing loose as relief finally hits.

"But I didn't," she says with a crooked grin. She pushes herself upright and wipes her mouth. "Okay," she looks at me. "Your turn."

Blythe plants her feet and presses her palms together. The green mist curls back toward her like it is being reeled in, sinking into her skin until only hairline fractures glow faintly in the stone. She exhales once, steadying herself, then turns fully to face me.

"Hold still," she says, already moving.

"I am not the one flailing vines at my own throat," I mutter, but I do as she asks.

She crouches in front of me, eyes sharp now, the lingering haze of pain burned away by focus. Her fingers hover inches from my collar, not touching it yet, as if she is listening to something I cannot hear.

"They keyed the enchantment to you," she says quietly. "Authority. Judgment. That whole… divine echo you carry."

"Can you break it?"

"Yes," she says, without hesitation. Then, softer, "It's going to hurt."

I huff a weak laugh, "That seems to be the theme."

She places one hand flat against the stone and the other against the chain at my throat. The moment she makes contact, the dungeon groans, deep and protesting, as if the walls themselves object. Green light bleeds from beneath her palm, flooding the links. Vines do not erupt this time. Instead, they seep, thin as veins, crawling along the metal, burrowing into the seams.

The collar tightens suddenly. I gasp as pressure clamps down, crushing. Fire lances up my spine. My vision goes white.

“Blythe,” I choke, and my eyes bulge.

“I know,” she snaps. “Don't pull away. If you fight it, it will lock.”

My hands clench uselessly at my sides. I grit my teeth, forcing myself to be still as the enchantment surges, sensing the challenge. The collar heats, burning my skin. I can smell scorched iron. The vines glow brighter.

“Now,” Blythe growls, and she twists her wrist.

The collar does not explode; it *unravels*. The metal peels apart like bark stripped from a dying tree, falling away in warped, useless fragments. The chain slithers loose and collapses to the floor with a dull, final clatter. I suck in air, deep and desperate, my knees buckling as sensation crashes back into my limbs. Blythe lunges forward and catches me before I hit the stone.

"Easy," she says, bracing me. "I've got you."

For a heartbeat, I let myself lean into her, wrapping her in my arms, breathing in the familiar sweetness of jasmine. Then the world crashes back into place.

"Do you remember what happened at the veil? Or have any idea where Nyx is? I cannot sense him."

Blythe's ears turn down. "No, everything is such a blur. Osiris most likely wants to keep you two separated. His ego can't take on *that* type of power all at once," she smirks. "I'm sure Nyx is okay. We will find him," she says, pulling me tighter.

I pull away. "We have to get to Windemere," I say quietly. "We need to warn the king about Osiris's plan."

"Fucking prick," she growls.

"Blythe," I hesitate, then force the words out. "I need you to go to Windemere. I have to go to Helheim."

Her head snaps up. "Absolutely not. We handle this together. We warn the king, then…" she breaks off with a frustrated groan. "Then we find Endricks."

"It is safer this way," I snap, sharper than I mean to be. "You are safe. I have already dragged you into too much."

"This isn't up for discussion, Edin." Her fox ears dip, flattening against her hair. "I won't let you do this alone."

She looks at me with nothing but love, and I know I have already lost. I sigh. She knows it too. Straightening my shoulders, I push myself to my feet. My legs tremble, weak and unsteady, but they hold.

"Alright," Blythe says briskly, already scanning the dungeon. "Up and out, before someone notices the missing chains."

A shiver runs up my spine. The dungeon feels wrong now. Too quiet. The air is thick and damp, like the stone itself is sweating. Torches burn low, their flames sputtering as we pass. I stretch my senses outward, listening for footsteps, for steel, for raised voices, but all I hear is the distant groan of the castle settling around us.

"This way," I murmur, guiding us toward the service stair.

We climb fast, boots striking stone far too loudly in the silence. Blythe stays close, one hand brushing the wall, her magic coiled tight beneath her skin. Every turn sends a spike of tension through me, waiting for a shout, a blade, a locked door, yet nothing comes. I shove through the door at the top. It skids across the stone, echoing down the hall. I freeze, bracing for chaos. Nothing.

The castle above is dim and abandoned, as though everyone has fled or is hiding. Doors stand ajar. Banners hang slack, their sigils barely visible in the low light. The deeper we go, the colder the air grows, threaded with something old and metallic that prickles against my skin.

"The lower passage," I whisper. "It leads to the labyrinth. I saw it when the goons carried me back. They did not realize it was a shortcut."

"That's reassuring," Blythe mutters.

We duck through and descend again, this time into tighter, older stone. The carved grandeur of the castle gives way to rough rock and narrow corridors worn smooth by centuries of passage. My magic hums faintly here, tugged forward by something deep and patient. The labyrinth greets us without ceremony.

The moment we cross the threshold, the air thickens. Sound dulls, swallowed whole. The walls begin to shift, not suddenly, but deliberately, stone sliding against stone with a slow, grinding sigh.

Blythe exhales through her teeth. “I hate when it does that.”

“It is deciding,” I whisper. “Whether to let us pass.”

We move carefully, following turns that feel right rather than logical. Passages stretch or narrow ahead of us, guiding, testing. The weight of judgment presses against my chest, not accusation, but recognition. Then, without warning, we are allowed through. The corridors widen. The stone smooths beneath our feet, etched with faded sigils older than the castle itself. It feels as though the labyrinth understands and knows the realms are in danger. My magic stirs, tingling in my fingers, sparks snapping faintly at the tips.

"The veil is close," I say.

We turn the corner, and the torches flare to life one by one, illuminating the path to the Room of Revelation. Relief floods through me so fast it nearly knocks the breath from my lungs. I grab Blythe's hand and pull her down the hall. The doors stand wide open. Everything is exactly as we left it.

Lavender mist spills across the catwalk from the veil, shimmering on the dark water below. We walk hand in hand, each step tightening the knot in my gut. Magic ignites beneath my skin, crawling up my arms as purple veins streak along them and climb my neck. I reach toward the swirling vortex, fixing Windemere in my mind. Blythe steps closer, ears twitching with anticipation. She squeezes my arm, then lets go and moves ahead.

I force out a slow breath, loathing myself.

"I am sorry, Blythe."

Before she can even register what is happening, I shove her through the veil. I clamp my palm shut instantly, tearing the seams between me and home, shredding the connection until the rift seals completely, until I know, without doubt, that she is safe.

A faint black shadow catches my attention. I watch it seep into the veil as it snaps shut with a sound like bones cracking. The lavender mist recoils violently, collapsing inward as the image of Windemere fractures and vanishes. The sudden silence is deafening. No hum. No pull. Just the echo of my own breathing and the burn of magic screaming through my veins. I stagger back a step, fingers curling into a fist as the last threads sever.

The moment stretches empty, wrong. My chest tightens so sharply I have to brace myself against the railing to stay upright. I can still feel her warmth on my arm, the phantom pressure of her hand squeezing mine, and the memory makes something inside me tear loose.

“I am sorry,” I whisper again, pushing off the rail. I bring my hand back up to the veil and set my intentions on Heleheim.

Chapter 12

Endricks

***

Screams of terror and pain ring out all around me. I can not make out exactly where they are dragging me to, but from the rising temperature, I assume we are headed deeper into Greybar. Rocks scrape and dig into my spine as the guard pulls me across the stone floors. Every turn, I am pulled against the sharp corner of a wall. *Hospitality at its finest.* The wails begin to fade as we descend until I am left only with the sound of footsteps and my heartbeat.

The guard comes to a halt, dropping my wrists with a thud. “Home sweet home, bastard,” he laughs.

I sigh, unamused with his antics. The old rusted iron door skids open against the rough floor, and the smell of copper and mold invades my nostrils. The scent is familiar, even without my vision, I know where we are. They pull me over the threshold and toss me to the ground. Hands grab at my chained wrists, jerking them up tight above my head. My shoulders burn in pain at the uncomfortable position. Something cold slams into my throat, knocking the air from my lungs. Choking, I hear the click of a lock behind me, and the soft hum of a rune coming to life.

I slam my eyes shut as the sack is yanked from my head. Squinting, I look around my new room. Two guards stand in front of me, arms crossed, with a smug look of satisfaction smeared across their faces. The guards do not speak at first; they do not need to. Silence does the work for them.

The room is smaller than I remember. Stone walls slick from humidity, carved with sigils so old they have been worn smooth by blood and time. Chains dangle from iron rings like the remains of failed prayers. The rune at my throat hums steadily, vibrating against my skin, restraining my power.

One of the guards steps closer. He does not bother hiding his smile. “Still breathing,” he says. “Won’t last.” He drives his knee into my ribs.

Pain shoots through my side, sharp and blinding. Air tears from my lungs as I fold forward, gagging. The chains bite deeper into my wrists as I struggle uselessly, vision swimming. I hear laughter, low, casual, almost practiced.

“Commander said no interrogation,” the other guard adds. “Just make it slow.”

They release the chains without warning. I hit the floor hard, bones rattling as the world tilts. My body screams to curl inward, but the rune flares hot against my throat, searing heat spreading like fire under my skin. I choke, clawing at my neck as my muscles lock, every breath scraping like broken glass.

One of the guards circles me slowly, boots scraping against the stone, each step deliberate, measuring, waiting for my breathing to betray me.

"Careful," the other says mildly. "If he dies too quickly, you'll replace him."

That earns a nervous laugh. The chains are wrenched up again, this time lower, pinning my arms behind me, forcing my chest open. Exposed. Vulnerable. The rune at my throat flares once, hot enough to blister, then settles, extinguishing what magic I have left.

The guard crouches in front of me. I can see his eyes now, flat, uninterested. This is not anger, just procedure.

"You've died before," he says. "More than once, if the records are accurate."

I refuse to respond, knowing that is what he wants: panic, fear, a rise in me.

"That makes you dangerous," he continues. "Men who expect death stop fearing it. So we teach them something worse."

The other guard steps forward with a thin, hooked instrument, etched with markings that crawl when the light hits them. He presses it against my ribs, not hard, just enough to promise what is coming.

"Don't scream," the guard says calmly. "It makes the timing difficult."

The first cut is shallow. It burns rather than slices, heat searing down into the muscle. I jerk instinctively, breath hitching, and the marks respond instantly. My chest locks mid-inhale, lungs screaming for air I am not allowed to take. I sink my mind elsewhere, anywhere, to endure the pain. My thoughts land on shining golden eyes, and I settle in.

That night in the shack, I never slept a wink, though she thought I did. I lay there in the dark, listening. Watching. Memorizing the way her breathing shifted once sleep finally claimed her, the way she mumbled half-formed thoughts under her breath, nonsense words, and soft complaints that made my chest ache. When she turned in her sleep, her long black hair spilled over me, brushing my skin, carrying the faint scent of vanilla and clove with it. Warm. Comforting. Dangerous.

He drags the blade again, never deep enough to kill, but always deep enough to hurt. New blood begins to drip from the corners of my mouth and nose. Each line ignites another wave of fire, another stolen breath, another moment teetering on the edge of black. They pace it carefully. Pain. Suffocation. Relief. Repeat.

Training my body to crave the moments between agony. My vision tunnels. My heartbeat stutters. My limbs shake violently as the rune tightens its hold, shutting me down piece by piece. Just when the darkness finally surges close enough to touch, he stops. The rune cools. Air floods my lungs in a brutal rush. I gasp, choking, every nerve screaming as sensation crashes back in. Then I sink back in.

She was beautiful, even here. Even in a place so bleak it tried to swallow the light. Morning crept in slowly, gray and unwelcome, but it could not touch her. When she stirred and opened her eyes, they were still that impossible shade of gold, bright and sharp and alive. She caught me staring and gawked, like I had been caught doing something criminal.

Squatting down, he watches me breathe, then jerks me up by my collar. A smile creeps across his face, knowing the amount of torment I refuse to show. I blankly stare back, meeting his gaze. His eyes narrow, and his lip begins to twitch, anger boiling inside him. He tightens his grip and slams my head, crashing into the wall. Pain radiates through my skull, sounding off like a canon. The tip of my horn cracks, flying across the room. I can no longer fight the darkness as my world begins to spin, black specks shrouding my vision. He smiles again, finally content with himself, his ego full. I faintly watch them nod to each other in satisfaction and stride out, the door locking shut behind them. Darkness floods my sight completely. I choke for air, coughing up blood. I lean my head back, sinking back into thought, hoping it will drown me.

I smiled before I could stop myself. Every quick-witted remark she threw my way sent my heart skipping, each one landing like a promise and a warning all at once. She did not know it then, but I was already lost. Already counting the ways the world might put out her flame, and already deciding it never would.

Chapter 13

Osiris

I step out of the mist at the summit of Castle Elysia. For a heartbeat, I do nothing but stand there, truly honoring this moment. The highest tower rises above all others, its circular chamber bathed in gold and old magic. Light spills through the arched windows, catching on gilded stone and glittering draperies, illuminating dust that has not settled in centuries. Metal sconces line the walls, and thick pillar candles burn steadily, as if they have been waiting for me. Everything is exactly as I remember it, exactly as it should be.

I inhale deeply, filling my lungs with the familiar air of my homeland. Power hums beneath the marble floor, thrumming up through my boots and into my bones. This tower was built to house power, to anchor the veil between realms, and soon, it will be mine.

My lips curve slowly.

"Gods," I murmur, reverent and amused. "It is good to be home."

Only then do I draw my sword, the steel whispering free. Fallon steps in beside me without a word, perfectly aligned, while the veil behind us fractures wider. My unjudged souls pour through in a silent tide, flooding the tower, flanking us on either side, patient, obedient, and lethal.

My army moves like a living organism, a mass of worker bees with a single purpose: overtake the castle and place me on the throne. Chaos magic threads through each of their minds, bending will and thought to my own. They think as I think. Move as I move. Kill as I kill. Together, we are unstoppable, an inevitability no one will see coming until it is far too late.

The first guards stationed within the tower barely have time to react. Steel rings out, and screams are cut short as we advance downward, step by step, carving our way through the spiraling staircase. Blades clash briefly before bodies fall, blood streaking the stone as those meant to protect this tower are cut down by the very general they once served.

Nostalgia gnaws at the edges of my thoughts.

How many of these men once fought beside me? Learned from me? Broke bread with me before my banishment? Now they will witness the fall of the city they helped steal from me with front-row seats to its undoing. Too bad most of them will not live long enough to see my reign.

At the very least, they will know who ended them. Their part in my exile will flash through their minds just as death takes them. In the end, all realms will fall under my rule, and the soldiers I grew up with will become part of my army once more. Everything will come full circle.

I will finally be seen for who and what I am.

The rightful king.

The ruler of all realms.

We descend relentlessly, my army flooding each level behind us, overtaking corridors and checkpoints with brutal efficiency. By the time the alarm bells begin to sound, it is already far too late. Taking the castle from the inside is one of the most brilliant strategies I have ever devised. The strongest divisions of my army hold the outer walls and gates. While Elysia scrambles to defend its perimeter, I am already at its heart.

We slip down the halls and into the castle proper, silent and lethal. My soldiers melt into the shadows along the walls, leaving the corridors eerily empty. I reach outward with my mind, my form splitting and multiplying as I take shape behind each of the five guards stationed at the throne room doors.

One by one.

A hand clamped over a mouth. A dagger is driven up beneath the ribs, piercing straight into the chest cavity. Clean. Efficient. Fatal. The guards crumple in unison, faces frozen in shock. My minions catch their bodies before they strike the floor, easing them down without a sound.

This is what an army should be: mindless killing machines, nothing more, nothing less. And to think... this is what I was exiled for.

The irony nearly makes me laugh.

The doors to the Great Hall loom ahead, massive slabs of reinforced wood and iron meant to withstand sieges.

I smile.

"Knock, knock."

My soldiers surge forward, slamming themselves against the doors with the force of thousands. The impact reverberates through the castle, echoing down every corridor. Again and again they strike, bodies shattering against the wood, skulls cracking like eggs, blood painting the stone, but they do not stop. The doors splinter, iron buckling as the wood finally gives way, crashing inward with a thunderous boom. Dust and debris billow into the hall beyond, screams following close behind.

The sea of bodies parts as Fallon and I stride forward, stepping through the wreckage and into the Great Hall.

Into my destiny.

CHAPTER 14

EDIN

Please forgive me, Blythe.

Electricity crawls down my arms as I step through the purple mist. My chest seems to fill with the strangest sensation, as if a swarm of moths have made their home deep inside my ribcage. Then warmth tingles in my fingertips, slowly making its way up my forearms. My foot lands on the dark obsidian stone floors as I take in the room. Runes burn along the stone walls, violent, shifting sigils that crawl and rewrite themselves in streaks of ember-red and sickly violet. The floor is veined with slow-moving crimson light, as if lava pulses just beneath the surface, trapped under a thin skin of stone.

I slowly push through the large iron double doors, finding lit torches that hang along the walls between portraits of stone-cold-looking men. I squint my eyes, trying to see an opening at either end of this long hallway. Without a single window, the darkness seems perpetual. Faint, tortured screams echo from both ends, sending shivers down my spine. The smoky air fills my lungs, catching in my throat. My stomach clenches as I turn left and begin down the corridor, praying to the gods that I do not come face to face with King Adonis.

Quietly, I slip down the hall, swallowing the foreboding ache in my gut and the creeping feeling that I am being watched. Each portrait feels as if their eyes track my every move. Most of the paintings depict King Adonis; his cruel ego radiates from his smug face, making me grimace. His dark brown, almost black eyes seem to bore straight into my soul. Long raven hair falls around his smooth face, framing a deep scar that extends from his temple to his chin. He stands tall in front of the gates of Helheim, clothed in a tailored black suit with an intricate gold crown that reminds me of thorns. A deep blue mist emits from his large stature, and thousands of souls surround him, kneeling in his presence, making my stomach churn. My hair stands on end at the thought of him and his vile plans.

A glimpse of blue pulls me to the next frame, where flames flicker around a silhouette, and my gaze lands on a young Endricks. I run my hand over the portrait, wiping away the smoky film. The warmth I felt in my fingertips travels further up my arms into my chest, accompanied by a faint pounding. He looks remarkably young, and his eyes have a spark of life that flourishes within them. My heart drops as I take in the owner of the arms that seem to wrap him so lovingly. A woman with long opalescent hair and large black horns embraces him. Her face is completely burned through to the stone wall behind the frame. Tears brim in my lids because I know this can be only one person. *Endrick's mother.* I drag myself away, pushing forward to find Endricks before he meets the same end.

The smell of smoke and brimstone grows stronger as I reach the end of the hall. My ears begin to ring, and the room spins. The faint pounding in my chest turns to an undeniably slow, steady beat. *Endricks.* I lay my hand across my heart, and my eyes water, feeling our bond again. Footsteps echo from around the corner, jerking me from my small victory. I press my back against the stone wall, sliding as far as I can towards a protruding torch to hide myself, begging the gods to become one with the stone. Taking in a shallow breath, attempting not to make a single sound, smoke fills my lungs. My eyes burn, and my lungs plead for air as I try to hold back a cough. Tears stream down my cheeks as the footsteps grow louder. *Please just keep walking.* My vision goes spotty, and I can barely see the shadow cast down the hall. *Keep walking.* The blurry, short silhouette of a figure comes into view and continues by. I throw my head up, silently thanking the gods. *Finally, the* footsteps fade off, and I slide down the wall, exhaling. My throat burns from the smoke, and a cough escapes my lips. I slam my hand over my mouth, not daring to move.

"Hello?" the figure calls out. "State your business." Footsteps begin moving towards me again, but far more quickly.

Shit.

I jump to my feet, swiftly moving to the other wall and conjuring all my magic into one palm, while my other hand rests on the hilt of my dagger. I steady myself, ready for whatever hellish beast awaits me. A shadow casts down from around the corner, and I lunge forward. A grunt echoes through the corridors as my magic wraps around his shoulders, and I shove him into the wall. I press my dagger to his neck, and a yelp escapes his lips.

"Please!" he chokes out, waving his hands in defense. Fire spits and sputters from smoldering cracks along his skin.

The cry for help startles me, and I blink twice as I look the small figure over. He barely reaches the height of my hips. "Tell me where Endricks is," I demand, pushing the blade harder against his throat.

"Lord Endricks?" the fire sprite stutters out.

"Yes! Tell me where he is!"

The sprite shakingly pulls his head up to my gaze. "Edin? Goddess of Purgatory?"

I turn my nose up. "Yes, and I demand you tell me where Lord Endricks is!"

The sprite slouches and exhales, steam puffing out of the cracks across his face. "Oh, Miss Edin, it is so pleasant to be in your presence finally! I have waited so very long for this moment! I have heard nothing but the kindest of words about you."

Dumbfounded, I stare down at him. "I do not understand," I grind out, still holding the dagger.

"My apologies, let me introduce myself." He looks down at my dagger, then back up to me.

I roll my eyes with a huff and jerk my dagger away, slipping it back into my thigh holster. He straightens his bow tie and swipes the dust from his blazer. "I am Oren, fire sprite, and footman of Lord Endricks," he says with a bow. "I can take you to Lord Endricks, but…brace yourself."

My heart sinks, "For what?"

Oren fidgets with his hands, stuttering out, "Since his return…King Adonis has been quite…*upset* with his failure."

"*Failure?* Failure to what?"

"To secure *you*, Miss Edin. You may be his fated mate, but you must willingly choose him as your partner, and from the looks of how he returned to Helheim…it would seem he failed."

"And where is he now?" Oren stares up at me, his lip quivering. "Oren!"

"In his old cell…in Greybar…Helheim's Prison. As I said before, King Adonis was very disappointed at his return without you, Goddess."

Rage builds within me, "*He* did not want *me* as his partner!"

"Even if that is true, King Adonis demands it, and he does not take well to not receiving what he wishes."

"Take me to Endricks," I growl

"As you wish, Your Highness."

"Do *not* call me that."

"Yes, Miss Edin," Oren stutters out as his cracks smolder.

Chapter 15

Edin

"This way," Oren beckons to a small door at the other end of the hall. "Pull your hood up to shroud your identity."

I lower my head, squeezing myself through the sprite-sized door. The narrow passage connects to a tunnel system within the walls of the castle. Bells hang periodically along the raw stone walls. I cover my ears as they ring off by the hundreds.

"These are the servant tunnels; they connect to the entire castle. Each bell that rings is a demand from an upper rank, and they are…very demanding as you can see," Oren says with a shrug.

"Clearly," I roll my eyes. I could not fathom demanding so much from Sera, or even looking at her as a servant. She has become family. We squeeze past bustling sprites and duck under trays carrying steaming plates of food. Whispers bounce off the walls, and I feel eyes glued to my back.

"Oren?" I whisper, pulling my hood farther over my head.

"Yes, Miss Edin?" Oren says, looking back at me over his shoulder.

"How long have you served Endricks?"

"Oh, I have served the royal family for thousands of years, and my father and grandfather before that. I personally changed Lord Endricks's soiled under garments myself." He snickers, but then his face turns gloomy. "Before that, I was Queen Atraya's personal footman. She was so kind." He shakes his head, looking down at his feet.

My heart clenches in my chest, "Endricks's mother?"

"Yes, ma'am. She was so very lovely, and I was honored to serve her." Oren cuts himself off as he stops abruptly at a metal door, and I almost topple straight over him. "We have arrived," he says, pulling a large set of skeleton keys from his vest pocket. He inserts the key, and the pins begin unlocking one by one, the rusted hinges squealing to life.

Chapter 16

Blythe

***

"Edin!"

The scream rips out of me as I hit the ground hard, palms slapping stone, knees screaming in protest. The sound echoes once and is swallowed whole, torn apart by the mist that surges in from every direction. It crawls into my mouth, my lungs, cold and metallic, stealing the air from my chest.

"What the *fuck*," my voice breaks, shredded and useless.

I can't see. The walls, floor, and ceiling are all gone. The world is nothing but white mist and choking silence. I drag myself forward on my hands, nails scraping across smooth stone, slick with cold. Marble. Of course it is. This place never does anything halfway. My hands shake as I claw through the fog, stirring it into wild, frantic spirals.

Where is it?

Where is the seam?

There has to be a tear, some fracture in the air, some wrongness I can *feel*. I push myself to my feet and stagger forward, hands outstretched, heart hammering so hard it hurts.

If I can just get back through before the veil seals.

If I can just reach her.

The mist thins. Not gently. Not mercifully. It pulls away like a curtain ripped from a stage, and the truth slams into me with bone-crushing force. There is nothing there.

No shimmer.

No veil.

Just an unbroken wall of pale stone where escape used to be.

"Damn it," I breathe, the words empty and useless.

My back hits the wall, and my legs give out beneath me. I slide down until I'm sitting on the floor, the cold seeping straight through my clothes, into my bones. My chest feels like it caves in as despair floods me, slow, suffocating, and inescapable. I press my hands to my head as if I can physically hold myself together, but the tears come anyway, hot and humiliating, spilling through my fingers.

My breath stutters. Once. Twice. Again.

What the hell was she thinking?

The thought lands sharp and vicious, then guilt follows close behind, wrapping around my ribs like barbed wire. Edin gave herself up for me. *For me.* To Osiris. To that manipulative, power-drunk bastard. She burned her principles, her freedom, *maybe even her life,* just to pull me out of a dungeon.

She traded herself for my survival. Anger flares, bright and sudden, scorching its way through the grief. I curl my hands into fists, nails biting into my palms. *Damn it, Edin.*

Thousands of lives hang in the balance because of that choice, because of *me*. The weight of it presses down until I can barely breathe. For one horrible moment, I let myself sink into it, into the atrocious possibilities, the self-loathing, and the useless ache in my chest.

Then I snap.

"No," I mutter, dragging in a harsh breath. "No."

I scrub my hands over my face, smearing tears away like they're a weakness I can't afford. My movements are rough, angry. I shove myself upright, forcing my spine straight even as my legs tremble.

Focus, Blythe.

Edin is a big girl.

She made a choice, and if she's in danger, falling apart here does nothing to help her.

The veil room of Swindon Castle comes back into focus around me in all its obscene splendor. Marble floors gleam beneath my feet, seamless and pristine, stretching into towering walls that rise toward a vaulted ceiling etched with gold filigree. Statues of the gods loom overhead, perfect, polished, and untouchable, watching in silent judgment.

Opulence bleeds from every inch of the space. It's beautiful in a cold, blinding way. Sterile. Lifeless. Everything here is carved, gilded, and preserved, frozen in perfection. It makes my skin crawl. I need warmth. Earthiness.

Wood and firelight and things that *breathe*. This place doesn't live, it merely exists.

My jaw tightens. Fear still coils in my gut, but it's changing now, sharpening into something harder. Purpose. Resolve.

If the veil is sealed, then I need to find another way. If no one knows what's coming, then I make them listen.

If Edin walked into hell...

... Then I will tear heaven apart to get her back.

I lift my chin, breathe steady at last, and turn toward the doors.

Time to move.

I take the stairs two at a time, lungs burning, boots slipping on polished stone. The landing comes up fast, and beyond it, a set of heavy double doors. I don't slow, I shoulder through them and spill into a long corridor, my footsteps cracking too loud against the silence.

Painted eyes follow me as I run. Portraits line the walls, generations of rulers frozen in their finery, crowns heavy with implied authority. I don't look at them for long, but I feel them, judging, watching, *measuring* whether I belong here. Whether I'm worth the trouble I'm about to cause.

Too late now.

I cut left, then right, then straight through a room I don't register beyond shelves and shadows. Another doorway. Another corridor. My pulse roars in my ears, drowning out everything else. Every wrong turn feels like time bleeding out of me.

Where the hell is everyone?

I'm running blind through a never-ending maze of marble, and it's getting me nowhere.

Everything looks untouched. Unlived in. Like a stage set waiting for actors who never arrive. I burst through a set of doors and nearly skid to a halt as light floods my vision. Green. Warmth. Living things. For half a heartbeat, my body betrays me, relief flares, sharp and aching. Plants crowd the space, leaves glossy and alive, flowers climbing marble like they're trying to reclaim it. I hate how much it hurts to leave, but I tear myself away and keep running.

The silence shifts, and then it breaks.

Voices. Footsteps. People.

I stumble into a wide hall crowded with motion, servants and courtiers weaving past one another, arms full, minds light. They move like the world is safe, like nothing is wrong. The normalcy of it punches the air from my lungs harder than any blow.

They don't know.

They have no idea.

I grab the nearest woman by the wrist and spin her toward me. "Where is the king?"

My voice slices clean through the room. Conversations falter. Heads turn. She freezes. Up close, she's pale, unnaturally so, her skin nearly translucent, her gray eyes dark and storm-deep. She lowers her gaze immediately, tension snapping through her posture.

"I'm sorry, my lady," she says carefully, "but the King's whereabouts are not-"

I cut her off, gripping her shoulders. "Take me to him. Now."

Shock flickers across her face, then something harder. Appraisal. Suspicion. The seconds seem to stretch too long, my pulse hammering.

"What do you mean, my lady?" she asks. "Why such urgency?"

Because Edin is gone. *Because Osiris is moving. Because the realms are already splitting at the seams.*

"There is no time," I snap, then, forcing the words out slower, sharper, "Windemere is not safe. The realms are in danger, and I will explain it to King Thayer myself."

She hesitates. I don't give her the luxury of deciding. I catch her arm and pull. "Please. Move."

Something in my voice must cut through, because she finally nods and turns, gliding toward a narrow side door half-hidden behind a statue. She slips it open and ushers me through with a speed that feels… wrong. Too smooth. Too light.

The air changes instantly. Rough stone replaces polished marble. Heat curls around us. Sound crashes in, metal on metal, voices overlapping, laughter. The smell hits next. Fresh-baked bread. *Home*.

My stomach twists painfully, but I keep moving. The kitchen barely registers. Women are dusted in flour, hands busy, eyes lifting in mild curiosity as we pass. No one stops us. No one questions the ghostly woman leading a frantic stranger through their space, as if this is an everyday inconvenience.

Outside again. Sunlight. Steam. Women bent over washbasins, fabric slapping wet and heavy. They glance up, startled, and I murmur an apology without slowing. My legs scream. My vision narrows. I stop just long enough to brace my hands on my knees and drag in a breath. She doesn't pause at all.

"How are you not winded?" I rasp.

“I do not breathe as you do, my lady.”

I huff a breath that might be a laugh. It dawns on me that she is a wraith, half mortal, half spirit. *Figures*.

“We’re close,” she adds gently. “Just beyond the next foyer.”

“Of course he is,” I mutter, forcing myself upright and pushing forward again.

The doors ahead are taller, heavier, gilded in white and gold. We pass through them into a long chamber dominated by a single table. King Thayer sits alone at its center, buried in papers. He looks up sharply as we enter.

“How did you get in here?” his voice snaps like a lash. “Where are my guards?”

His gaze pins me, then slides to the wraith beside me. His hand slams down on the table, the sound cracking through the room. “Well? Answer me at once!”

The wraith bows deeply, smooth and reverent. “Forgive the intrusion, Sire. We found no guards posted. This woman carries an urgent message.” Then she steps back.

Suddenly, it’s just me. I straighten, spine locking into place, fear still burning in my chest, but beneath it, something harder. Determination. If he won’t listen, I’ll make him.

“Your Majesty,” I begin, steadying my breath before it can betray me. “There is no time to spare. Osiris is already in motion. He is planning to overthrow Elysia, and if we hesitate now, it will be too late.”

I pause, just long enough to gather myself. My chest tightens, but I force the words forward.

"Twenty-four hours ago, I was held captive in the dungeons of Purgatory." I press my tongue to the inside of my cheek, anchoring myself before the memory can surface. "I did not expect to survive. And Edin…" My hands curl slowly into fists. "Edin surrendered herself to Osiris to save my life."

I take a measured step forward.

"Thousands are at risk. Entire realms, whether they know it or not. If we do not act now, there will be no stopping what comes next."

The room feels too large, too still, but I continue. "The veil was sealed behind me. I have no way back. I was thrust here by Edin, Goddess of Purgatory, because I needed to reach you, to *warn* you." I lift my gaze to meet his. "My people, *your people,* are unprepared. They walk blindly with peace, while Osiris prepares for conquest."

My voice wavers, but I brace a hand against the table and hold my ground.

"I did not come here lightly with this information," I say. "I came because I had no other choice. You must believe me."

I draw in a slow breath, willing my hands to stop shaking. Hunger and exhaustion twist in my gut, but I ignore them.

"Everything is shifting, Sire. The veil. The magic. The armies. Osiris's plans are already unfolding, and the longer we wait, the less chance the realms have of surviving what he intends."

I fall silent, the weight of my words settling heavily between us.

"Elysia is already under threat," I add quietly. "We must act. Now."

The silence that follows is suffocating. He studies me with furrowed brows, unreadable, as though weighing my words rather than hearing them.

"Did you hear me?" The question slips out before I can temper it. I wince and add, more carefully, "Sire."

His mouth finally opens.

Then the door slams open.

A guard storms in, armor clanking, breath sharp. Relief flickers in me for half a heartbeat, gone almost before I can grasp it.

"Where were you?" the king snaps at him, irritation flaring. Then his gaze flicks back to me, dismissive. "These two waltz into my quarters, unannounced, unchaperoned, spouting nonsense."

The words land like a blow to my gut.

Nonsense?

"Wait," I step forward, anger clawing up my throat. "Everything I said is true. You can act now and help save Elysia, or you can sit here and watch it fall."

I glance at the wraith. She's staring at her clasped hands, shoulders drawn inward, suddenly small.

The king exhales through his nose. "Get them out of here. I have important matters to attend to."

The guard strides toward us, grabbing my arm.

I rip free, disbelief burning hot and sharp. Disgust floods me, thick and choking. He thinks I'm just another frantic woman, spinning stories for attention.

"What the fuck is the matter with…"

Pain explodes.

The back of the guard's metal-clad hand connects with my jaw, and the world tilts violently. I hit the floor in a useless heap, breath knocked clean out of me as darkness crashes down.

Light stabs into my eyes when I come to. I blink hard, groaning. Pain radiates through my jaw, white-hot, my skull throbbing like it's been split down the middle. It takes a moment for the world to stop swimming, the edges blurring in and out like a bad dream. Everything looks wrong. Tilted. Then it clicks, I'm on my side, staring up at the guard looming over me.

Ah. Of course. What a strong, brave male. Hitting a woman who dares to speak.

The king rises from his chair, moving with the slow, deliberate confidence of someone used to absolute control. He stops just short of me and the wraith, arms crossed, eyes cold as ice.

"She will not ruin this," he mutters, voice low but venomous. "Osiris, the narcissistic bastard, always so arrogant. He was never very good at tying up loose ends."

The words hit me like shards of glass, sharp and bitter.

The guard shifts, glancing between me and the wraith. "What shall I do with them, my Lord?" His gesture toward us is casual, but the menace in it is absolute.

The wraith doesn't look at him. Her hands are still clasped, but now tears streak down the bridge of her nose, landing silently on the polished floor. She knows they've revealed too much, said *too much* in front of her.

Panic claws at me, hot and urgent.

We need to do something. Now.

I try to rise, to grab at the guard, to do anything, but the edges of my vision smear into darkness, the room tilting and fading. My knees wobble. My strength drains like water from a broken vessel. The guard's grip clamps around me, hauling me upright despite my protests. I can barely focus, the light pools and fractures in my eyes, and the sounds of the room become distant and distorted. I taste bile, my stomach twists, and fear threatens to swallow me whole.

We cannot let this stand.

Chapter 17

Edin

The air itself seems to sweat as the metal door slowly screeches open on rusty hinges. The cloud of smoke intensifies, burning my eyes. Tortured screams pour in, jerking at my heartstrings. My stomach drops as I step out.

"Welcome to Helheim, Goddess," Oren says with a bow.

I rub my eyes in shock. The City of the Abyss rises like a cathedral of defiance in the heart of Helheim. Black skyscrapers, forged from obsidian and volcanic glass, drink in the dim light. They tower like monoliths carved from night itself. Every surface is smooth, reflective, and impossibly sharp, as if the buildings were grown rather than built. Threaded through the darkness are veins of molten gold, pulsing like the city's lifeblood. These luminous streaks run vertically up each tower, forming patterns that shift subtly, almost as if the structures were breathing. At night, if such a place even has a day, the gold burns brighter, outlining the skyline in a halo of shimmering fire. Rivers of fire flow through the streets in controlled channels, casting dancing reflections onto the obsidian facades. Bridges of black iron arch over them, inscribed with runes that glow faintly in the same molten hue. The air hums with heat and distant echoes of chanting, as though the city itself whispers to those who walk its streets. Demons, lost souls, and flame-forged soldiers move through the avenues with purpose, their shadows long and distorted by the golden glow. In this Hadestown, grandeur and torment seem intertwined. A place where dangerous beauty gleams through the darkness, and even the light feels sinister.

"It is," I stutter out, "Magnificent. I read the stories of Helheim, but this? This is far beyond what I ever expected."

"Come," Oren says, pulling me away by the arm. "We must make haste."

We slink along a narrow trail, pressed close to the castle walls. I hold my breath, pulling my cloak higher to hide my face. My stomach knots tighter with every step, my heart aching as screams echo out, each one sounding closer, louder, more desperate. Rounding the corner, my breath catches. My eyes widen, and my jaw drops; I nearly forget how to breathe. The sight before us steals every coherent thought from my mind.

Oren turns, catching my expression, a small, knowing smile tugging at his lips. "Impressive, is it not?" he murmurs.

A field of flowers spread across the grounds of hell like a beautiful mistake. Their blossoms are pale and elegant, soft purples fading into sickly whites, drooping on thin green stems that look too fragile to survive the heat. Yet they thrive. The air around them shimmers, heavy with warmth and a sweetness that almost masks the sulfur beneath it. From a distance, the field looks calm, inviting even, as if it does not belong in a place of punishment at all.

"Belladonna," Oren says.

My heart drops. "Excuse me?" The words slip out before I can stop them.

Oren steps closer, brushing his singed fingertips over the dark petals. "Wondrous, are they not? Belladonna, also known as deadly nightshade, is native to Helheim." He lets out a soft giggle. "Quite ironic, really. *Belladonna* means *beautiful lady*, yet the plant itself is highly poisonous."

"Yes… funny," I murmur, though my thoughts are already unraveling. The world tilts as memories of Endricks surge forward, his smile, sharp and knowing. I stumble back, breath catching.

Oren's hand closes around mine, steady and insistent. "My apologies," he says gently, "but we must hurry before we are discovered, Miss Edin."

I shake my head, blinking rapidly, forcing the visions of Endricks's smirk back into the shadows where they belong. When I look up again, my voice is steady, resolve hardening every word. "Yes," I say, determination dripping from my lips.

Stepping slowly into the field, the belladonna closes around us like a hush. The flowers brush our legs as we walk, their petals cool against the heat-soaked air. Each step stirs up a sweet, heavy scent that makes the atmosphere feel thicker, almost syrupy. The ground beneath is soft with ash. The glow of hellfire reflects faintly off the dark leaves, turning them glossy and ethereal.

The flowers tilt as we pass, not quite moving, not quite still. The silence presses in, broken only by the faint crackle of distant flames and the whisper of mine and Oren's footsteps. An uneasy feeling crawls up my spine that the field is paying attention. It is as if the flowers know we are here and are simply lying in wait. Tension pulls tight in my chest, making it hard to breathe. Nothing attacks, and a lump builds in my throat, intensifying the sensation.

Ahead, the belladonna thins and the trees begin. They rise crooked and close together, their trunks twisted like frozen smoke. No leaves grow on their branches, only long, splintered limbs that claw at the dim red light. The air changes as we approach, losing its sweetness and turning cold and dry, as if the trees drink in warmth instead of water. Stepping out of the flowers and into their shadow, the ground hardens beneath us. I glance back at the field with a sickening feeling. It looks too calm now, too perfect, like something wants me, no, *needs* me to turn back. The trees creak softly, although there is no wind, and their branches lean inward, narrowing the path ahead. It feels less like entering a forest and more like stepping into the maw of a waiting beast. My hair stands on the back of my neck. Swallowing hard, I slip into the shadows.

"It is not much farther," Oren begins rambling. He nearly skips along the path, slipping easily beneath every low branch thanks to his short stature. "This is only a sliver of the Weeping Thicket. The forest stretches far beyond the eye's reach, west of Helheim. You needn't worry here, Goddess. No creature can survive long enough to threaten us. The forest has its own defenses."

"Defenses?" I cough, swatting hanging limbs from my face.

"Oh, yes. The trees here are very much alive."

"Oren, you do know we have living trees back in Windemere, right?"

He laughs. "But are they carnivorous?"

I stop short. "Come again?"

"With no true sunlight in Helheim, the trees have…adapted," he says lightly. "They feed on any creature foolish enough to wander in."

I blink. "Oren?"

"Yes, Goddess?" he replies, beaming, utterly oblivious.

"Why, in all of Helheim, are we walking through a man-eating forest?"

"Ah! Because it is the quickest route, of course!" He finally stops and glances back at me. "I suggest you keep moving. They say the slower your pace, the faster your death."

My eye begins to twitch.

I could snuff out his smoldering little life without any effort. No. No, Edin. You need him. He is the only one who can lead you to Endricks.

I force a smile, even as the twitch refuses to fade. "Thank you for the advice, Oren," I say. Something coils around my boot. I snap my gaze downward just as thick vines slither up my calf, rough and cold, tightening as they climb. More follows, weaving around my knees with deliberate slowness. The pull is not violent; worse, it is steady and relentless.

"Miss Edin," Oren squeals. Smoke and fire sputters from his cracked skin as he reaches for my hand, and vines jerk him in the opposite direction.

The ground softens beneath my feet, swallowing the soles of my boots inch by inch. I try to step back, but the earth does not let go. I snatch the dagger from my side and slash wildly at the vines. They only tighten in response, coiling tighter as my feet begin to tingle and fade into numbness. My blade is useless against them; every strike splits fibrous flesh and releases thick, dark-green sap that bubbles from the wounds. The sap hisses as it spreads, eating through the leather of my boots. My heart slams against my ribs.

So this is how it happens. Slowly. Methodically. Consumed piece by piece. How can I come this far only to be ended like this? And if I truly am immortal, what does that mean here? Dragged beneath Helheim's soil, conscious forever, buried just bounds away from Endricks?

That would be true hell.

Panic claws up my throat. I reach down instinctively, and a haze of violet mist coils from my palms. The sap clings to my fingers, burning, biting into my skin. Tears blur my vision as the pain creeps through my nails, relentless and sharp. "I am too close," I whisper, forcing the words through clenched teeth. Then I push, power surging from my palms, raw and desperate, spilling into the ground beneath me, and the earth answers. The mist thickens, rolling from my hands in violent waves. The soil beneath me shudders, then cracks with the sound of splitting bone. The vines recoil, thrashing as if burned, their grip faltering for the first time. I scream, not in pain, but in effort, and drive my palms deeper into the earth. Light flares from my hands, casting deep shadows down the path, and the sap begins smoldering before evaporating into smoke. The vines shriek as they unravel, snapping back into the ground like wounded serpents. Their pressure vanishes all at once, and I tear my hands free as I stumble forward, collapsing onto my hands and knees, unable to stop myself as adrenaline pumps through me. The soil continues to churn behind me, and I slowly drag myself clear of its reach. The ground caves inward where I stood, swallowing the last writhing remnants of the vines as if nothing had ever been there. Then silence crashes down. My breath comes in ragged gasps. Smoke curls from the scorched earth, the scent sharp and bitter. My hands burn, skin raw and trembling, veins glowing faintly beneath the surface as my magic fades.

"Edin!" Oren squeals, gripping my shoulders, hauling me upright before my legs give out. His face is pale, his eyes wide with a mix of awe and fear. "Are you okay?" he pants. "Stars above, that is some power you have."

I nod weakly, staring at the crater behind me. “Just take me to Endricks.”

He swallows. “Helheim does not like being defied.”

“Neither do I.”

My gaze lifts, locking onto the twisted path ahead, where the land darkens, and the air grows heavy with intent. Somewhere beyond the trees, Endricks waits, close enough now that I can feel it, a pressure just beneath my skin.

Chapter 18

Edin

We follow the twisted path as it coils deeper into the trees. Branches claw at my cloak, their bark blackened and split. Whispers swirl in a language I do not understand. The light thins with every step, turning sickly red, as though the forest itself is bleeding it away. The pressure beneath my skin grows tighter, more insistent, guiding me forward whether I want it to or not.

The screams fade as we move, only to return minutes later, louder, layered, no longer distant echoes but a constant, living chorus. My pulse stutters, skipping a beat. Oren slows beside me, his shoulder brushing my hip, a silent reminder that I am not alone.

Then the trees end, not gradually, but abruptly. The path spills out onto bare stone, and the forest breaks apart like a curtain being torn open. I stop short, breath ripping from my chest.

Before us sprawls a vast prison seemingly carved into the mountains of Helheim. Jagged towers rise from the ground like broken teeth, connected by iron bridges and spiked walkways. Cells are stacked upon cells, cut directly into black stone walls that plunge deep into the earth. Chains hang everywhere, some still, others swaying gently against the windless sky.

The air is thick with heat and ash. Rivers of lava glow beneath cracked stone, casting a hellish red light that flickers across iron bars and the twisted silhouettes within. Figures cling to the bars of their cells, some silent, some screaming, some too broken to do either. Magic hums through the structure, heavy and suffocating, pressing down on my lungs with every breath.

This is no place for redemption. This is a place designed to hold someone for eternity.

Oren exhales slowly. “Welcome to Greybar,” he says under his breath.

My hands curl into fists as my gaze sweeps the prison, dread and fury knotting in my chest. My skin feels stretched to its breaking point, as if the pressure inside me could shatter bone. A deep thump reverberates through my chest, knocking the air from my lungs. Inhaling slowly, a low hum begins to spread through my body, flowing down my arms and into my fingertips, drawing my pulse back into rhythm. Then it strengthens, steadier, louder, pounding in my ears. I would know that beat anywhere. Somewhere within the prison's monstrous labyrinth, Endricks is waiting, and he knows I am here.

"Oren," I growl.

"Yes, Miss Edin," Oren says, his lip quivering. Steam begins to pour from the cracks along his skin with stress.

"You need to get as far from here as possible. Find us in the aftermath."

"Yes, Miss Edin," he nods knowingly.

"Thank you, Oren."

I watch the little fire sprite skid off back into the trees until I can no longer see the dim light glowing from his fractured skin. "Endricks," I whisper, "I am here." Turning back around, disgust fills me, and the ground trembles. Slamming my hands to the ground, a hum surges outward, spilling from my palms in waves of violet mist that roll across the stone like living smoke. Runes carved into the prison walls flare violently, their light stuttering as my magic presses against them. Chains rattle, and iron groans. The very air seems to recoil. I press my hands down harder, my shoulders screaming with pain, letting every ounce of rage flow through me, and power answers.

"Rise."

At first, it is subtle, a shiver beneath the soil, a tremor that ripples outward like a held breath finally released. Cracks spiderweb through the ground, splitting stone and ash. From beneath the prison, beneath Helheim itself, shadows begin to rise. Dirt lifts and collapses as pale light leaks from below, veins of magic threading through the ground. Fingers punch through the soil, then hands, dragging themselves upward with grim determination. The dirt seems reluctant to let them go, clinging and sliding as bodies force their way free. One by one, they rise. I stumble back, unsure of what I am actually seeing, unaware that I was even capable of wielding such a power.

Figures pull themselves from shallow graves and forgotten pits, coated in ash and dust. Bones knit themselves back together beneath tattered armor. Rust flakes away as metal reforges itself, bending to a will older than death. Blades long buried scrape against stone as they are reclaimed. Shields surface, cracked but whole once again. The army assembles itself with eerie precision, ranks forming without command, bodies straightening as if memory alone guides them. Empty eye sockets ignite with a deep purple light as heads lift in unison.

The earth seals behind them, as though it has merely returned what was borrowed. Hundreds of glowing eyes fall on me, unwavering. An army of the undead now stands before me, awaiting my command. Fear strikes through me with thoughts of failure, and I jerk my fist shut, nails digging into my palms. *Not today, Edin. You are the Goddess of Purgatory, and you will be victorious.* I straighten, heart hammering in time with my magic. I throw my hand up towards the prison. "Forward!" I command. I watch as they turn on their heels without falter, and their destruction begins.

The prison answers with resistance. Hidden runes blaze to life along the walls, their light screaming as it flares brighter, harsher. Iron sigils snap into place across the gates, locking with a thunderous clang that shakes the ground beneath my feet. Heat rolls outward in punishing waves, and the air thickens until breathing feels like pushing through molten glass.

I bare my teeth, "So be it."

My hand drops, and the undead move as one. They surge forward in a silent tide, boots pounding stone that fractures beneath their weight. The first wave collides with the gates, and the impact rings through the prison like a bell struck by a god. Or *goddess*. Fire and wind magic detonates outward, hurling bodies back, but they rise again, reforming, relentless. I step forward, power roaring now, no longer a hum, but a storm. Violet energy coils around my arms as I thrust both palms out. "Shatter," I command, and the ground splits wide. The gates buckle, iron screaming as the earth beneath them collapses. Chains snap like brittle thread. Runes flicker, fail, and then crumble in a cascade of dying light. With a final, deafening crack, the gates tear free and crash inward, swallowed by dust and fire.

The undead pour through the shattered gates, surging forward in disciplined silence, boots striking stone in perfect unison. Somewhere inside, something ancient and furious stirs, but it is too late to stop what has begun. The prison erupts into chaos. Across the courtyard, the guards respond instantly, hulking figures of horns and shadows, armored in blackened steel etched with infernal sigils. Their eyes burn like coals as they draw blades wreathed in hellfire.

My lips turn upward into a sickly sweet smile. I stride through my army, each soldier stepping aside in my presence. I use my power to amplify my voice across the courtyard, "You have something very dear to me, and I have come to reclaim it. If it is a war you want, then I shall strike the first match." Power pulses through me in a way I did not know was possible. I flick my wrist, and the first clash rolls out like thunder.

Steel meets claw, and hellfire collides with necromantic force. The sound ripples through the prison walls, a shockwave of impact and rage. Demons roar as they charge, swinging massive weapons meant to crush bone and spirit alike. The undead do not flinch. They do not feel pain or sorrow or fear. All the undead feel, all the undead *know,* is my will. Blades pass through them, shattering armor and scattering bodies, only for the fallen to knit themselves back together moments later. Broken limbs reattach. Cracked skulls reform. They rise again and again, relentless, tireless, immune to all worldly concerns.

My undead magic flares through the ranks, violet light pulsing like a shared heartbeat. Shields lock, and spears thrust. Deathly sharp swords find openings in demon armor, their enchanted edges biting deep into infernal flesh. Fire explodes across the courtyard, consuming stone and shadow alike. Wings unfurl as some take to the air, raining molten strikes from above. Everywhere, magic collides, and wards begin to shatter, towers crumbling with our advancement. Chains snap loose, crashing from battlements as prisoners cry out from behind their cells. The prison trembles under the strain, its ancient defenses buckling beneath an enemy that cannot be intimidated or exhausted.

At the center of it all, the undead press forward, advancing step by step, an unstoppable tide of bone and will. Then silence falls over chaos, and the guards begin to fall back, not from defeat, but from the realization that this is not an army meant to be slain; it is an army meant to endure.

"Leave not a single one of these bastards alive."

There is no room for failure.

Chapter 19

Edin

***

The dead push deeper into the prison, and Greybar itself seems to recoil, realizing too late that it is being overrun by something it can not control. Striding through the ruined halls, smoke curls around my boots, and heat bites at my skin. I knock over every still-lit torch as I walk, leaving a blazing inferno behind me. The pull is like a blade beneath my ribs, dragging my attention downward. It yanks at something old and instinctive, something I should have learned to stop questioning a long time ago.

My pace quickens, boots striking stone in a relentless rhythm that matches the pounding in my chest. Walls crack as I pass, sigils flaring and dying. Every ward meant to keep us apart splinters like glass under my pressure. The taste of blood and ash fills my mouth, and something familiar. *Acceptance.* Not mine. The look Endricks gave me as the veil closed around him flashes through my mind.

"Hold on," I whisper, the words torn from me like a promise well overdue.

The prison screams as I descend, stone collapsing, corridors caving, shadows fleeing from the heat that follows me. Somewhere ahead, something precious is breaking, and I am done being late. Flames race along the ceilings, devouring old banners and rotted beams as Greybar collapses in on itself. Stone fractures with deafening cracks, entire corridors folding like brittle bones. Smoke chokes the air, carrying screams, some terrified, some triumphant, as the dead and the living surge through the ruins together. Glancing back, I catch glimpses of the undead still loyally following. My ears ring, and my singed skin feels as if I have been set alight.

Keep moving forward, Edin.

The fire parts for me, curling away from my body as if it knows better than to try to touch my skin. Every step closer sharpens the pull in my chest until it hurts to breathe around it.

Endricks.

His name beats through me, louder than the destruction, louder than the roar of collapsing prison. I feel him, faint and battered, still burning stubbornly against the dark. The bond between us stretches tighter still, guiding me through falling walls and ruptured floors as if the prison itself is being peeled open just for this. A tower buckles ahead, crashing down in a storm of debris. I throw up a hand, magic screaming out of me as it tears a path through the rubble. Ash coats my tongue, and my lungs scream in burning pain, but I can not stop.

Cells blur past, doors hanging open, chains dragging uselessly across the ground. Prisoners flee in every direction, eyes wide as they take in the sight of the world ending behind as I pass. Some recognize what I am and scramble out of my way. Others stare, frozen, as if afraid I will vanish if they blink.

My heart jumps, like it will claw its way right out of my chest. I slide to a halt, the hall breaking off into three directions. Panic runs through me, and my vision speckles from lack of oxygen. With shaking hands, I take a deep breath and close my eyes. *Reach out, Edin. Feel it.* The pull jerks me hard to the left. I turn sharply, boots skidding on stone slick with soot and blood, and sprint down a collapsing stairwell. Each step caves in behind me, the prison desperate now, panicking as it tries and fails to bury us both.

The heat spikes, taking my breath away. My vision blurs at the corners of my eyes. Sweat runs down my face, dripping off my chin. I grit my teeth and push forward. I burst into a long corridor already half-consumed by fire. The ceiling is gone, open to the night sky so far above, and embers rain down like burning snow. Suddenly, I feel it, and the world re-aligns. *There.* The stone walls have crumbled under the pressure of my destruction. Beams lay toppled and burning down the hallway. At the end of the chaotic scene lies my worst nightmare, and I take off in a dead sprint, shoving columns and rusted iron doors out of my path.

"Endricks," I choke out through the smoke.

My heart shatters into a million pieces, and a lump rises in my throat. He is slumped against the wall of a demolished cell, chains hanging loose from his wrists, blood dark against the stone. His head is bowed, shoulders pulled almost from their sockets, not quite, but close enough that my chest tightens painfully.

"Endricks!"

He does not move, and for a heartbeat, the world freezes. I crash down onto the floor in front of him, ignoring the pain that grinds through my knees. Frantically, I grab his chin, lifting his head to me. "Endricks!" I plead, pushing his blood-matted hair from his eyes. "Endricks, please! Do not lea-, please, Endricks!" Tears finally break free; I am no longer able to contain them. His head sags, and his skin, usually burning, feels icy, dead beneath my hands. "No!" I yell, gripping his shoulders, shaking him as if my strength alone could drag him back. "Endricks, you stubborn asshole, I did not come all this way for you to die here! Not like this! Not now!" He does not move, not a twitch, not even a flicker. Dread coils in my stomach. I clutch his face, my nails digging in, and violet mist erupts from my palms, swirling around us in a shimmering, desperate haze.

"Endricks! Wake. *The fuck.* Up."

I jerk my head around as the walls start to collapse. Stone splits apart with a shriek, and fire tears through the upper levels, raining heat and ash down on us. The air scorches my throat. My heart pounds so hard it hurts, each beat frantic and wild.

"No, no, no, NO!"

I shove my arms under him, wrapping around his chest. He is heavy, too heavy. I scream as I strain, muscles burning, teeth grinding as I haul him upward. My legs give out with a sob, and I slam back into the ground, Endricks ripping from my grip. The impact rattles my bones. I claw at him, at the floor, at *anything*, rage tearing out of my throat in a broken, animal scream.

"Get up!" I scream at him. "Get UP!"

Tears stream down my face, hot and blinding, mixing with soot as the ground shakes beneath us. I pound my fist against the stone, my voice shredding itself raw. I grab him once more, hauling with everything I have, fury and terror bleeding together. Yet my efforts are fruitless.

I collapse over him, shaking, sobbing, screaming into his shoulder as fire roars closer, and the walls begin to crumble around us. Then a cough splits through the chaos, *his* cough. It shudders through Endrick's chest, violent and guttural. His hand slides across my back, fingers digging into my shoulder as if he is trying to stay conscious from his grasp alone. The world is screaming, but I no longer hear it. Slowly, I open my eyes to a soot-streaked face and a striking set of blue eyes. Disbelief flickers across his expression, quickly chased by something raw and unguarded.

"Edin," he breathes, like saying my name is the only thing keeping him here, keeping him alive.

My whole body relaxes, and I feel like I can breathe again. Rubbing his cheek, I lock eyes with him, every emotion inside me churning in utter turmoil. "You are such an asshole, trying to die on me like that," I whisper, leaning in.

"I guess, I *am* the damsel in distress this time," he coughs out, attempting a smirk, but his mouth twists into a pained grimace.

My forehead brushes his, horns grazing against each other, our breaths mingling together. Smoke burns my lungs, but beneath it all, I smell him, familiar and grounding, and it steadies me. My lips press to his with more feeling than finesse, like I am trying to pour everything I cannot say into this single touch. It is instinctive, desperate. He responds immediately, a soft sound catching in his throat as his hands grip my sleeves, anchoring himself to me.

The kiss deepens just enough to make my pulse stutter, warm, real, and overwhelming. He tastes like blood and fire. I kiss him like I need him to know he is still here. That he made it, and that I did too. Finally, I pull back, it is only by inches. My thumb brushes the corner of his mouth, wiping away blood without thinking, my touch lingering longer than it should. For a moment, nothing else exists, not the burning prison, not the chaos, just him, and I refuse to let that go.

Another tremor ripples through the floor, ending our moment and pulling us back to reality. I meet Endricks's gaze as he stiffens beside me, breath catching sharply. His grip tightens on my sleeve, not in pain this time, but recognition.

"Valker," he says.

The name means nothing to me, but the way he says it, hoarse and urgent, does. "Where?" I ask, already shifting, already listening.

"Lower tiers. West Wing," he swallows, jaw tightening. "They dragged him past me. He was… conscious."

I straighten, violet mist curling instinctively around my hands. "Lead the way," I tell Endricks, looping his arm over my shoulders before he can argue. My magic trails across his chest, helping me withstand the weight of his large form. He leans into me, stubborn as ever, refusing to put his burden fully on me, and his body trembles under the strain.

The west wing is in ruin, its cells gape open, stone split and blackened by fire. Failed runes flicker weakly along the walls, their magic unraveling as Greybar eats itself alive. Smoke presses low, thick enough to choke on.

There, by a shattered support beam, is a Satyr chained upright, head bowed, and long white hair streaked with soot and blood. One arm hangs wrong, contorted in a way that makes me wince. His chest rises in shallow, uneven pulls of air.

"Valker," Endricks breathes.

The man's head lifts at the sound of his name. One eye is swollen shut; the other fixes on Endricks with startling clarity. "You look like shit," Valker croaks.

Endricks lets out something halfway between a laugh and a sob. "You are not allowed to die before me."

I do not wait for reunions. Violet mist pours from my palms as I tear into the chains. Metal shrieks, runes fracture, and the links give way with a sound like bones breaking. Valker slumps forward, and Endricks catches him on instinct, teeth gritted as pain rips through his own ruined shoulders.

"Easy," Endricks mutters, bracing him. "I got you." He grunts as his face twists with pain that he tries and fails to hide.

Valker exhales, forehead dropping briefly against Endricks's shoulder. "Knew you would."

The ceiling groans ominously above us."Save it for later," I snap, already hauling Valker's uninjured arm over my shoulders. He stiffens at my touch, surprise flashing across his face as he looks at me properly for the first time.

"Who…"

"Edin," I cut in. "And if you wish to keep breathing, shut the fuck up and start walking."

He studies me for half a second; horns, magic, the prison burning behind us, then nods once. "Fair."

Boots thunder in the distance. Shouts echo closer. Valker looks Endricks over, quickly realizing the state he is in, and switches spots, sliding under his shoulder. Together, we stagger down the corridor, Endricks between us now, stubbornly upright, supported on both sides. Every step is a fight. Fire rains from above as the underground gate looms ahead, its runes flickering erratically, barely holding. I raise a palm, using the last ounce of my energy, forcing my magic into the iron doors. The gate does not shatter; it groans. The ancient iron trembles as the bars slowly squeal open on their hinges against my magic. Greybar finally gives way behind us, runes flickering erratically as the prison devours itself from the inside out. Fire roars through the upper tiers, heat pressing down like a living thing, and the corridor collapses with a deafening crack.

I glance towards Endricks, who looks like he is hanging on by a thread. My heart sinks as self-doubt creeps through my bones. "My magic will not hold this for long!"

"We will make it," Valker rasps, bracing Endricks's weight against his side.

I nod, trusting him, then slip out from under Endricks as Valker takes all his weight. There is no time for anything else. A few undead soldiers flank around me, rushing ahead. I reach the gate just as another tremor throws me sideways. I slam into the hard metal door, breath ripping from my lungs, but I keep my footing. The gate's runes flare bright and defensive, meant to keep things in.

"Help me," I snap, shoving my shoulder into the iron.

They finally reach me, and Valker joins in, teeth bared as he grunts through the pain. Endricks wedges himself between us, using his body like a brace despite the way his arms tremble violently with the strain. The gate screams and metal warps. Hinges tear loose from the stone that has been burning for hours. With one final heave, it rips free and crashes outward, sending a plume of ash into the air.

We spill out of the gates and collapse just beyond the threshold. My soldiers begin to rot at the release of my magic, falling piece by piece to the ground, dissolving back into the earth. Greybar does not follow. The prison convulses behind us, stone folding inward as the inner tiers finally collapse. Screams echo once, then cut off abruptly, swallowed by fire and crushed by falling rock. The gate slams shut again on its own, sealing with a thunderous finality that sends a shock through the ground.

For a long moment, none of us move. Valker is the first to break the silence, coughing hard as he spits blood onto the ash-covered stone. "Next time," he rasps, "we're burning the whole damned place down *after* we leave."

Endricks huffs a weak laugh, then inhales sharply as his pain catches up with him. He slowly sits up with a wince, breath coming shallow now that the adrenaline is gone.

I am beside him instantly, steadying him as his weight sags. “You still with me?” I ask quietly.

He nods, eyes half-lidded, but focused on my face. “Yeah. Just…do not let me sleep.”

Valker looks between us, recognition dawning, not romance, not jealousy, just understanding. History. He shifts closer, planting himself solidly on Endricks’s other side. “She won’t,” he says with a grin. “I won't let her. She saved me, and now she has to deal with the consequences.” He winks, and a small laugh escapes him between heavy breaths.

I meet his gaze for the first time, urgency no longer clawing at my ribs. He is battered and bloodied, but sharp as broken glass. “I did not do it for you,” I say.

He smiles anyway. “Feisty, I like it. Exactly what someone needs to deal with this one,” he nods towards Endricks.

I can not help but laugh. I throw a hand out, “Edin.”

“Valker,” he says, with a bow.

CHAPTER 20

ENDRICKS

Groaning, I prop myself against a fallen log at the forest's edge, spine screaming every time I shift. Edin walks over and kneels in front of me to retie the wrap around my ribs. Her fingers are stained with ash and blood. Her jaw is tight, focused. No magic now, just cloth, pressure, and stubbornness. Valker paces off, sword barred, watching the treeline as if it has personally offended him. *The woods are too quiet.* I open my mouth to say something, anything, when light flashes through the underbrush.

"Incoming," Valker snaps.

I force myself upright despite Edin's sharp intake of breath. A streak of flame breaks from the trees and skids to a halt in front of us, scattering sparks across the leaves, small, burning, and familiar.

"Oren," I rasp.

The fire sprite doubles over, hands on his knees, glow flaring and guttering rapidly with his panic. "You…are…alive," he pants, then looks at all of us like he has not yet decided if that makes things better or worse.

"Talk," Valker orders.

Oren straightens, his fire burning hotter. "Elysia has fallen."

The words hit harder than the prison ever did. Edin goes still, keeping her eyes fixed on the ground, and the color drains from her face.

"They breached the veil," Oren says quickly. "Inner wards collapsed. The council is gone. The King's banners were torn down." His flames burn blue at the edges with fear. "They are calling it a restructuring. A coup."

"Who?" I grunt.

"We do not know yet, My Lord," Oren stutters.

Valker exhales through his teeth, slow and sharp. "And Verenia?"

Oren nods. "Last seen in the eastern quarter of the castle, causing quite a ruckus."

Valker does not hesitate. He steps past Edin and crouches in front of me, gaze hard and searching. "You going to make it?"

"Unfortunately," I mutter.

Valker's mouth twitches. "Good." He rises, already turning on his heels. "I'm going back for Verenia."

Edin looks up, fumbling with her finger. "Alone?"

"If that's what it takes," Valker says. "King Adonis better hope there isn't a hair out of place on my sister's head," he pauses, then looks back at us, really looks. "They'll be hunting anything tied to you and Edin." His eyes flick to me. "You two vanish," he continues. "Heal. Think. If you're still breathing when this settles, we burn our way back in."

I swallow against the pain. "Go find Verenia."

Valker gives a single, sharp nod. "Count on it." Then he is moving, melting into the forest with the kind of purpose that does not allow for second thoughts.

Oren's flames dim slightly. "I know places they will not look," he offers. "Old tunnels. The Dead Grounds."

Edin shifts closer to me, steadying my weight as my legs threaten to give out. Her voice is low, controlled. "We could go dark."

"Seriously?" I ask.

She meets my eyes, with no fear now, only intent. "Just until you can stand without shaking."

I snort weakly. "Ambitious."

Her mouth curves despite herself. "Necessary."

I nod once, feeling the weight of Elysia's fall settle into my bones alongside the pain. "Then we head to the Dead Grounds," I say. "And we plan."

Oren hesitates, fire flickering as he looks between us and the dark where Valker vanished. Then he makes a sharp decision. "I can track him," he says. "Fire remembers heat. I can keep up."

"Do not be seen," I command.

Oren grins, fierce and bright, with a wink. "No promises."

He turns and sprints after Valker, flames streaking low through the brush before disappearing entirely. The forest swallows the last glow, leaving only shadow and the soft crackle of cooling leaves. The silence that follows is heavy. I push myself upright, teeth clenched as pain lances through my ribs. Edin is already there, steadying me, but I angle us away from the path Valker took.

"This way," I say.

Edin glances in the direction I indicate. "Are you sure?"

"You are in my territory now, Your Highness," I reply.

That earns me an exasperated look and an eyeroll, but then she nods and starts off beside me.

Chapter 21

Endricks

I lead us off-trail, choosing ground that looks uninviting, with thorn-choked brush, uneven stone, and fallen limbs that break lines of pursuit. Every step costs precious time, but I know where the forest thins, where sound dies, where magic begins to feel…tired. The change comes gradually. The air dries, and the night grows too still. The trees pull away from one another, bark paling, leaves turning brittle underfoot.

This forest feels like a living punishment. Shadows cling to the gnarled trees, their twisted trunks blackened as if scorched from some eternal fire, branches clawing at the sky like skeletal hands. Silence is a weapon here. Every sound carries, bouncing off the blackened trunks, but the deeper you move, the more the forest swallows it whole. It feels like leaving the material world behind, an uneasy space between reality and nightmare, where the living and the dead twist together in thorn and shadow, and the air itself seems alive with menace.

The farther we make our way into the shrouded woods, the more my nerves begin to settle. The steady rhythm of our pace forms a quiet pattern beneath the canopy, lulling me. With each step, my thoughts drift inward, replaying the chaos that led us here and the uneasy silence left in its wake.

Elysia has fallen, but by whose hand? My father is arrogant enough to believe himself capable of such destruction, yet this feels beyond even his reach. And Edin... why did she come after me? Why go through all of this when she had already been rid of me? She knows something. It is written plainly across her face.

Edin's arm brushes against mine, drawing me reluctantly out of my own head. I am not sure how long we have been walking in silence, but judging by the density of the trees around us, it must have been quite a while. The forest feels thicker here, the air heavier, as though the forest is consuming us whole.

I glance down at her. Her eyes are fixed straight ahead, unfocused, as if her thoughts are somewhere far beyond the trail. Her mouth is drawn tight, and she worries at her finger, a small, nervous habit that betrays whatever she is trying to keep hidden.

When she senses my gaze, she finally looks up. Our eyes meet, and for a brief moment, the silence deepens, charged and expectant, as if she is deciding whether to speak or keep whatever weighs on her locked away.

Edin breaks first, her attention snapping back to the path as if she is afraid of what might surface if she holds my eyes any longer. The moment passes without a word between us, the silence stretching on, heavy and deliberate. Our footsteps fall back into rhythm, the only sound not muffled by the forest.

The trees begin to thin just enough for something to take shape ahead. A small cottage emerges from the shadows, half-swallowed by the forest, its warped wood dark with age. A single lantern hangs beside the door, its flame steady and bright despite the stillness of its surroundings, casting a warm glow that feels strangely out of place so deep in the woods.

Perched atop the sagging roof is a crow, black feathers glossy in the lantern light. It watches us without blinking. As we draw closer, I notice something pale tied carefully around its leg: a folded piece of parchment, secured with thin twine, swaying slightly as the bird shifts its weight. I give the crow a nod, and it swoops down, landing on my outstretched arm. I wince at the weight as I slowly untie the twine and take the small note.

My Lord,

I have made a bargain with the earth sprites and secured this cottage for you and Edin. I apologize for the condition of the cottage and beg your forgiveness. The cottage has been warded with defensive enchantments; you may rest and heal here without fear.

I regret that I have no further information regarding Elysia at this time, but please know I am exhausting every avenue available to me. Valker has located Verenia and is escorting her to a healer in the western caves of Helheim, where they will remain until your next instruction.

- Your humble servant,

Oren

I tuck the letter away and give Edin a nod, tipping my chin toward the cottage to urge her forward. I lead the way to the door, the lantern's glow shrinking the shadows just enough to make them bearable. The crow takes flight as we pass beneath the eaves, its feathers whispering against the night before vanishing into the dark.

Chapter 22

Endricks

The door opens without protest. The air inside is warmer than the forest, carrying the scent of old wood, ash, and something faintly sweet. Dried herbs, maybe, or magic settling into the building's bones. As soon as we cross the threshold, the world outside seems to recede, as though the cottage has sealed itself shut behind us. I feel it then, a subtle pressure along my skin, wards knitting closed, unseen hands drawing lines of protection through the air.

Edin exhales softly. I had not realized she had been holding her breath.

The interior is small but deliberate. A single room opens around a stone hearth, its embers still alive, casting low, steady light across worn furniture. A narrow table stands near the wall, two chairs pulled close together as if expecting us. Shelves line the far side of the room, cluttered with jars, bundles of dried plants, and a few objects I do not recognize: smooth stones etched with runes, a vial of black sand, and a mirror clouded with age. A thin curtain divides the space, concealing what I assume is a sleeping alcove.

"Oren?" Edin murmurs, trailing her fingers along the doorframe.

"Yes, apparently he has quite the connection with the earth sprites," I reply. The magic hums quietly beneath my words, tired but stubborn, like a wounded guard refusing to stand down.

She steps farther inside, boots soft against the floorboards. Only once she reaches the hearth does she stop, shoulders slumping as the tension finally drains from her posture. For a moment, she looks smaller, caught in the firelight with shadows hollowing her eyes.

I pull off my tunic, the motion tugging painfully at my side, and I hiss before I can stop myself.

Edin turns instantly, “Let me help you. You are hurt.”

“I have been worse.” A lie, or close enough to one to count.

She does not argue. Instead, she moves with quiet purpose, searching the room. She kneels beside a low chest near the hearth. When she opens it, the faint scent of iron and crushed leaves fills the room. She pulls out a bundle of linen, a small knife, and a jar sealed with wax.

“Sit,” she says, not a request.

I comply, lowering myself onto one of the chairs. The fire pops softly, filling the silence left between us. Edin works without meeting my eyes, fingers steady as she breaks the wax seal and dips the linen into the salve.

"Edin," I say quietly.

Her hands pause.

"You have been carrying something since we left the city. Something you have not told me."

She swallows. The firelight catches the tension in her jaw as she resumes her work, pressing the salve gently against my ribs. It burns and then cools, sinking deep into the ache.

"You do not need to know everything," she says at last.

"I need to know what will get us killed."

Silence answers me.

She binds the linen carefully, each wrap deliberate, as though she is stalling. When she finally meets my gaze, her eyes are darker than before, reflecting more shadow than flame.

"You should not have come after me," I growl. "You were safe back in Purgatory."

"Safe," she snorts.

"Yes, safe. You were safer with that egotistical meat sack than you will ever be here with me!"

"You have no idea what nightmarish torture I have endured in your absence," she snaps.

I clamp my mouth shut, teeth grinding. Rage, at anyone, *anything* that laid a hand on her, and at the secrets she keeps buried, churns violently in my chest.

"Elysia was not just attacked," she says. "It was unmade. Unraveled from the inside out."

My chest tightens. "That kind of magic…"

"Does not belong to your father," she finishes. "It belongs to me."

Silence stretches again, but this time it feels different. Thinner. Fragile. Edin looks away, no longer able to meet my gaze, her face twisting with disgust and despair.

"After the veil closed, everything unraveled. Osiris…" She winces. "He was not who I believed him to be."

I bite back my response, allowing the silence to seep back in while she gathers herself.

"Blythe and I were thrown in the dungeon, chained, and tortured."

I shift, unable to sit still.

"He used his chaos magic to break into my mind," she says, voice shaking, "shaping himself into you, convincing me *you* had come to save me." Her composure fractures, her voice cracks, and tears spill freely now. "I thought it was you, Endricks. He, you," She drags a hand through her hair in frustrated disbelief. "You took me upstairs and fucked me, and then reality clawed its way back in, and it was Osiris on top of me." Her breath stutters. "I never even made it out of the dungeon." She pulls her cloak aside, exposing the welts, bruises, and burns marred across her neck. "I am so sorry, Endricks."

The fury inside me surges, wild and blinding. I drop to my knees in front of her, hands gentle as I cup her face, thumbs brushing away her tears until she is forced to meet my eyes.

"Do not apologize," I say, my voice low and unyielding. "Not for *his* crimes."

"Elysia has fallen because of *me*! He went after Blythe," she grabs her arms, pulling herself inward, disgust running across her face. "I could not bear the thought of his hands on her, Endricks. I could never live with myself. He…"

"Enough," I cut in softly but firmly, grabbing her hands. "You do not need to justify your choices, not to me."

I sit back on my heels, still holding her hands, letting the firelight dance across both of us. Silence stretches, but it is no longer oppressive; it hums with unspoken fear, grief, and a fragile trust.

"You survived," I say finally, voice low, almost a growl. "That is what matters."

Edin shakes her head, the motion slow, exhausted. "I do not know if I survived *myself*," she whispers. "Every moment since…the veil, Osiris, the chaos… It is as if part of me is stuck there, chained in that dungeon." Her eyes glimmer in the firelight, haunted. "And now Elysia… Blythe… they are out there, and because of *me*, they are vulnerable."

"Where is Blythe now?"

“I cast her back to Windemere when we escaped the dungeon,” she sniffles. “To warn the king. To keep her safe.”

I lean closer, tilting her chin back up.“You did what you had to, and Blythe will understand that.”

Her hands tremble in mine, and for a moment, I allow myself to feel the full weight of her presence, her fierceness, and the damage that the world tried to imprint upon her.

“I should have been stronger,” she mutters, barely audible.

“You were strong enough to survive Osiris,” I correct her. “And strong enough to find me. That is all the strength we need right now.”

She nods, pulling closer to me.

Needing to change the subject before my frustrations consume me, I lean over to the chest by the hearth, pulling out the salves and clean pieces of fabric Edin found earlier. She shifts to let me lean away, though her shoulders remain tense, her hands fidgeting in her lap. The firelight flickers across her bruises, burns, and welts, painting every mark in sharp relief.

"Stay still," I murmur, settling behind her. My hands are steady despite the fury still thrumming beneath my skin. I dab the salve onto a clean cloth, pressing it gently against the worst of her burns. She flinches at the sting but does not pull away.

"I am fine," she says softly, but there is no defensiveness in her voice, only exhaustion.

I wipe away dried blood and dirt, working carefully around her neck and shoulders, making sure the linen wraps are snug but not tight. Every touch is deliberate, careful, and an unspoken promise that she is safe here for tonight.

She lets out a shuddering breath, leaning back further against me as I work. For the first time since we have been together today, her body fully relaxes.

"You should sleep," I say quietly once the worst of the wounds are cleaned and bandaged. "You have been through a lot."

She hesitates, eyes fixed on the fire, but the weariness in her posture betrays her. "And you?" she asks.

"I will rest in a moment," I reply, working my hands into her shoulders until the tension in them slowly melts away. She tilts her head back, letting her eyes close, and the firelight softens her face.

I kiss her forehead and drag a blanket over us both, careful not to jostle her. I make no attempt to move us to the bed; the simple comfort of her presence is enough for me here on the floor. Edin's breathing slows, each exhale deeper than the last. Even in sleep, there is a fragility about her that makes my chest tighten. I keep watch, hands resting lightly on her arms, until my own eyelids grow heavy. I shift, letting the warmth of the fire and her presence anchor me, and finally, exhaustion pulls me under, too.

CHAPTER 23

EDIN

The first light of dawn filters through the thin curtains, pale and grey, cutting across the floorboards like sharp knives. The forest outside is quiet, too quiet. The kind of silence that carries the weight of waiting. I shift under the blanket, every muscle stiff, every nerve screaming that yesterday is not yet behind me.

My neck aches where the burns and welts still mark me. I glance down at the linen wraps. They are clean, dry, and carefully applied. *I must have dozed off before Endricks was finished.* My chest tightens at the thought that he has been carrying my weight alongside his own.

He stirs beside me. The light glints off his features, casting half his face in shadow. He reaches for the spare blanket, draping it over my shoulders without a word. A small gesture, quiet and caring. I blink back a surge of something I do not want to name, something that has nothing to do with safety and everything to do with trust.

"Morning," he says, low. His voice carries a steadiness I desperately want to cling to.

"Morning," I murmur, voice hoarse. I pull myself up, wincing at the tenderness across my body. He is instantly alert, arms shooting out to support me. I do not protest, not now, not when it matters. We sit in silence for a moment, the fire somehow still sputtering away, and the cottage holding our fragile peace. The wards hum faintly around us. I can feel them, the subtle pull of their magic threading through the walls, creating a net of safety for now.

"The crows," I say.

"What about them?"

"Can you summon one here so I may send a letter to Blythe?"

He rubs my arm as he stands, kissing the top of my head, and snaps his fingers.

I blink, and a black shape materializes out of the twilight. A crow, impossibly large, impossibly real, lands gracefully on the sill. Its feathers gleam even in the dim light, glossy as wet obsidian. It tilts its head toward me, watching, unblinking.

"Thank you."

"Your wish is my command, Your Highness," he says, with a wink.

The comment brings a smile to my face, knowing the old Endricks is still in there somewhere.

Blythe,

If you are reading this, know that I am safe, for now, and so is Endricks. I am so sorry. Everything I did was meant to keep you safe, even if it did not seem that way. Have you alerted the King of Windemere? I have received word that Elysia has fallen, and the world has grown far more dangerous than we feared. Still, trust that we are preparing to reclaim what has been stolen. Wait for me in Windemere. I will find you.

- With love,

Edin

I fold the letter and hand it to Endricks. Leaning back in the chair, I watch him tie the small note to the crow's leg with twine he found inside the wooden chest. It jumps off the windowsill, flapping its wings once, and then disintegrates into a mist, traveling beyond the realms. The thought of sending it gnaws at me… *Will she understand?*

The hours pass slowly. We do not speak much, but the way our hearts beat in rhythm builds a tension that crawls across my skin. I rest against the wall, feeling the ache in my shoulders ease just slightly. Endricks tends to small chores, stoking the fire, shifting the embers. I try to close my eyes, to let sleep pull me under, but my mind refuses to quiet.

Eventually, I hear a soft thump against the wooden chest. Endricks looks at me, eyebrows raised. I approach cautiously. Inside, neatly stacked, are bread, fruit, dried meat, and a small note written in Oren's careful hand.

My Lord,

Food and fresh water have been left for you. The cottage will maintain these supplies for as long as you remain. Rest, heal, and take counsel. You are safe here, for now.

- Oren

A flicker of relief runs through me. Simple sustenance and a reminder that someone is still working on our behalf. I gather the modest meal, and we eat in silence, the act almost sacred after the chaos of the last days. The warmth of the cottage, the smell of the fire, and the taste of real food all feel like luxuries I once had in Windemere with my family.

We spend the day in quiet recovery. I tend my wounds, clean and rewrap them with Endricks's help, and he allows me the space to rest without intrusion. He does not press me to speak, but when I glance at him, I catch the watchfulness in his eyes, and the tension intensifies.

Hours stretch into the afternoon. The fire burns with a low, crackling heat. I drift in and out of sleep, comforted by the soft hum of the wards around us and Endricks's quiet company. The cottage feels alive in its own quiet way, as though it knows we are trying to heal, and in knowing that, it embraces us.

The sky fades from a pale grey to charcoal, and the shadows begin to crawl out of their corners for the night. I sit near the window, watching the light filter through the trees, the mist curling around the roots. Endricks joins me, leaning against the wall, quiet, patient. I realize we have spent the day here, healing, resting, and existing somewhere between safety and the world beyond. I lean back, letting the warmth of him seep into my bones, a striking difference from yesterday. The letter to Blythe remains on my mind, a tether to hope. The note from Oren, the food, the fire, all small proofs that we are not entirely alone.

The grey finally turns to night, and shadows stretch long across the floor. The day is ending, and with it, the fragile peace we have found. Outside, danger awaits, but for now, in this small cottage, I allow myself to breathe.

Endricks moves towards me, startling me and pulling me from the calm trance. He lifts me without a word, his arms solid around me. The world narrows to the warmth of him as he carries me to the bed, each step deliberate and silent. When he lays me down, he does not pull away; he settles on the other side, close enough that the space between us pulses. My breath catches at the faint brush of his hand against mine, at the steady thrum of him so near, and for a heartbeat, the silence feels like it could break into something neither of us is ready to name.

His gaze sweeps across me, soft, urgent, a warning and an invitation all at once, making my pulse drum in my ears. I shift, letting my shoulder brush against his arm, a whisper of contact, and he responds with the faintest tilt of his body toward mine.

The air between us feels taut, as if it could tear at any moment. I lean closer, daring him. His breath catches, and his hand moves, tentative at first, brushing my fingers. The simple touch ignites a storm beneath my skin, and I can not stop the small shiver that climbs my spine.

***

I trace the line of his jaw, as if memorizing the planes of him, the angles I have come to know in fleeting glances and quiet moments. Endricks does not pull away. His hand finds mine again, fingers curling, holding, grounding, and the tension that has been simmering all day, the pull, the unspoken need, presses against my ribs until I can barely breathe.

"Edin…" he murmurs, voice low and rough, and it makes my chest ache.

I respond with nothing but movement, leaning in, letting our foreheads touch, lips hovering just shy of connection, tasting the heat that has built silently, relentlessly in the space between us.

The fire flickers, throwing shadows across the walls, dancing over our skin. Every small motion feels monumental, every brush of hand or sigh of breath charged with everything neither of us has dared to say. I feel the tremor in his chest mirrored in my own. Every nerve is alight, every glance loaded with something dangerous and exquisite. The moment hinges on the edge of all restraint.

"Endricks," I whisper.

He brushes his nose against mine. I can feel his reserve, treating me as if I may fall apart.

"Endricks, I need you to take *that* fucking memory," I say, breathlessly, "break it, shatter it, make it your own."

"Edin," he says, locking eyes with me, concern running across his face.

"I am not fragile, you know that better than anyone. All of the torture, all of the chaos, take it," I beg, grinding against him.

He takes one final moment to make sure that I mean every word that falls from my lips, then he grabs my neck and shoves me onto my back. I look up at him in awe as he releases his hold, leans back, and pulls his shirt up and over his head. My eyes drag down his chest, following the intricate tattoos that dip below his waist. Grabbing his belt, I glance up, and he gives me a satisfied smirk, flicking his eyes downward.

I tug his belt free, sliding it from each loop before letting it drop to the floor. He motions for me to sit up, and I do so without hesitation. Our lips crash into each other, needy and frantic. His hands glide down my waist, igniting my skin as they go, until they catch at the hem of my gown. He tears my gown up and over my head, the suddenness stealing my breath as fabric gives way, and then our lips collide again, fierce and urgent. A shiver races up my spine as my heart pounds wildly in my chest. The bed creaks under our weight as I drop back down, taking Endricks with me. I wrap my legs around him, pulling him, needing his body against mine.

I run my fingers through his hair and up his horns, then bite down on his lip. He lets out a growl, grinding his dick against the single layer of cloth between him and my pussy. Letting out a moan, I push back, the small distance making me feral. He yanks my arms up above my head, pinning them, and leans back, continuing his tease. A throbbing ache pulses in my clit, and I bite down on my own lip.

"Please," I moan, breathlessly.

He chuckles, grinding into me again. "You will have to do better than that."

"Please, Endricks!" I beg.

"Not quite, Your Highness."

He effortlessly lifts me from the bed and carries me to the center of the room, where a wooden column stands. Slowly, he lowers me to my feet and yanks my hands above my head again.

"Do not move," he says, running his thumb across my lip.

I am wound so tight I could cry, but I hold myself motionless, every nerve straining in anticipation. I watch him stride across the room, then return swiftly, belt in hand, a mischievous glint dancing in his eyes. He loops the belt around my wrist and the column, pulling it taut until it bites into my skin. He plants kisses on my neck, beginning his descent down my body at an agonizingly slow pace. I rub my thighs together, needing more, until he is kneeling before me.

He drags his eyes over my body hungrily. "A true goddess."

He pulls out his dagger and presses it against my inner thigh. Methodically, he runs it up my skin, his knuckles brushing over my undergarments, then curves towards my waist. A soft moan escapes my lips, and I push my hips forward. He steps to his feet, pulling the blade up my side. Red welts begin to form, and goosebumps run across my body. I jerk my head forward, wrist screaming against my weight, urgently needing his mouth on mine.

"You want more?" he says into my lips.

"Harder," I say, nipping his lip, drawing blood.

Applying more pressure, he drags the blade back down my side, setting my body alight. He stops just above the fabric, the only barrier between me and his cock. My body begs for release. He locks eyes with me, then he slides the dagger below its seams. With one swift movement, he jerks the blade down, completely exposing me.

Thin, crimson droplets run down my side. Endricks slides down my body, leaving a trail of kisses in his wake that leave me panting. He tosses the dagger aside, running his tongue up to my center. I throw my head back in relief. His hands wander up my stomach, smearing blood across my chest. His fingers find my nipples, twisting them till I yelp, and he dips his tongue deep inside me, leaving me teetering on the edge. I wrap my legs around his neck, not allowing him to break free. He welcomes it, sucking on my clit. I grind against his face, desperate and hungry.

"Such a needy girl, you are, Belladonna," he growls.

Endricks reaches down and begins stroking himself, letting out a low groan. The sound of his own pleasure sends me into a frenzy. Every nerve coils tighter, my body trembling as tears brim and threaten to spill, caught on the edge of release. Suddenly, he stops, and frustration crawls across me. He grabs the knife, releases me from my restraints, and lifts me. We crash down onto the bed, mouths interlocked, feverishly grabbing at each other. I slide my hand up his shaft, counting all six of his piercings, and then he pushes into me.

A pulse runs through my body as we connect, and for this moment, everything is right in the realms. He slams into me with no mercy, like his life depends on it. I weave my fingers through his hair as my eyes roll back. No longer able to contain it, I surrender, allowing waves of pleasure to crash over me. My pussy clamps down, and he pumps into me harder, faster, chasing his own release. Colors flare and dance behind my eyelids, bright and blinding, consuming me. Endricks falls forward, wrapping his hand around my neck. A low moan spills from his lips, and his grip tightens on my throat as he is met with his own gratification.

He kisses my forehead and brushes a silver strand of hair from my face, lingering just long enough for our eyes to meet. The steady pulse of our fated connection hums, sending warmth rippling across my skin. He does not say a word, and he does not need to. The warmth of the bond tightens, no longer soothing, but purposeful, like a current snapping taut. As it does, something inside me *loosens*. The screaming edges of my thoughts dull. The images I have been bracing against, the fire, the restraints, *his* voice that never stopped, begin to blur. They do not vanish all at once. They *fade*.

Painful memories drift away like ash in water, their sharpness dissolving into distant echoes. The weight I have been carrying in my chest lightens, breath by breath, until the terror that once clawed at my ribs retreats into silence. I gasp, startled, not by fear, but by the sudden absence of it. Endricks feels it, too. His eyes darken, not with concern, but with resolve. The bond pulses once, strong, deliberate, and understanding floods me.

He is taking them.

Not erasing them... but pulling them out of reach.

Endricks gently slides off of me, easing onto the bed as though afraid to disturb what he has gathered back into me. He keeps me close, one arm curved around my shoulders, the other steady at my waist. I fit there like my body remembers its place, even if my mind is only just learning it.

The bond hums faintly now, no longer pulling, no longer buzzing. It feels satisfied and complete. Exhaustion seeps in where fear once lived. My eyelids flutter, the last remnants of tension draining away with each slow breath. I listen to the rhythm of his heart, steady and unyielding, and let it set the pace for my own.

He presses one last kiss into my hair, a promise without words. Then, sleep takes me. There are no dreams of fire, no sudden jolts of terror: only darkness, soft and unbroken, and the certainty of warmth at my back. Somewhere in the quiet, Endricks's breathing deepens, his hold tightening just enough to keep me anchored as he follows me into sleep.

Chapter 24

Endricks

I wake to a darkness that is not quite night. The walls of the cottage are dim and gray, shadows crawling along them as though alive, moving with the pulse of something unseen. The smell of smoke and damp earth hangs heavy, sharp and acrid, carrying the taste of ash that never fully leaves the air.

Edin lies beside me, still encumbered by the soft haze of sleep, her chest rising and falling with even, calm breaths. The bond hums faintly, steady and sure, a tether that reaches across the weight of this nightmare. Even here, where the air tastes of decay and shadow, she is radiant, a small defiance against the gray that presses against the windows.

I reach out, brushing a lock of hair from her face, and the bond hums stronger, recognizing the connection I guard. Her fingers twitch against mine, even in sleep, and I tighten my hold, drawing her closer. *I will not allow this chaos to consume her, not while I still draw breath.*

She stirs, a small, fragile movement that pulls me back from the edge of sleep. Her eyelids flutter, and I watch her take in the dim room, the curl of her hands, the rise and fall of her chest. Every careful breath she takes reassures me that the remnants of her pain have retreated, muted echoes that I can feel but she cannot.

"Good morning," she whispers, giving me a soft smile. The word trembles in the gray, fragile against the air that presses through the cabin walls.

I shift closer, resting my hand over hers, feeling the familiar warmth. "Good morning, Belladonna," I reply, my voice low. I can see her relax slightly, letting the small trust between us settle.

Her gaze drifts to mine, cautious but unafraid, and for a moment, I allow myself to simply look at her, at the fragile curve of her cheek, at the line of her jaw softened by sleep. Even here, in the woods that belong more to shadows than to life, she is mine to protect.

A crow cries off in the distance, its harsh, jagged call cutting through the stillness of the cabin. She tenses, wrapping the blanket around her shoulders, and rises, moving toward the window with quiet urgency. My hand hovers, hesitant to touch her, because this hope, this cautious anticipation, is hers alone. I watch her frame in the dim light, the shadows of the cottage soft against her skin, her gaze fixed on the woods beyond.

She presses her hands to the glass, her fingers pale against the gray of the morning. The forest lies twisted and dark, the trees gnarled like frozen screams, yet her eyes are bright, waiting, expectant.

"Endricks…" she breathes, not looking at me, voice threaded with something fragile and yearning.

I rise and step into her back, setting my hands on her shoulder. "I am here," I murmur. The warmth of her hope brushes against me as I rest my chin on her head. We stand in silence, eyes fixed and waiting. The crow cries out again, but further, shrouded in the forest. Her shoulders drop, and she pushes off the windowsill, all hope draining from her face. She looks up at me with concern. I instinctively touch her face, and tears begin to fall.

"Something is wrong, Endricks," she mumbles. "Blythe has not responded, and that is… very unlike her."

I wipe her tears, tightening my grip on her face. "Then we shall return to Helheim Castle and go check on her ourselves."

"But King Adonis?"

"Will be handled once we know Blythe is safe, and we speak with the king of Windemere about Elysia. I am sure Father will be more understanding of your… destruction once we have information about this rebellion."

She nods, sniffling.

"I will send word to Oren and Valker to wait for us near the edge of the Weeping Thicket."

I pull her close again, planting a kiss on her forehead, and then break away with a soft sigh. The parchment waits, smooth under my fingers, the ink glinting like liquid night. I snap my fingers twice, and the crows land in a flutter of wings, black shadows against the dim light. I dip the pen in ink, letting the first stroke of words ripple across the parchment. Their eyes glint in anticipation, as if they already know what I am about to write.

My pen scratches across the paper, and the crow's wings stir impatiently, eager for the command. They descend from the shadows, black eyes glinting with sharp intelligence. I hold up each letter in turn, feeling the weight of what I am sending into the world.

"Take them," I murmur.

One crow rises with the first letter, the other with the second. I toss each a generous piece of bread as a token of thanks and then watch as they take flight, wings beating once before their forms unravel. Mist curls around the space they leave behind, swallowing the beat of their wings until even the echo is gone. I remain still for a moment longer, listening, an old habit, though I know the message is already in motion. Words, once sent, have a way of growing teeth.

"How soon are we returning?" Edin asks, still staring at where the crows departed.

"As soon as we can gather supplies, I suppose."

She turns and glides over to me, eyeing me up and down. "And your wounds?"

"They will buff out," I say, rubbing the back of my neck.

"Do not give me that bullshit," she says, with an eye roll, pulling me from my seat and over to the chest. "Sit."

Chapter 25

Edin

I settle beside Endricks, close enough to feel the heat of his body. When I loosen the bandage at his shoulder, his breath hitches, and his body tenses in response. The wound is still angry and red at the edges, but it is clean. That, at least, is something.

"Hold still," I murmur, trying to focus.

I clean the wound with steady hands, easing away the worst of the ache before pressing the salve in gently. He exhales under my fingers, tension loosening, and something in my chest tightens in response. I focus on the work, on making sure he heals, because letting my mind wander anywhere else may send me into a spiral.

When he tends to me in turn, his care is just as deliberate. He unwraps my bindings slowly, pausing whenever I flinch, his thumb brushing reassuringly over my skin. The salve stings, then soothes, and I exhale, letting the tension bleed out of my shoulders. His touch lingers, and I find myself leaning into it before I can stop myself.

Once the last bandage is secured, I gather what supplies remain: herbs, a clean cloth, and a nearly empty vial. I pack them away into a small satchel and grab my cloak. Endricks gathers what is left of the food and water before wordlessly handing them to me to put in the satchel as well.

We take one last glance over the cottage, our haven, and I let out a sigh. Endricks interlocks his fingers with mine, and we step out the door. Outside, the forest greets us with a bone-chilling silence, sending goosebumps across my skin. He squeezes my hand, giving me a nod of reassurance. I throw him a smile, draw my cloak over my head, and fall into step beside him. My stomach begins to twist as we reach the forest. Helheim Castle waits somewhere beyond the trees, dark and unavoidable.

The moment we step beneath the twisted canopy, the air shifts, cooler, heavier, carrying the forever-present scent of ash and damp earth. Shadows cling to the roots and branches, stretching long and watchful, but I do not slow. I twinge as my freshly wrapped wounds pull with each step. I adjust my grip on my pack, mindful of the pace Endricks's has set. Neither of us says it, but we are measuring each other constantly, watching for a falter, ready to catch each other.

The ground crunches softly beneath our boots. Somewhere deeper in the trees, something shifts and then stills. The Weeping Thicket is never quiet without reason. I brush my fingers against his sleeve, a small, grounding touch, and feel him angle subtly toward me in response. It is enough, a promise without words.

The path toward Helheim Castle is half memory, half instinct. The forest resists us the way it always does, branches clawing, roots twisting underfoot, but we move through it together, steady and unyielding. Behind us, the cottage vanishes into shadow. Ahead, the dark thickens. I draw a breath, square my shoulders, and keep walking. Whatever Helheim has waiting, we will meet it side by side, wounded, weary, and still choosing each other.

Chapter 26

Osiris

The impossibly black floors reflect my boots as I step into Helheim. The veil parts at my command without hesitation, as though it has always known me as its master. The air is acrid, thick with smoke and the suffering of others. I breathe it in anyway, savoring the promise in it. My plans are aligning. Nothing and no one will stand in my way now.

Portraits of King Adonis line the long hall. *The man loves the sight of himself.* The first decree I issue when I take this throne will be the removal of his face from these walls. No one will forget who their rightful king is.

Six soldiers follow at my back as we make our way down the long hall toward the main corridor. Echoes of pain mingle with the sound of clanking chains through the smoky air. Cries of misery sweep through the halls, close enough for guests to hear. A charming first impression. I almost admire it. Fear is a useful tool that I intend to keep sharpened.

"State your purpose," a hellion guard growls as he approaches, chest puffed in forced authority.

"Take me to your king. I have urgent business."

His eyes rake over me. "Name?"

I square my shoulders and lift my chin. "King Osiris, Ruler of Elysia."

The color drains from his face, and he drops to one knee. "Forgive me, Sire. King Adonis will require your purpose before granting an audience."

"I bring opportunity. My enemies multiply by the day. I will soon have a surplus of traitors in need of… accommodation. I believe your king would enjoy hosting them."

The guard hesitates only briefly before a slow grin spreads across his face. He snaps his fingers. A fire sprite materializes, charred skin split with glowing veins of molten light. The guard leans down, speaking low to him. The sprite's eyes flare, then it vanishes in a snap of heat and ash. *A messenger.*

The guard spins on his heels, shoulders pulled back once again, and waves his arm, directing us, "Right this way, King Osiris."

The sound of my title settles over me, bringing satisfaction.

We move through the castle. Obsidian walls swallow the firelight, spitting it back out in fractured, blood-red spears. Smoke clings to the vaulted ceilings. Helheim is shadows, shaped into architecture, brutal, unapologetic, and honest in its cruelty. It is nothing like Elysia. Elysia gleams. Golden spires pierce an endless sunset sky. Marble halls glow in perpetual sunlight. Laughter carries on the warm wind. The air smells of citrus blossoms and sweet wine, not ash and iron. It is radiant. Celebrated. Worshipped... And *suffocating*.

Helheim does not pretend to be anything other than what it is. Elysia smiles while sharpening a blade behind its back. Strangely, both realms suit me. One reflects what I show the world. The other reflects what I am.

Banners bearing Adonis's crest hang outside his chambers. Even in private, he cannot resist spectacle. Wards pulse along the carved sigils lining the door. Strong magic meant to keep most aggressors at bay. I am not *most aggressors*. The guard knocks, the hollow boom of his fist echoing down the hall. We wait, and my patience begins to thin. Then, footsteps approach from within, and the doors open. Adonis appears flanked by guards, offering me a smug nod.

"I hear congratulations are in order." King Adonis smiles, but it never touches his eyes. He does not invite us in. He stands in the doorway dressed in casual attire, deliberately disrespectful. His every move is calculated.

"These formalities are unnecessary," I reply smoothly. "I propose a treaty. One that benefits us both."

A flicker of interest sharpens his gaze, and navy smoke begins to swirl around him. "I am listening."

"My reign has created… unrest. Rebels," I scrunch my nose in disgust, "are gathering. I will eliminate them; do not worry about that. Every dissenter will be sent here for your… *recreation*. I hear Greybar has vacancies."

His arrogance falters, just slightly. "I will consider it," he says at last. "You may show yourself out."

For a moment, I simply stare at him. *Dismissed.* The insult burns. I signal my soldiers, flicking my wrist to my own guards. "Adonis," I spit, rage curling in my throat. "I do not think we are quite done here."

He turns slowly, guards closing ranks before him. "Greybar has lovely accommodations," he replies, fire lighting his eyes. "I could reserve you a cell."

I draw my sword, my men follow in unison, and we push forward. Steel sings through smoke. I step back from the clash and focus on the wards. Chaos coils through my veins. I drive it into the carved sigils. My magic twists down my wrist into the blade. Stone cracks and fractures under the pressure of the countering arcane pulsing through it. The wards shatter with a thunderous boom. Power surges through me, unhindered. I split it outward, duplicating my forces. Six becomes twelve, and confusion erupts. Hellion guards fall quickly beneath disciplined blades. Adonis steps forward, and what is left of his guards shift around him, but he lifts a hand, and they retreat to the walls. He wants this witnessed.

"You came here with six men and a threat dressed as an offer," he smirks. "Did you think I would not smell blood in those arrogant words?"

I smile slowly. "Did you?"

The air changes. Moisture gathers along the floor first, thin, almost imperceptible. Then the temperature drops. Firelight dims as steam curls along the ceiling. Water beads across the obsidian walls. Adonis flexes his fingers, and the droplets rise. They spiral upward, twisting into hovering ribbons of liquid that coil around him like living serpents.

Ah. So that is his trick.

The water lashes forward. I barely have time to pivot before a whip of liquid cracks across my chest. The force slams me backward into a pillar, and pain explodes through my ribs. He does not give me a second to breathe. Another whip strikes my legs, sweeping them out from under me. The floor floods instantly, water rising to my boots as if the room itself is bleeding. My soldiers charge, but a crashing wave hurls them aside, bodies smashing into walls.

Adonis advances through the rising tide, perfectly balanced, perfectly calm. “You are ambitious,” he says. “But ambition without discipline is merely suicide.”

He flicks his wrist, and the water surges upward, wrapping around my throat like a tightening noose. It forces its way into my mouth, my nose. *Drowning inside a castle.* I snarl and send chaos ripping outward. The water trembles but does not weaken its push. I drive my magic into the runes along the walls. The wards flare, intertwining with my own magic. A shockwave cracks through the chamber, disrupting Adonis's concentration for half a heartbeat. It is enough, and I split myself. One of my illusions tears free of the water's hold while the other lunges forward. Adonis reacts instantly, liquid hardening into a shield, my blade screeching against it as if striking glass. He thrusts his hand toward my clone. The water condenses into a spear and punches straight through its chest. The duplicate dissolves.

He learns quickly.

A torrent crashes into my side before I can recover. I feel something give in my shoulder as I am thrown across the chamber. I hit the overturned desk hard enough to splinter wood. Blood fills my mouth. Adonis does not mock me this time. He gestures sharply, and the water on the floor spikes upward into jagged, icicle-like shards. One grazes my thigh, slicing through my armor. Another punches into my side, making me stagger. He is not just controlling the surge of water. He is *weaponizing* pressure, density, and temperature, down to its very molecule.

"You should have stayed in your golden paradise," he says, voice echoing through the chamber. "Helheim devours men like you."

I wipe blood from my lip and grin. "Then let it try."

I slam both palms against the soaked stone and send chaos ripping through every molecule of water in the room. The liquid convulses violently, and Adonis's control wavers. I charge through the collapsing tide and crash into him before he can reassemble it. My sword slices across his ribs, drawing blood. He grunts, retaliating instantly, water hardening around his fist, which he drives into my jaw. My vision flashes white. He follows with a surge that slams into my wounded side, forcing a roar from my throat.

We are both bleeding now. *Good.* He summons a towering wall of water and brings it crashing down on me. I brace, pushing upward with raw force. The impact caves the floor beneath us, cracks spiderwebbing through obsidian. I split again. This time, not to distract, but to overwhelm. Three of me begin circling him now. The water lashes out wildly, striking one, then another, but the third reaches him. I seize his wrist, forcing his magic to stutter, and drive my blade deep into his ribs. He gasps, but he does not fall, and blood begins to drip from the corners of his mouth. With a snarl, he grabs my collar and releases every ounce of compressed water he has left. It detonates outward. The blast sends us both crashing in opposite directions. I land hard, ribs screaming, pain burning in my abdomen where one of his earlier shards lodged itself.

Across the chamber, Adonis struggles to his feet, blood soaking his side, but his eyes still burn bright. Water gathers again, thinner now. Slower. He is weakening, but so am I. I do not give him the chance. I hurl chaos like a spear. It shatters what remains of his control, ripping the moisture from the air itself. The water drops uselessly to the floor.

Before he can recover, I launch myself across the room and drive him backward into the wall. My blade punches through his chest, through his spine, and into the obsidian. Pinning him against the wall of his own chamber, impaled by his own need for gaudy displays even in private. His body jerks, and blood spills, mixing with the last thin sheets of water at our feet.

He grips my wrist weakly, grinding his teeth. "You… will not… rule here…"

I lean close, breathing in salt and iron. "And yet I have defeated you." Then I jerk my sword back through him, twisting as I pull it out, tearing flesh and dislodging bone.

His strength leaves him, coughing wetly as blood drips from his lips. He lets out a slow exhale, and the chamber falls silent except for the ragged pull of my own breath. I gather myself, pushing red locks from my face, then spin around towards my men.

They fall to their knees. "Osiris, King of Elysia and Helheim," they say in unison.

A smile creeps across my face at the sound of their chant. "You will stand guard here, in Helheim Castle. I will return to Elysia to clean this," I grimace, looking down at myself, "putrid, unholy blood from my armor, and I will return with an army to announce my reign with Fallon by my side." I leave my men with that, exiting the chamber, making my way back down to the veil, striking down anyone in my path.

Things are coming together quite smoothly. King Adonis clung to the notion that another would bar my ascent. Even in death, he fails to grasp the lengths I will go to secure what is mine.

Chapter 27

Endricks

The silence feels wrong as the last line of trees comes into view. I know Helheim by heart, every corridor, every contour of stone. What rises before us does not match my memory. The wards along Helheim's perimeter should greet me, subtle, familiar, a pressure at the back of my skull. Instead, there is only fractured silence, like a spell cut mid-breath. I slow, instinct tightening my grip as the trees thin and the castle comes into view.

Towers that once stood immutable now lie collapsed, their broken crowns scattered across the blackened ground. Runes along the battlements flicker weakly, some burned out entirely, others warped into symbols I do not recognize. Smoke coils upward in thin, exhausted spirals, carrying the stench of ash, blood, and ruined magic.

Edin stops beside me. I can feel her attention sharpen, cataloging every detail as I am. We finally turn to each other, confusion and fear swirling together. Before a word can leave my mouth, a shift at the treeline catches my attention. Instinctively, I grab Edin, jerking her behind me. Three figures emerge from the shadows, weapons lowered but not sheathed. Even battered, they are unmistakable: Valker, Verenia, and Oren.

Relief hits fast and quietly. All three of them, alive. Valker's armor is cracked along the shoulder, Verenia's sleeve is dark with drying blood, and Oren's expression is tight with the effort of holding himself together.

"They came through the veil," Oren says before I can ask. His voice is hoarse. "Like they have walked the path before."

"Who?" I snap.

"Elysians, My Lord."

"Osiris," Edin mutters.

"As soon as I received your letter, I made my way out of the castle to await your arrival. The sounds of chaos and destruction rang out as I reached the outer wall." Oren flicks his eyes towards the castle, "Yet, it has been eerily quiet for some time now."

I lock eyes with Valker, then Verenia. "Are you both healed?"

They both nod, jaws clenched.

"Then let us see what all the commotion is about," I say.

I grab Edin's hand before she can pull away, threading my fingers more firmly through hers, anchoring us both. Up close, the sternness on Edin's face is almost convincing: jaw set, eyes fixed forward, shoulders squared like she is bracing for impact, but the tremor betrays her. It runs through her fingers first, a faint shiver I might have missed if I were not holding her hand. Then it travels up her arm like a suppressed storm. The realization lands heavier than the chaos around us.

I shift half a step closer, angling my body so I am between her and the broken rise of stone ahead. Not shielding, *she would be livid*, but present, solid. Something that remains unchanged when the world around us does.

"Hey," I murmur, low enough that only she can hear. My thumb rubs slow circles over the back of her hand, grounding, steady. "I got you."

Her stern demeanor melts for only a moment, and she gives me a small smile, then the mask slips back on.

The castle looms closer with every step, warped but still standing, its once-pristine sigils scorched and half-erased. Each mark tells a story

I do not like reading. The air grows thicker as we pass beneath the gate, heavy with the residue of broken wards and spent magic.

I keep Edin close, my awareness split between the ruined courtyard and her steady presence at my side. Valker and Verenia fan out ahead, weapons ready, while Oren lingers just behind us, eyes tracking the shadows along the walls.

Stone is torn and cratered, as if the ground itself resisted and lost. Scattered debris crunches beneath our boots, fragments of rune-etched masonry, splintered weapons, blood darkened to nearly black. I recognize too many of the fallen sigils, their purposes unraveling in my mind as I pass them. Valker leans around the corner, scanning ahead, then nods in approval. I take the lead, making our way towards my father's quarters.

We move deeper, step by careful step, every sense straining for a sign of life. The silence presses in on us, deafening in the long, broken hall. Our boots pass over fallen Hellions, bodies strewn where they made their last stand, armor split and busted. Anger floods my veins, hot and relentless, but I feel no remorse for the pathetic bastards.

A low sound echoes through the halls ahead. I raise a hand, and the group stills. Edin shifts closer, her shoulder brushing mine, and I draw a slow breath to steady myself. The first blade comes without warning. I feel Edin tense beside me a heartbeat before I see it, white steel catching the ruin-light as an Elysian guard lunges from behind a shattered column. I shove her back on instinct and bring my arm, magic snapping into place just as the blade strikes. The impact rattles through my bones.

"So they stayed," I growl.

More of them step into view, four, then six, in golden armor, marked with the sigil of the heavens. Their eyes track us as if we have already been judged and found guilty. Edin does not wait; she moves as she always does, decisive and lethal. Steel flashes as she closes the distance, striking low and fast, forcing one guard back before he can raise his shield. I follow, weaving fire through the air and slamming it into another's chest. The magic detonates outward, hurling him into the stone hard enough to crack it.

They adapt instantly. One breaks for Edin, spear sweeping toward her ribs. I twist the flame, sending it with a flare. Space folds just enough for me to intercept, my blade catching the spear and wrenching it aside.

"Stay with me, Your Highness," I wink.

"I am," she answers, breathless but fierce.

We fight back-to-back, instinct taking over where words fail. I break their formations, sending out a sheet of ice across the onyx floors, just enough to throw them off balance while Edin exploits every opening, every misstep. Her blade finds joints, throats, and the narrow weaknesses that armor cannot protect.

One guard slips past me through the mayhem. I hear Edin grunt, pain, not fear, and something cold snaps loose in my chest. I turn and unleash what little control I have left, driving an ice shard straight through the guard's shield. It collapses inward, taking him with it, with a sound like stone grinding against bone.

Silence crashes down just as suddenly as the fight began. Bodies lie still across the frozen floor, golden armor smeared dark with blood. My breath comes hard, uneven. I turn to Edin immediately. She is still standing, bleeding...*nothing new*, but upright, eyes sharp, blade steady in her hand. When our gazes lock, relief hits harder than the fight ever did.

"You hurt?" I ask.

"Not enough to stop," she says, with a wink.

I can not fight the proud smile that creeps across my face.

Chapter 28

Edin

The corridor leading to the king's quarters feels no different than the rest of the castle: cold stone, broken wards, the stench of violence. I know we have reached it when Endricks slows, not from hesitation, but from recognition.

The doors stand open. Inside, the damage is deliberate. Furniture shattered, banners torn down, sigils carved through with practiced precision. This was not *just* chaos. This was the intent. Osiris came here to be seen and to leave nothing untouched.

Then I see him, the King of Helheim, lying sprawled across the obsidian floor, crown discarded at his side like an afterthought. Blood darkens his chest, the fatal strike clean and unmistakable. Power still clings to him in faint, unraveling threads, old magic refusing to release its hold even now.

I look to Endricks instinctively. He does not rush forward, does not freeze. He simply stands there, arms loose at his sides, eyes fixed on the body with an expression I can not immediately name. It is not shock, nor sorrow, but something colder.

"So," he says at last, voice level, almost detached. "Osiris did what I never bothered to finish."

The words land hard. I step farther into the room.

"I am sure he made it costly," Endricks continues, no pride, no mourning, just fact. "Adonis always did."

The silence stretches, thick with things that were never said. I can feel it now, the weight of years between them, sharpened into something jagged and unresolved. This death did not close a wound. It split it open.

"Osiris wanted Helheim leaderless," Valker finally joins in.

Endricks's gaze never leaves the body. When he finally speaks again, there is steel beneath the calm. "Then he miscalculated." He steps past me into the room, not to kneel, not to touch, only to look down once, final and unyielding. "My father ruled through fear," he pauses. "Let history remember him that way." Then he turns away from his father's corpse without another glance.

A chill runs down my spine, and I realize that it has nothing to do with the castle's cold. Whatever the Elysians started here did not end with the king's death. It forged something far more dangerous in his son.

"Oren," Endricks snaps, "Update the troops that still stand, and see that all of Helheim knows King Adonis has fallen."

Oren stiffens at the name, the weight of it settling like bricks on his shoulders. He nods once and turns on his heel, already barking orders to the nearest runners. Horns begin to sound across the castle, low and mournful, carrying the truth faster than any blade ever could.

Endricks closes the distance between us. "I have business to attend to." His arm circles my waist, pulling me into a lingering kiss. "Come find me in the throne room this evening."

I stiffen for half a heartbeat before the warmth of him seeps in. The kiss is brief but deliberate, a promise rather than a farewell. When he pulls away, his eyes search mine as if weighing what he is leaving unsaid.

Valker coughs and Verenia giggles.

"Assholes," Endricks mutters into my lips, then spins around. "Yes, *Valker*, let us go and strategize." Then he is gone, boots echoing down the corridor, the scent of smoke and cedar lingering where he stood.

I touch my lips, steadying myself. *The throne room this evening...of all places. Whatever business Endricks has, it is not just politics.*

I jump as Verenia grabs my arm, pulling me from thought.

"We were never properly introduced. I am Verenia, Valker's sister," she smiles. "Come, let us go get cleaned up. I am sure we can find you something else to wear, too."

I let Verenia guide me down the quiet corridor, my boots leaving faint marks on the ash-covered stone. The castle feels different away from the main halls. Muted, almost kind. Steam curls from the bathing chamber as she pushes the door open, warmth brushing my face.

The bathing room is hauntingly beautiful. Veins of gold run through the rock, catching the low torchlight and throwing it back in soft, wavering reflections. The ceiling arches high above, lost in shadow, with iron chains suspending lanterns that glow like captured embers. At the center of the chamber rests a deep stone tub, its rim worn smooth by generations of use. Warm water is fed into it through the open mouths of stone wolf heads set into the wall, steam curling from their fangs as if they breathe. The air is thick with the scent of heated stone, pine resin, and bitter herbs meant to draw pain from tired flesh. Along one wall, wooden shelves hold neatly folded linens and stoppered glass bottles; oils, salves, and crushed leaves suspended in dark liquids. Despite its purpose, the room is not gentle. Everything in it speaks of endurance rather than indulgence, a place to restore the body so it may be broken again.

"Sit," she says gently, already moving with practiced ease. She pours an ember bottle into the tub, the scent of herbs blooming in the air; lavender and something sharper beneath it. Comfort, bottled and poured. "This one was always my favorite."

I perch on the edge, shrugging off my clothes, suddenly aware of every ache I have been ignoring. I slip into the bath with a hiss, muscles protesting before finally giving in. The heat seeps deep into my bones, loosening knots I did not know how to name. My shoulders sag as the water rises, the sound of it filling the room where words do not. Verenia tests the temperature with her hand, nods, and then she begins removing her own clothes. She slides in across from me. Her hooves briefly brushing against my toes.

"So," she chirps, "Fated to the king of Helheim."

"King?" I gasp.

"Well," she giggles, "Endricks *is* heir to the throne."

Through all the chaos and death, it had not dawned on me. I dunk my head, letting the water swallow my ears for a heartbeat. *Elysia has fallen. Still no word from Blythe. Endricks is now the king of Helheim.* The world is duller under the water, reduced to the thrum of my own pulse. When I resurface, Verenia is watching me as if she has decided my panic is amusing, but also inconvenient.

"You are spiraling," she says.

"Of course, I am spiraling."

"He is still Endricks," she continues. "Same scowl. Same ridiculous sense of honor. Same habit of pretending he does not care while rearranging the world to protect what he does care about."

The water laps as I shift, knees drawing closer to my chest. Somewhere beyond the bath, the room creaks softly, old stone settling. I think of Endricks as I last saw him, bloodied, furious, gentle in the moments he thought no one noticed.

"I do not know how to kneel beside a king," I say quietly.

Verenia's teasing expression softens. She reaches out, nudging my ankle with her own. "Good. Helheim does not need someone who knows how to kneel. It needs someone who knows how to stand."

I nod, thoughts crowding my mind.

"Also," she laughs, "*Someone* has to keep Endricks in line. Gods know I have had my hands full between him and Valker. You look like somebody who can put him in his place."

"You do not know the half of it," I giggle.

"It will be nice to have another female." Her eyes flick to mine, bright with memory. "He and Valker grew up together, practically inseparable. Same tutors, same punishments, same bruises." She smiles to herself. "They used to sneak out of the citadel at night. Valker would *swear* he knew the tunnels better than the guards. He never did."

A picture arises in my mind unbidden: Endricks, younger, less carved by war, laughing in the dark with someone at his side. The image twists something in my chest.

"Valker was the only one who treated him like a person," Verenia continues. "Not an heir. Not a symbol. Just… Endricks. They were best friends long before swords ever came into it."

The water laps softly as I shift again, fingers tightening beneath the surface. "Are they still…?"

She tilts her head. "Close? Yes. The same?" Her mouth quirks. "No. The throne has a way of carving space between people, whether you want it to or not."

I swallow. I think of the way Endricks watches Valker, measuring, trusting, and wary all at once. The way his shoulders ease just a fraction when Valker enters a room. I had noticed, but I had not understood.

"He loves deeply," Verenia adds, quieter now. "But he learned early that loving something means it can be used against you."

My throat tightens. Heat presses in from all sides, but goosebumps still rise on my arms. "That is why he keeps himself locked down," I whisper. "Why he tried to push me away."

Verenia nods. "Exactly."

I stare at the rippling water between us, at my reflection fractured by steam. "I do not want to be another weakness," I say.

Her gaze sharpens, but there is warmth there, too. "Things are different now, Edin. Valker told me how you destroyed Greybar just to find Endricks. Thank you for saving my brother as well, by the way. Adonis is dead. He no longer has any hold over Endricks."

I close my eyes, Endricks's face flashing behind my lids, his rough hands, his careful distance, the way his voice softens when he says my name like his life depends on it.

Verenia's hoof brushes my foot again, deliberately this time. "You are not a weakness," she says firmly. "You are a choice. One he has already made, whether he is brave enough to admit it or not."

The air hums around us, holding the silence that follows. I breathe in, allowing myself to feel the truth settle, heavy, frightening, and achingly tender all at once. The water clings stubbornly to my skin as I rise, steam curling around me like a cloak I cannot shake off. Verenia follows behind me, slipping behind a wooden screen. I pad to the shelves, picking up a linen cloth to dry myself. The fabric is coarse, familiar, but comforting in its simplicity. My muscles protest with every motion, reminding me of battles fought, roads traveled, and sacrifices made. The mirror across the room catches my reflection, red-rimmed eyes, damp hair clinging to my shoulders, the way my jaw tightens almost unconsciously.

Verenia emerges from behind the screen, already dressed in a pale-blue gown, the fabric flowing and soft, cinched at the waist. She glances at me with an approving nod. "Taking your time?" she teases, "Or are you trying to impress me with how long you can sit and brood?"

I grimace, rubbing my damp hair back. "You already know me too well."

She steps closer, tugging the folds of her gown in place. "Better to know you than to have to guess."

I make my way across the room where a row of dresses hangs, brought in by a small water sprite. I find a sleeveless gown in a deep shade of violet that seems to drink in the light, shimmering subtly with every movement. The water left my skin warm, flushed, and sensitive to the touch of fabric, as I pull it over my head. The fabric clings effortlessly to my waist, sculpting an hourglass silhouette, before cascading into a long, flowing skirt that brushes the floor. The neckline plunges daringly, while the back dips low, tracing a graceful arc below the small of my back, exposing just enough skin to be enticing without losing its sophistication.

Verenia adjusts a clasp on her shoulder and watches me, expression shifting from amusement to something softer, more calculating. “The bath helps,” she says. “But the mind needs more than warm water. Remember that.”

I nod, fastening the clasp of a choker around my neck, fingers fumbling over the metal.

“You look like someone who might make him pause,” she observes. Her eyes flick to mine, keen and assessing.

I catch my reflection again. My hair has dried into soft waves, almost reaching my hips. Color has bloomed back into my lips, and my eyes are wide, shadowless. Verenia moves toward the door, and I follow, the gown brushing against my legs. The stone floor is cold underfoot, a reminder that warmth fades and steel waits outside this chamber, but for the first time, I do not feel fear pressing down on me, only a steady pulse of purpose. I feel the weight of what comes next: standing beside a king, holding my own place in a kingdom that does not yet know my strength.

"You ready?" she asks, hand on the heavy wooden door.

I nod. "As ready as I will ever be."

Together, we step from the bathhouse, the scent of herbs and steam fading behind us, carrying the quiet promise of endurance into the world beyond.

Chapter 29

Edin

The throne room is still standing.

That surprises me more than the ruin we have already seen. The ceiling arches overhead, scarred but intact, its sigils dimmed rather than destroyed. The great throne remains at the far end of the hall, black obsidian veined with ancient runes, its steps stained dark with old and new blood. I meet Endricks's eyes from across the room, and he winks, then strides toward his new seat without ceremony, no hesitation, no reverence.

The Hellions who remain gather in uneasy silence, wounded and ash-streaked, watching him from the edges of the chamber. No herald announces his name. No oath is demanded. Helheim does not need the ritual; it recognizes power when it sees it.

He stops before the throne and looks at it for a long moment. I can not read his expression. *Not contempt, nor triumph.* Something harder than either. Then he turns.

"My father is dead," he says, voice carrying easily through the ruined hall. "And with him, his reign."

There is no mourning in his words, only finality.

"He ruled through fear and called it order. He bled this realm to keep himself untouchable." Endricks's gaze sweeps the room, settling briefly on each of them. "That ends now."

A murmur ripples through the Hellions, not in protest, but recognition. Endricks steps up onto the dais and lowers himself onto the throne. The moment he does, the room changes. The runes etched into the obsidian flare to life, responding to him alone. Power surges outward in a controlled wave, not violent, not demanding, but *claiming*. The throne accepts him. Helheim accepts him, and I feel it deep in my bones.

Endricks leans back, one arm resting loosely against the throne's edge, posture relaxed in a way that feels dangerous. He looks nothing like a king crowned by legacy. He looks like a king forged by refusal.

"Helheim still stands," he says calmly. "It has been invaded, wounded, and tested. We will answer."

The crowd cheers.

"We will rebuild," he continues. "We will ascend on Elysia, and they will learn what it means to challenge a realm that bows to no one."

The Hellions, together as one, drop to one knee. I stay where I am, watching Endricks as Helheim's power settles around his shoulders like a mantle he never asked for yet never feared.

This is not inheritance. This is conquest, claimed with blood, sealed by will, and for the first time since we entered the forest, I am certain of one thing: *Helheim has found a far more dangerous king.*

His eyes find mine across the chamber. Just for a moment, something unguarded flickers there, resolve sharpened by trust. The chamber is still ringing with celebration when Endricks rises and lifts his hand. The sound does not fade so much as *submits*. Helheim's citizens, warriors, shades, and ancient houses bound to him in iron and oath fall quiet, faces alight with triumph and awe. Their king stands before them, power settled cleanly into his frame now, no longer raw or borrowed. Claimed. *Chosen*, in the only way Helheim understands. I remain where I am, half a step behind the line of the court, a shadow among shadows.

Endrick turns, not toward the throne, but toward me. "This kingdom knows of the prophecy," he says, voice steady, carrying to the farthest arch. "It has been whispered in fire and carved into bone since before my name was spoken," he pauses, a deliberate breath. "The fated mate of Helheim's king. The one who walks between ending and absolution."

The air tightens. Every gaze swings to me.

"Edin," he says, and my name rolls through the hall like a bell tolling at a threshold. "Goddess of Purgatory."

A murmur rises, reverent this time, not surprised. Recognition flickers in their eyes. Relief. *Rightness.*

"She is not a prize," Endrick continues, and steel enters his tone. "Not a symbol. Not a consort kept behind my throne." His hand clenches at his side. "She is balance, judgment, and mercy earned through fire."

My pulse hammers, but my face remains still, carved from ice. *Goddess. Queen. Mate.* Each title presses against me from the inside, threatening to crack something open. I lock it down. I will not be undone before a kingdom.

"She stands beside me," he declares. "Helheim demands two forces to rule it, conquest and consequence." His gaze finds mine, unwavering. "And I will not rule without her."

The chamber erupts, not in chaos, but in unity. Hellions slam fists to chests. Blades strike stone. A roar of approval surges upward, shaking the rafters. They are joyful and certain. Helheim has its king, and now, its queen.

Endrick turns fully to me and extends his hand. "Edin," he says, quieter now, though the power behind the word still hums. "Stand with me. Rule with me."

I step forward. Each stride toward the dais is measured, unhurried. I feel the realm itself recognize me as I move, the air parting, the shadows bowing low, the magic within me curling along my skin like a familiar breath. I do not rush, but I also do not hesitate.

As I ascend the steps, the runes flare, not in challenge, but in acknowledgment. At the top, I stop beside him and spin around. The noise fades again, as if the kingdom itself is holding its breath. I lift my chin, eyes sweeping over the crowd with calm, merciless composure. Inside me, emotion churns, fate tightens its grip and power answers power. Something dangerous anchors me to the man at my side: *unwavering love*. None of it touches my expression.

If I am their goddess, I will not soften.

If I am their queen, I will not yield.

Endrick's presence is a constant heat at my shoulder, unbreakable and chosen. When he speaks my title, it settles into my bones as if it has always belonged there.

"Queen of Helheim," he says.

The Hellions answer. The roar that follows my title is not wild, but it is *sure*. Approval rolls through the chamber like thunder that knows exactly where it will strike. Helheim does not question this moment. It accepts it the way it accepts death: inevitable, necessary, and final.

Endricks turns to me, and for a breath, the kingdom disappears. His hand finds mine, a claim made without possession, a promise made without words. My power answers his. Where his power burns like forged iron and surges like a current, mine flows, inexorable, like the quiet pull of judgment at the edge of the abyss.

He lifts our joined hands. “Kneel,” he commands.

The Hellions move as one. Hundreds of knees strike stone in a sound that reverberates through my ribs. Even the shadows bend, pooling low and submissive. A shiver runs up my spine in awe as I look over the kneeling Hellions. *My people.*

Endrick speaks again, his voice carrying iron and fire. “You will honor her as you honor me. You will answer her summons as you answer my call. Her judgment is final. Her mercy is earned.”

He pauses, dangerous and deliberate.

“Those who stand against her, stand against their king.”

A shudder passes through the hall.

I step forward, just enough that our shoulders no longer touch. The movement is small, but it shifts the balance. "My people," I say. The title feels strange on my tongue, but I do not soften it. "I am not here to be adored," I continue, my voice steady, as cold as the space between realms. "I am not here to be loved." A flicker of heat coils beneath my skin. "I am here to ensure that every soul who enters Helheim receives what they are owed, no more, no less."

Silence stretches, taut as a blade's edge.

"Purgatory is not cruelty," I say. "It is *truth.* Under my watch, no soul will be lost to it unjustly, and I will do the same for Helheim."

I let my gaze sweep the kneeling masses, unflinching. Inside, something trembles, not weakness, only magnitude. Fate has locked into place. There is no stepping back from this.

"I will stand beside your king," I finish, "not as ornament, but as reckoning."

For a heartbeat, nothing moves. Then Helheim responds. The runes blaze. The shadows bow deeper. The realm exhales, long and low, as if relieved. Approval thrums through the stone, the air, and then my bones.

Endrick steps back to my side, his presence solid and sure. His voice drops, meant only for me. "You were always meant for this."

I do not look at him. "Then Elysia should be afraid," I murmur back.

Chapter 30

Endricks

The moment Edin finishes speaking, Helheim *moves*. I feel it before I see it, the deep, tectonic recognition of a realm that has accepted its balance. The stone beneath the dais groans, old mechanisms stirring after centuries of waiting. This was always meant to happen. I simply arrived a bit late.

A low, resonant sound rolls through the chamber as the floor to my right splits along a seam etched with runes older than any crown. Heat breathes upward from the fracture, not violent or wild, but measured and controlled. I keep my gaze forward, but my awareness stays anchored to her.

From the opening, a second throne rises. It is not a mirror of mine. Mine is carved from black obsidian veined with iron, sharp lines and brutal angles, a seat made for conquest and command. Hers emerges in dark stone shot through with pale ember-light, smooth where mine is severe, curved like a threshold rather than a blade. Runes of judgment spiral up its back, glowing soft gold and ash-white, the language of endings and second chances intertwined so tightly they cannot be separated.

A murmur ripples through the hall, reverent and hushed. No one questions it. No one would dare. The realm itself has spoken, and Helheim knows better than to argue with inevitability. The throne is settled into place beside mine, aligned. Equal. The space between them is narrow enough that our arms could brush, wide enough to make a point.

I turn then, finally, and look at Edin. Her expression is carved from stone, fierce and unyielding. A goddess and queen in perfect, terrifying harmony, but I feel what she keeps locked beneath it. The pull. The weight. The gravity of a destiny that has just closed its jaws around her.

I extend my hand again, and she takes it. The contact sends a familiar, grounding warmth through me, not power this time, but certainty. Together, we turn and sit. The instant we do, Helheim seals the bond. The runes flare. The thrones resonate a low harmonic hum that vibrates through my chest and into my bones. The realm aligns around us, conquest and consequence locked together at last. I have never felt so dangerous or more *whole*.

The Hellions bow deeper, fists to stone, heads lowered in absolute fealty. Then, slowly, carefully, the court begins to withdraw. Blades are sheathed. Banners lower. One by one, they rise and back away, never turning their backs on the dais. The massive doors at the far end of the chamber groan open, spilling torchlight and shadow across the floor.

As they leave, I feel the shift, the difference between ruling an army and ruling a *realm*. The noise fades, and footsteps echo, then disappear. The doors close with a final, thunderous boom that reverberates through the now-empty hall.

Silence settles.

I lean back slightly, my throne answering me like an old weapon reclaimed, and glance sideways at Edin. Even seated, she radiates control, her presence bending the air subtly toward her.

Helheim is mine... ours, and for the first time since I took the crown, I know with absolute certainty... I will never sit alone again.

The great doors open without a sound this time. Oren steps into the throne room alone, his presence quiet but weighted, like a blade still in its sheath. He wears no armor, only a ceremonial black robe, layered with gold chains etched in sigils of binding and sovereignty. In his hands is a narrow obsidian case, cradled with reverence.

Edin's gaze sharpens the instant she senses him. Mine never leaves Oren.

"My Lord," he says, and drops to one knee, not in submission, but in acknowledgment of a rite older than kneeling. "Queen." He dips his head to Edin with the same gravity.

"Rise," I command.

He does, and approaches the dais, boots echoing softly in the vast chamber that now feels smaller, more intimate. This room has seen blood, betrayal, and coronations that ended in screams. What is about to happen is no different. This is not about an oath, but a *binding*.

"It is time," Oren says simply.

I nod and stand.

The motion ripples through the thrones; mine goes still, hers hums faintly, answering the shift. I step forward to the center of the dais, removing my gauntlets and setting them aside. The air tightens, expectant, and all of Helheim leans in.

Oren opens the obsidian case, and inside rests my seventh and final piercing. It is forged from star-iron pulled from the deepest fault beneath Helheim, dark metal threaded with a vein of molten silver that pulses faintly, as if alive. Runes spiral along its curve: oaths of protection, dominion, and endurance. This is not a mark of beauty. It is a mark of survival.

"The king of Helheim does not wear a crown alone," Oren intones, voice slipping into ritual cadence. "He bears the realm upon his body, where it may draw blood if he betrays it."

There is no hesitation. No fear. I have bled for this realm countless times. This is simply the acknowledgment of it. Oren steps closer, his focus absolute. I feel Edin's presence at my side, her power a steady pressure against my spine.

***

I raise my hand to Oren. "It would be an honor for my queen to grant me the final piercing,' I say, my eyes briefly finding Edin's.

Edin's eyes flare wide.

"As you wish, My Lord," Oren states with a nod, then hands off the obsidian case.

Edin nods to Oren, and she takes the case, her fingers trembling slightly. Oren makes his way out of the throne room, giving us the privacy we so desperately need. The doors shut, and her eyes snap to me. I wrench open my belt and slide down my trousers, leaving only my black robe. I cross the dias and sit down on the throne, legs spread wide.

I raise an eyebrow and flick my eyes downward. “Come.”

Edin scrambles to gather her thoughts at my demand, but she steps towards me anyway.

“No,” I say.

Edin stops, confusion crossing over her face.

“Crawl,” I growl.

She lowers herself to the stone, unbothered by the cold, and begins to crawl toward me. The sight of it pulls the air from my lungs. A goddess reduced to deliberate, reverent movement. Each slow advance tightens something deep in my chest.

I sit motionless on the throne, hands braced against the carved arms, careful not to break the tension. Her eyes never leave mine as she comes closer, dark with intent, yet gleaming with promise. She reaches me and pauses at my feet, close enough that I can feel the heat of her presence. She tilts her head up, a knowing curve to her mouth, and in that moment, I am no longer just king. I am hers, and she is mine, and the bond between us hums, quiet and fierce, in the space between us.

Her hands reach me first, fingers curling around my ankle as she draws closer. The contact sends a quiet jolt through me, claiming me. I feel it everywhere. I straighten slightly on the throne, the instinct to reach for her burning in my palms, but I hold still. This moment is hers to command.

She lifts her gaze to mine, close enough now that I can see the flecks of light in her gold eyes. There is reverence there, and something fiercer beneath it, a need wrapped in devotion. When she rises on her knees before me, the world seems to narrow to the space between us. Her hands slide up over my thighs, inch by inch, my cock growing harder by the second. She leans in and licks up my shaft. Jaw clenched, I squeeze the arms of the throne, refusing to steal her thunder, no matter how badly I would love to switch roles.

Every hair on my body stands as she slowly licks her way up, then slides her lips over the tip. Her head tilts up, locking eyes with me, then she sinks her mouth to the hilt. I throw my head back, and a low groan crawls up my throat. She sucks in her cheeks as she withdraws slowly, then slams back down. The throne arms fracture under my grip, fighting the urge to have my way with her and the pleasure she is bringing me. She reaches up and cups my balls, giving them a slight squeeze. The movement sends me into a tailspin, and I grab the back of her head, taking a fistful of her hair. I shove her all the way down my dick, forcing her to gag. She looks up at me with watery eyes.

"You make me so proud," I growl.

Edin gives my balls another tug, and I thrust into her mouth. She follows the motion, suctioning her lips around my cock with every stroke. I pull her head back, allowing her a breath. Drool drips down her chin, and tears streak her cheeks. I clinch my jaw, looking at every inch of her. She has never looked so enticing. She gives me a wink and jerks her head forward, back down onto my dick. Her pace picks up, swirling her tongue up my shaft with every rise. Pressure builds at the base of my cock. I thrust my hips forward, hitting the back of her throat, sending me over the edge. Groaning, I slowly pump into her mouth, and she lets out a moan of satisfaction in response.

I brush the top of her head in awe of her performance, but she is not done. She grabs my shaft, licking the cum that drips from the head, then all the way down. Running her tongue over each piercing, she counts, and the memory of her enlightenment flashes through my mind.

"One, two, three, four, five, and *six*." She looks up at me from where she kneels, "Are you ready for number seven, *My Lord*?"

"Only by your hand," I say, lifting an eyebrow.

Edin flicks her tongue one last time over my head, sending shivers up my spine, then reaches for the obsidian case. I straighten in my seat as she prepares. Letting out a slow, deep breath, gathering her own nerves, she reads out the words carved into the lid.

"This binds you to Helheim," she says, lifting the needle. "Its pain will remind you that rule is not mercy. Its heat will remind you that power is never free."

The bevel touches my skin and slides through.

Fire.

Then she slides the piercing through the fresh hole with a searing precision that steals my breath, but not my control. I do not flinch. I do not growl. I let the pain write its truth into me, allowing Helheim to drink from it. The rune-light flares, and I feel the bond snap into place, my pulse syncing with the realm's, my senses sharpening until I can feel the far borders of my kingdom like distant limbs. The piercing settles, warm and heavy, humming with contained force.

"It is done," Edin murmurs.

The pain fades to a low, constant heat, a reminder, but not a wound. I exhale slowly and slide back, power locking into place around the new anchor point. I look down, meeting Edin's eyes, something fierce and dark flashes between us, recognition, approval, and something dangerously close to pride.

"Endricks," she says, laying her head on my thigh, "I would also like a piercing." The same devilish smile creeps back across her face.

"Oren," I shout.

The door swiftly swings open as if he had been standing just outside.

"Yes, My Lord?" Oren says, averting his eyes.

"Bring us a piercing fit for my queen."

"As you wish," Oren clips, a small smile forming, then he rushes off.

I look back at Edin returning her smile and lunge out of my seat, grabbing her face. We crash into the stone, a frenzy of limbs grabbing at one another. Our lips meet, tongues sliding between them. I tear her dress straps down her arms and quickly rip her gown off.

A soft knock echoes through the throne room, halting our celebration. The door slowly slides open this time, and Oren steps in, eyes covered. He makes his way across the room, stumbling and tripping. Quickly, he sets the opal case down beside me and scurries out of the room. Edin looks at me and bursts into laughter. I can not help but join in. I stroke her hair, joy filling me for the first time in centuries. Resting my hand on the stone next to her head, I lean in, pressing my lips to hers, then continue my descent, kissing every inch of her. My head settles between her thighs, and I run my tongue over her clit, returning the favor.

Her head dips back, and a sweet moan breaks from her lips, already begging for release. I slip two fingers into her pussy, pumping upward. Her legs shake just as I find the spot that sends her into ferality. She grabs the back of my head, pushing my face further into her. Pulling my hair, she begins grinding. I meet her movement, licking and sucking, sending my fingers deep into her cunt. Her walls squeeze tight around me, and her hips thrust forward as she crashes into ecstasy. Her body shudders with release, and she wraps her legs around me, riding out the waves.

She pants, and her body goes limp, her legs sliding from my shoulders. I kiss her lips one last time, sending a final shiver through her body, then move my way up her body. I brush a stray hair from her face, tucking it behind her pointed ear, and kiss her cheek.

"Are you ready?" I whisper.

She nods, still regathering herself.

Reaching behind me, I grab the case. The heat at my throat is still humming when I turn to her. This is not tradition. This is a choice. *Her choice.* I open the case. The piercing meant for her is different. Forged from pale star-metal drawn from the boundary between realms, it glows faintly, soft and steady. Runes of passage and judgment curl along its surface, finer than those carved into mine, but no less absolute. This is not a symbol of rule over Helheim alone. This is a mark of *between*.

"For the Goddess of Purgatory," I intone, settling back between her legs. "Queen beside the King. Keeper of the Threshold."

I take the piercing from the case. The moment it touches my palm, it warms, answering my blood, my bond, and answering *her* in unison. Helheim does not stir this time; this is not its rite. *This belongs to us.* I lean closer to Edin. Close enough that the rest of the world recedes, the throne room is vast and empty despite its size. I meet her eyes, searching for hesitation; there is none.

"Tell me to stop," I say quietly.

She lifts her chin a fraction, gaze burning. "I will not."

I raise my hand, slow and deliberate, and brush my knuckles along her jaw, barely a touch, but grounding. Not claiming, never that, only acknowledging the weight she carries, the line she walks.

"This binds you to me," I say, voice low. "It binds you in a way beyond our titles, beyond our fated prophecy."

Her lips curve, not soft. *Certain*. "Do it," she says.

I guide the needle into place with steady hands, hovering just above her clit. The point barely kisses her skin, and already I feel the tension coil through her. For a heartbeat, I hold it there, then I push. The resistance is immediate, but I feel it give in slow increments, her body fighting the intrusion even as she forces herself to stay still. Her breath fractures, dragged in like it cuts on the way down, and her entire frame locks beneath my hands. She does not pull away, but it is clear the pain hits her.

I watch it crash through her control, the way her back arches despite herself, the way her thighs tense so hard they tremble. A tear slips free, carving a bright path down her cheek. Her fingers curl, nails biting deep into her own skin as if she needs something, *anything*, to anchor her through it. A broken sound slips past her lips before she can stop it, quiet and raw.

The needle slides completely through. I feel every fraction of it, the way her pulse stutters violently, the way her body tries to recoil, and the way she fights it. Another tear falls, faster this time, her control cracking just enough for it to slip out. Her breathing turns uneven, each inhale dragged in like it costs her something, each exhale stuttering no matter how hard she tries to steady it. Pain floods her, all-consuming, and for a moment I think… *No.*

She lifts her chin. Her glassy eyes find mine, rimmed in the kind of hurt that would drop anyone else, and there it is again, no surrender, only defiance. The bar slides into place, and I feel her body seize. A sharp, strangled breath tears free, and then I watch her drag herself back.

Tears trail down her cheeks, but when her lips part again, it is not a cry that follows. It is a smile, tight and shaking, but undeniably fierce. A new power answers her pain. It surges up from somewhere deep, rolling off her in a controlled, violent wave, barely contained, like she is holding it together with her last shred of stubbornness. The air distorts around us, trembling with it, reacting to her instead of the act itself. Lights flare, cutting through the space with a blinding clarity, as if something inside her has been carved open and *revealed,* rather than broken. When it fades, she is still there, breathing harder now, skin flushed, tears still clinging to the curve of her jaw, and smiling like she won.

I smile down at her, feeling it all lock into place, a new tether forming between us, not a fated chain, but a line drawn straight and true. Her power settles, and the piercing cools against her skin, humming softly in harmony with mine. The bond is complete. I lower my hand slowly, aware of how close I still am, how the space between us feels charged and intentional. When I look at her now, something has shifted, not ownership, not possession, only recognition.

Goddess. Queen. Equal.

I take her into my arms, lifting her from the stone floor, and set her at her rightful throne. When I resume my place beside her, the space between our thrones hums, alive with shared purpose. We sit, taking in the moment, the emotions, and the chaos that will soon unfold.

The thrones answer us immediately, stone warming, runes dimming to a steady glow as Helheim settles into the shape we have given it. The bond between us pulses, low and constant, no longer demanding attention, simply *there*. Right. *Permanent*.

I rest my forearm on the arm of my throne, running my finger across her hand, a reassurance that through everything, I will stand by her side. The silence stretches just long enough to remind the realm, remind *me,* that peace has never been Helheim's natural state. I rise from my seat, snatching my pants from the stone and Edin's gown in the process. I watch her pull the deep violet dress up over her hips, and it sends a shiver up my spine as I pull my own clothes on. She stands and turns for me to retie her corset. I lean in, kissing her back as I pull the strings tight. She spins back around and I plant one final kiss on her forehead. We return to our seats and only then do I speak.

"Oren." The name carries.

The doors at the far end of the chamber open at once. Oren returns alone, already moving before the echo of my voice fades. He drops to one knee at the foot of the dais, head bowed, posture sharp with readiness.

"Summon the militia," I order. "Every legion. Every Hellion blade. I want commanders in the war hall before the hour turns."

Oren's jaw tightens, not in surprise, but anticipation. "It will be done, My Lord."

"And then," I continue, eyes lifting toward the towering glass doors that seal the far wall of the throne room, "Open the gates."

Oren looks up now, just briefly. He follows my gaze.

The glass doors loom tall and vast, forged from blackened crystal shot through with veins of ember-light. They overlook all of Helheim, the spires, the rivers of fire, the endless layers of the realm stretching toward the horizon. They are opened only for victory… or declaration.

Understanding dawns in his eyes. “Yes, My Lord.”

He rises and moves swiftly, signals already being relayed through the hall. I feel Helheim stir as the call spreads, steel waking, banners unfurling, ancient engines groaning back to life. This is a language the realm speaks fluently.

Valker and Verenia step in, giving us a nod, then make their way over to the far side of the room. The glass doors begin to part. Light floods the chamber, fierce and blinding. The red-gold glow of Helheim pours in, wind carrying the scent of ash and iron. The sound follows: the distant roar of the city, of armies assembling, of a realm bracing itself for what comes next.

I stand, and the movement ripples outward. Edin rises with me, seamless, her presence flaring at my side like a second horizon. Together, we step forward until the open doors frame us against the vastness of Helheim. Hellions scurry forward from below the terrace and the sound of sprites moving and dragging tables into place rattles behind us.

I raise my voice. “Helheim,” I call.

The realm answers.

The noise below shifts, funnels, and stills. Countless faces turn upward. Countless weapons pause mid-motion. Even the fires seem to lean in.

“Elysia has watched us bleed,” I say, my voice steady as stone. “They have whispered the prophecy while sharpening their blades. They have mistaken our balance for restraint.”

I pause, allowing my words to sink in.

"That mistake ends now."

Edin's power unfurls beside mine, quiet, lethal, and absolute. Purgatory stands with judgment, and conquest is forged in wrath.

"I do not declare this war for vengeance," I say. "I declare it for *truth*. For every boundary crossed. Every soul stolen. Every lie wrapped in light and called justice."

The wind howls through the open doors, carrying my words across the realm.

"Helheim will rise!"

The roar that follows is thunderous. I feel it in my bones, in my piercing, in the steady heat of Edin's presence beside me. Below us, banners ignite with sigils of war. Legions move as one, and the realm does not hesitate. I lower my hand slowly. Beside me, Edin stands unmoving, fierce as a verdict, gaze fixed on the horizon where Elysia awaits, radiant, self-righteous, and *doomed.* I take Edin's hand, giving Helheim one last glance, then we turn away, meeting Valker and Verenia's expectant gaze.

"Mobilize the troops," I order.

CHAPTER 31

EDIN

Valker and Verenia nod simultaneously, moving as one unit; they begin unscrolling parchment across tables for battle plans. Exhaustion creeps in, burning my eyes, but there is no time for rest. I inhale, holding it for a moment, then slowly blow out. Doors on opposite sides of the throne room swing open, and military leaders file in, awaiting their orders. I swallow the lump that builds in my throat as I look over the crowd.

I feel it, the weight of their stares, long before I let myself really see them. Steel-eyed commanders. Veteran sergeants with scars carved by decades of survival. Hellions who have buried kings and followed stronger ones. They fill the throne room in disciplined silence, armor dark, weapons at rest but never far. They are waiting to decide whether I am worthy of what Endricks has commanded.

Endricks steps forward, the motion alone sharpens the room. Conversations die before they can start. Even the scrape of parchment stills as Valker and Verenia pause, heads lifting in perfect unison.

Exhaustion claws at the back of my skull, a dull burn behind my eyes, but I lock it down. A queen does not show fatigue, not now, not ever. I step forward to the edge of the dais, meeting Endricks's side. For a heartbeat, I say nothing. I let them look, let them judge, let them weigh my scars against their own.

"If looks could kill," I say evenly, voice carrying without strain, "I would already be dead."

A few mouths twitch. A few shoulders ease. Not laughter, but recognition that I am not afraid of them. That matters.

Endricks speaks, and the room bends toward him. "At ease," he orders. "You were not summoned for ceremony," he pauses. "You were summoned because Elysia believes Helheim has grown complacent. That our balance has dulled our edge."

When he mentions divine interference, something cold and sharp settles in my chest. *Osiris.* Light-drenched lies. Mercy was offered only to the obedient. Souls stolen under the guise of salvation. I have felt his trespasses rip through Purgatory like hooked chains. This war is not new to me. It is simply no longer unavoidable. Endricks rests his hand on my lower back and nods to me to take over. I lean further over the dias.

"Osiris," my stomach twists, "Is a fallen Elysian and was once a prisoner of Greybar. He is the slayer of King Adonis and is now the ruler of Elysia. We can only assume the Elysian king has fallen as well. Osiris is a wielder of chaos magic, the ability to manipulate your mind and the world around you. You must all stay focused and alert." I look over each face, silently praying to the Gods for their safety. "The Elysian veil is located in the highest tower of the castle. I will open the veil, and from there you will follow Lord Endricks's orders." I turn to Endricks, giving him the floor.

He clears his throat. "Most of you have never traveled to the heavenly realm. I have only been a handful of times myself. As Edin stated, it is located inside the highest tower of the castle. That means narrow spiraling staircases as our entry and exit into the main halls. We need to move swiftly in organized lines, then fan out once reaching the halls. Osiris is a very…*egotistical being*. He believes no one would dare to challenge him. He also is under the presumption that I am dead, and Helheim is leaderless, which gives us the upper hand."

He pauses to ensure everyone is tracking.

"Take down all beings that align themselves with Osiris, Elysian and unjudged souls alike. Osiris has formed a small army of souls from Purgatory to help him gain access to Elysia. Do as you must, and know these beings will face their judgement once Edin has secured her throne in Purgatory."

He turns to me, and a flicker of pride sparks in his eyes.

"Edin, travel to Windemere, find Blythe, and notify King Thayer of our plans. Verenia will go with you. Then find me in Elysia."

I nod, my own pride filling my chest as I watch how smoothly he steps into his role as king.

The war council fractures into motion with brutal efficiency. Commands echo through the chamber, barked and relayed, parchment rolled and snapped shut as plans become inevitabilities. Valker and Verenia split the map between them, voices low and lethal as they divide legions, routes, and contingencies. No one questions the course set. Helheim has aligned itself, and now it moves.

I step forward when the noise thins. "Take me to the veil," I demand. My voice cuts cleanly through the remaining murmurs.

Endricks turns immediately, already anticipating the order. He dismisses the commanders with a sharp gesture, and they clear the throne room in disciplined waves, leaving behind the echo of boots and the faint scent of iron and ink. They crowd into the halls, awaiting our next move.

We walk side by side through the corridors of Helheim Castle, and the sea of soldiers parts. Verenia and Valker fall in line behind us and behind them, the soldiers follow. The stone here is older than conquest, veined with ember-light that pulses gently as we pass. Torches bow in their sconces, flames leaning toward us as if acknowledging the balance we carry between us. The closer we draw to the veil, the quieter the world becomes.

The veil chamber opens before us. It is vast and circular, its ceiling lost in shadow. At its center hangs the veil itself, a towering curtain of translucent light and dark, neither fabric nor flame, suspended between runes carved into the floor like a binding circle. This is where realms touch without colliding. Now, this is where wars begin.

I step into the circle. The veil stirs immediately, not in resistance, but in recognition. It thins, softening and waiting. Endricks halts at the edge of the runes, his army assembling behind him in silent formation, banners lowered, blades ready. The weight of what we are about to do presses in.

I turn back to him and for a moment, we are not king and queen, not goddess and conqueror, just two souls standing at the edge of something that will change everything.

"You will come back," I say quietly. Not a question.

His mouth curves, not with arrogance, but with certainty. "So will you."

I reach for him, fingers sliding up his jawline, grounding myself in the steady heat there. He cups my face, calloused thumb warm against my cheek, and when he leans down, the kiss we share is unhurried and soft, out of place in a room built for traveling between.

It is a promise.

It is trust.

As we part, his forehead rests briefly against mine, breath mingling, power humming between us like a living thing.

"I will hold the line," he murmurs.

"And I will find the truth," I answer.

I turn back to the veil and lift my hands. This time, there is no resistance. Purgatory flows through me like a familiar tide, and the veil parts smoothly, light folding back on itself to reveal Elysia beyond, radiant spires gleaming beneath an immaculate sky. The path stabilizes instantly, wide and unwavering.

"Go," I command softly.

Endrick does not hesitate. He turns, raises his blade once in silent salute, and leads Helheim's armies forward. They pass through the veil in disciplined silence, darkness pouring into light, until the last banner vanishes beyond the threshold.

I close the passage with a gentle sweep of my hand, and the chamber stills. Only then do I let myself breathe. Verenia steps up beside me, interlocking her fingers with mine, a silent understanding of fear and determination. I pivot and open my senses, tuning them away from war and toward something quieter, more fragile. Another veil responds, this one thin and gray, smelling of rain and salt and *memory*.

Windemere.

I carve the opening smaller, sharper, just enough to slip through. As the passage opens, cool air spills into the chamber, carrying the sound of life and the smell of freshly baked bread. I step toward it without looking back.

"Wait for me," I murmur, not to Helheim, not to Elysia, but to the man already fighting in another realm. Then we cross the threshold, the veil sealing behind me as war and fate split in opposite directions.

CHAPTER 32

EDIN

The veil opens, and Windemere hits me like a breath I have been holding for years. Cold, wet air floods my lungs with salt, rain, and old stone, and for a moment, I forget how to move. This is not just a place, it is home. The realization settles heavily in my chest, familiar in a way that aches more than any wound Osiris or Helheim has ever given me.

Verenia steps through after me, her boots whispering against pale stone. The veil seals behind us with a soft, breathless hush, and the pull of other realms drains away. We stand in the lower quarters of Swindon Castle, where everything is washed in white and veins of gray. The ceiling rises high, its marble beams smooth and colorless, the walls polished to a dull sheen that reflects light without warmth.

Frosted sconces cast an even, sterile glow across the stone, erasing shadows instead of deepening them. The air is clean but lifeless, carrying a faint chill that has never known the warmth of sunlight. This level was never meant to be inhabited; it is only crossed, only endured to get somewhere else. A place stripped of ornament and memory, where secrets persist not because they are hidden, but because the room itself feels too empty, too monotonous, to invite a second glance.

"I have not been able to return," I say softly. The words feel fragile, like they might splinter if I speak them any louder. "Not since they named me and sent me to Purgatory."

Verenia's gaze flicks to me, sharp and searching, but she says nothing. I take a step forward, my boots echoing too loudly in the narrow corridor. Every sound feels intrusive, like I am disturbing something that has learned to live without me. Once, there was warmth here. Safety. Now it feels like a memory I borrowed from someone else.

The staircase rises ahead, narrow, steep, worn smooth down the center over the centuries. I press my palm to the wall, fingertips grazing cold stone. Each step tightens something inside my chest. Windemere does not feel hostile; it feels… *indifferent*, like it went on without me, like it never noticed I was gone. Being named a goddess did not kill me… but it cleaved my life in two and left the first half behind like it never mattered. That realization hurts more than I expected.

The corridor closes in as we move, torchlight thinning, shadows beginning to stretch long and uneven along the stone. The hair at the back of my neck prickles. It is subtle at first, nothing I can name or see, but the sensation crawls beneath my skin all the same. I know this feeling too well, the sense of being observed without invitation. I keep my stride even, my face composed, but my awareness sharpens, every breath measured, every echo weighed. Windemere may be indifferent, but the dark between its walls is not. The shadows feel crowded, heavy with attention, as if the corridor itself has turned its gaze on me, curious and unkind. I do not look toward them. I refuse to give whatever is watching the satisfaction.

A low growl slips from the shadows, and I stop, not because it is threatening but because it is *familiar*. The sound curls through me, deep and resonant, carrying a cadence I have not heard in far too long. Recognition hits like a shock of lightning, sharp and sudden, stealing the breath from my lungs. Sweet. Impossible. My heart stutters painfully as the truth surfaces all at once.

I had forgotten.

Not erased, just buried beneath realms, trauma, and survival.

The growl shifts, softening at the edges, less warning than greeting, and something warm twists in my chest. I turn toward the darkness without thinking, the fierce composure I have worn since stepping through the veil cracking just enough to let the ache through.

"Nyx," I breathe, the word barely more than a whisper.

The shadows stir, heavy and familiar, and the weight of being watched changes shape, no longer predatorial, no longer hostile, but protective and loyal.

I am not as alone here as I thought.

The shadows ripple, and then part. Nyx steps into the torchlight. His massive form unfolds from the darkness like it was always meant to live there, obsidian skin drinking in the light, eyes glowing low like embers. Smoke curls lazily from his jaws with each breath, heat shimmering faintly around his shoulders. He moves with quiet grace despite his size, claws clicking softly against the stone as his gaze locks onto mine.

My breath catches, joy hits me so hard it is almost painful, bright and sudden and wholly unguarded. A laugh escapes before I can stop it, sharp with disbelief. “Nyx,” I whisper, and the sound of his name feels like coming home.

Verenia reacts instantly. Steel flashes as she whips a dagger free, stance snapping tight, body angling in front of me on pure instinct. “Edin, do not move,” she hisses, blade raised, eyes wide and tracking every measured step Nyx takes.

“It is all right,” I say quickly, reaching out without thinking. My hand presses gently to Verenia’s arm. “He will not hurt us.”

Nyx lowers his massive head, ears flattening, not in submission, but in recognition. His growl fades into a low, rumbling sound that vibrates through the floor, unmistakably pleased. His tail sweeps once behind him, stirring dust and shadow.

Verenia does not move, still pointing her dagger. "That is," she says tightly, "A black-flamed hellhound."

I can not stop the smile that curves my mouth. "Yes."

Nyx takes one more step forward and nudges his scorched nose against my palm. Heat blooms under my skin, familiar and comforting, and something in my chest finally loosens. "He is my familiar," I add softly.

Verenia glances between us, disbelief warring with resignation. After a tense moment, she exhales and lowers her blade, just a fraction of an inch. "You attract the strangest things."

I laugh under my breath, hand gliding across Nyx's smooth skin. "You have no idea. Though I am unsure how he is here in Windemere."

"Hellhounds are war creatures that can slip between the realms using the shadows. Though they follow commands, they will also take the initiative for whatever best suits their master. You said Blythe was here, yes?"

"Yes."

"It is possible Nyx has been with her, watching over her from the shadows."

Nyx's gaze slides past us, down the corridor toward the voices echoing faintly from above. His ears flick, posture shifting, alert, protective, restrained by will alone. The meaning clicks into place with a jolt of heat in my chest.

"You have been here," I breathe. "Watching."

He exhales through his nose, a soft burst of smoke curling along the floor. One heavy paw steps back into shadow, then stills, an invitation to look, not follow, but to *understand.* The relief is sharp enough to sting. I have crossed realms, worn crowns, raised the dead, and all this time, Nyx has stayed. Anchored here. A silent sentinel in the forgotten places of the castle, keeping watch when I could not.

"Thank you," I whisper, the words meant for him alone.

Nyx raises his head, nose brushing briefly against my shoulder, careful, controlled, and affectionate in the way only something powerful can be. The contact grounds me more than I expect.

Verenia finally lets her blade slip fully away. “So,” she says, eyes never leaving him, “That explains the growl.”

Nyx’s lips peel back just enough to show teeth, not a snarl, but a warning, aimed somewhere far beyond us. I straighten, hand brushing along Nyx’s flank, and signal to Verenia. The stairs continue to spiral upward, but this time I move with purpose. Nyx falls silently beside me, a shadow in motion, every muscle taut and alert. Verenia stays behind me, dagger sheathed but hand hovering, unwilling to relax completely. The corridor above is quieter now, the air thicker with the smell of iron. Then a voice cuts through the stillness, a sharp, crude bark of words that make my chest lurch with recognition.

“Don’t think locking me up makes you clever! I’ll tear your ears off before breakfast if you don’t watch it!”

Relief crashes into me so fast it is dizzying, tangled with disbelief and something dangerously close to grief. I swallow hard, forcing air back into my lungs.

Verenia pauses a step behind me. "That sounded… personal."

I let out a breath that shakes despite my efforts to control it. "That," I say quietly, "Can only be one person."

Nyx growls low, the sound vibrating into my bones. His tail stiffens, ears forward, eyes fixed on the next flight of stairs above. He has known, and has been waiting, watching.

I glance at Verenia. Her eyes widen as she catches my expression. "You know her?" she whispers, tone a mix of disbelief and caution.

"She is… usually like this," I murmur, a grin tugging at my lips despite the tension in my chest. "That is Blythe."

The crude words continue, sharper now, punctuated by the clang of metal against wood. She is clearly not alone; someone has locked her up, but the defiance in her voice makes my chest tighten with something fierce. Relief, yes, but also the familiar sting of guilt.

Nyx nudges me forward, quiet but insistent, and I step with renewed determination. The stairs are nearly spent, the corridor bends ahead, and the source of that voice, the living, infuriating, indomitable Blythe, is just beyond the next landing.

We reach the top of the narrow stairwell and spill into the dungeon corridor. The smell hits first: stale air, iron, and sweat. It pulls my stomach into tight knots. Shadows stretch long and uneven across stone walls, flickering from a single torch nailed crookedly to the far wall.

"Stay close," I hiss, my voice low but firm. Nyx pads silently beside me, growl rumbling in his chest, every muscle coiled like spring steel. Verenia's hand rests on her dagger, eyes scanning every shadow, every corner. The guards are halfway to reacting when Verenia moves. She is a blur, dagger slicing through the air with precision. One guard drops silently, chest caved in by the tip, never realizing what hit him. Nyx lunges in perfect tandem, massive paws and teeth making the second guard's protest short and brutal.

I barely blink, letting the clash of steel and shouts blur into meaningless noise as I move toward the chains biting into Blythe's wrists. Violence can wait. *She* cannot. Her voice reaches me first, ragged, disbelieving, still sharp with fight. Relief threads through it, fragile but unmistakable. She is alive. *Gods, she is alive.* The knowledge hits like a knife: alive *despite* me.

"Edin?" she breathes when my fingers curl around the iron, as if saying my name might shatter me. Her voice trembles, raw and incredulous.

"Shh," I murmur, though my own breath stutters. I wrench the shackles open, the locks giving way with a brittle click. The sound is too soft for how heavy the moment is. I lower her arms carefully, guilt burning through my chest as I take in the damage: raw skin, bruises blooming where the chains held her.

This is on me. Every mark.

She sways, and I catch her instantly, anchoring her before she can fall. Nyx rumbles low in his chest and presses his massive head against her waist, grounding her, guarding her, as if he, too, knows how close I came to losing her.

I glance back only long enough to see Verenia sweeping the corridor, blades ready, eyes sharp.

"Clear," Verenia whispers.

The word barely registers.

"I thought I'd never see you again," Blythe whispers. The words break apart at the edges, and something in me fractures with them.

My arms tighten around her before I can stop myself. I draw her against me, carefully, like she might dissolve if I hold her too hard. My forehead drops to her hair, and the apology tears free of my chest.

"I am so sorry, Blythe," I choke. My voice shakes, stripped bare. "This is my fault. I thought sending you to Windemere would keep you safe. I *sent you into this.*"

Her fingers curl into my clothes, clutching like she is afraid I will vanish. When she cries, it is quiet at first, the kind of sob that has been held back too long.

"King Thayer," she says through the tears, pressing closer to me, "he's aligned with Osiris."

The name lands heavy and cold, and the world shifts.

He knew, he knew long before I stepped foot in Swindon Castle. He knew when he grabbed my shoulder, comforting and reassuring me at the Enlightenment.

I pull back just enough to look at her, the final piece snapping into place with brutal clarity. This is not chaos; it is coordination, and it is far larger than I ever allowed myself to believe.

"Did you find Endricks?" she sniffles.

"Osiris was successful," I say quietly. "Elysia has fallen. Endricks spearheaded the Helheim army straight into the heavenly lands."

Her jaw tightens. Resolve steels her expression even as tears still cling to her lashes. "Then we have to take King Thayer out here, in Windemere, before the war spreads any further."

"Agreed," Verenia says, stepping forward at last.

Blythe turns at the sound of her voice. She studies Verenia for a moment, really looks at her, and something soft and unexpected flickers across her face. A small smile curves her lips, hesitant and almost shy. It is a look I have not seen on her before.

Verenia's lips twitch into a brief, almost imperceptible smile, her white hair brushing her cheek as she tucks it behind her ear. Then, just as quickly, the warmth vanishes, and her face hardens, eyes sharpening to the steel I know so well. "Let's move," she says, voice quiet but firm.

I nod, taking a step forward. Blythe stays close to me, still trembling slightly, but her resolve is already regaining its edge. Nyx pads silently beside us, massive and unyielding, a shadow in motion that makes the dungeon corridors feel safer despite their oppressive gloom.

The castle seems to sense our urgency. Shadows stretch and twist along the walls, torches flickering as we pass, the faint drip of water echoing like a heartbeat through the stone. Every footstep carries us further from the lower quarters, further from chains and helplessness, and closer to the source of the danger that has hidden in Windemere for centuries. We move with precision; it feels almost practiced. Verenia sweeps ahead, eyes scanning every doorway, every nook where a guard might be lurking. Nyx's ears twitch, alert to the shift in the air.

The corridors twist and turn, old stone worn smooth beneath our boots. Each step brings the echo of our purpose closer: King Thayer. The name tastes bitter in my mouth, heavy with all we have lost, and all we are about to reclaim. I swallow, steadying the storm inside my chest.

War is coming, but we will not walk into it blindly.

Chapter 33

Endricks

I shield my eyes as I step through the veil; the light that shines in swirls of orange is a stark contrast against the darkness that emerges. The veil sits high in the Elysian castle, overlooking the heavenly land. It stands arrogant and unguarded, as if this realm still believes it is untouchable. The air smells clean, sharp, and untouched by blood, an offense I intend to correct.

Valker appears at my side the instant my boots meet the marble. Solid. Steady. His presence is an iron-bound restraint barely leashed, his gaze already sweeping the tower with a general's instinct. No awe. No hesitation. Just readiness. Behind us, the veil shudders, and Hell pours through.

The Hellions emerge in waves, armor as dark as the void between stars, eyes burning with disciplined hunger. Steel rings against stone. Wings unfurl, scraping sacred columns as if daring the heavens to object. The tower fills with the weight of them, conquest given form, their allegiance absolute. This is not a raid. This is an arrival.

I feel it then, the realm reacting. Elysia recoils. The wards along the tower walls flare weakly, light stuttering as Helheim's power stretches its shadow across sanctified ground. Judgment coils beneath my skin, ancient and patient, measuring this place not by its beauty, but by how easily it will fall.

I lift my gaze toward the open arches at the tower's peak, where the sky gleams endlessly, unaware of what now stains its threshold. The corner of my mouth curves. "How blindly ignorant they are," I say, voice carrying through the tower as the Hellions fall into formation behind me, "Unaware that judgment walks on their holy land."

I take my first step forward into heaven, and Elysia, at long last, will learn what true fear is. A single gesture is all it takes. The Hellions move as one, falling into disciplined lines without a word spoken. Their armor is muted, blades sheathed, wings refolded tight as they begin their descent down the spiraling corridors of the tower. Columns of light slide past us as we move lower, the tower's vast windows opening to the heavens beyond. Outside, the sky burns gold, the sun sinking toward the horizon in a wash of divine color meant to inspire reverence. Instead, it becomes a backdrop for invasion.

At my silent signal, the winged demons peel away. One by one, then in darkening swarms, demons step onto open ledges and leap without hesitation. Wings snap wide mid-fall, catching the air with a thunderless grace as they rise into the golden sunset. Shadows cut across the clouds. Against that radiant sky, their silhouettes are unmistakable, wrong, and blasphemous. They fan outward in practiced formations, vanishing into the light to secure the city below, unseen and unchallenged.

Valker watches them go, approval flickering once in his eyes. “No alarms yet.”

“They will not come,” I murmur, continuing down the tower as the army flows behind me like a living blade. “Elysia still believes itself sacred.”

Ahead, the tower leads into the heart of the castle, wide halls, high doors, and the first thin tremor of fear threads through the stone. Conquest does not announce itself. It arrives quietly. I stop at the threshold of the grand hall. The castle opens before us in alabaster splendor, vaulted ceilings, sanctified banners, courtiers frozen mid-breath as they finally realize what has breached their sky. Shock ripples through them, disbelief cracking into fear as Hellions fan out with surgical precision, hemming them in without a single cry raised.

My voice cuts through the hall, calm and absolute. "End them. Any Elysian who dares to disrespect the Goddess of Purgatory, strike them down where they stand," I pause deliberately. "But Osiris," I growl, venom beneath the velvet, "He is mine."

The order lands like a death knell. I snap my fingers and my magic answers. Water seeps first from the seams of the marble floor, thin silver lines threading between celestial runes. Then it surges, violent and obedient. Fountains roar unnaturally to life, walls weep, and the polished stone vanishes beneath a rising tide. Screams finally break the silence as Elysians stumble back, robes soaking, wings dragging uselessly in the sudden weight.

The flood does not rage wildly. It moves with intent. It pours through archways and down stairwells, spilling into the courtyard below like a released breath. From the tower windows, I watch it cascade outward into the streets of Elysia. Holy avenues are transformed into channels of judgment. The golden city reflects itself in the water, distorted, drowning in its own perfection.

My Hellions advance. Blades flash. Wings beat. Any Elysian foolish enough to raise a voice in defiance or worse, speak Edin's name with scorn, falls where they stand, struck down with merciless efficiency. The waters rise another inch, and heaven learns what it means to drown.

A fitting baptism.

Valker steps closer, water lapping at his boots. "The city is sealing its gates."

I smile, slow and cold, eyes already searching the chaos for one presence alone. "Let them," I say, raising my palm high into the air, setting the rooftops alight. Flames rapidly spread from canopy to canopy and smoke plumes into the air. "I have no doubt Osiris will make his appearance very soon."

Chapter 34

Osiris

I sit high above the clouds, suspended in eternal sunlight. Elysia rises before me, a heavenly realm where divinity meets invention. A breeze drifts through, sending shivers down my spine. The air smells faintly of warm metal, incense, and fresh rain. The entire city gleams with golden architecture, its towers shaped like ornate spires and clockwork cathedrals. Every surface glows softly, not from reflected light, but from an inner radiance, as if the city itself is alive with celestial energy.

Gears the size of wagon wheels turn slowly along the sides of buildings, their polished brass teeth meshing in perfect harmony. Delicate steam vents shaped like angelic wings release curls of shimmering vapor, which drift upward and melt into the luminous sky. Throughout the city, a soft hum, part machinery, part choir, fills the air, creating an atmosphere both serene and mechanical.

"Fuck," I breathe out slowly, tossing my head back. I thread my fingers through Fallon's dark locks, turning my gaze back down to the floor as a moan crawls up my throat, turning into a growl. She sits on her heels between my legs. Fisting a wad of her hair, I jerk her head back, and her mouth pops off of my cock with a smacking sound. "Such a good girl you are," I grind out, smacking the side of her face. Fallon looks up at me in submission through her thick dark lashes. She leaves her mouth open wide, tongue hanging out. I dart my eyes down to my dick, and she takes the cue, sliding her lips down my length, making my hips buck.

My head dips back again, and my balls tighten, my eyes slowly closing. Echoed screams ring out, jolting me forward. I shove Fallon aside and jump to my feet, stepping on her hand in the process. A yelp escapes her lips as she hits the marble floor with a thud. Yanking my pants up, I lean over the balcony, gripping the stone rail until it splits beneath my hands. Cracks spiderweb through marble once thought unbreakable. Darkness spills across the sky like ink in water. The lazy gold of the sunset sky gutters and dies, swallowed by a bruised midnight gray. Smoke thickens the air, dense and choking, rolling over my pristine white kingdom like a curse laid upon holy ground.

"Guards!" I snap.

Below, the world is coming apart. Flames claw upward from the surrounding towers, devouring rooftops, licking at the heavens as if daring them to strike back. Black plumes coil into the sky, blotting out the last light.

I turn slowly, too slowly. Time fractures, each second dragging like it is caught in tar. The chamber doors burst open. Guards stumble through, soot-streaked, blood-slick, and armor dented, ringing with every unsteady step. Their mouths move, but the roar in my ears drowns them out. I just stare. One of them reaches me first. His hands clamp onto my shoulders, shaking, whether from fear or urgency, I cannot tell.

"Sire, are you listening to me?"

"What the *fuck* is happening?" The words scrape out of me, low and lethal.

"A man," he coughs, smoke tearing at his lungs. "Claiming to be the King of Helheim."

A brittle, unbelieving laugh ripples through the others.

I do not laugh. I seize him by the throat and lift him clean off his feet. His boots scrape uselessly against marble as my fingers crush into his windpipe. I hurl him against the wall. Armor slams stone. He drops hard, metal clanging, body crumpling face-first onto the floor. Without another word, I turn my back on them. My sword waits where I left it. I take it up and draw it free, steel singing.

Fucking Endricks.

Behind me, Fallon rises, blood on her lip, weapon already in hand. “Stay,” I bark over my shoulder. I stride from my chambers. The corridor throws my footsteps back at me in hollow echoes. Beyond the doors, the clash of battle erupts, steel against steel, armor buckling, men screaming. Hellions and Elysians tear into one another in a frenzy of flashing blades and splintering shields. Soldiers fall in my wake, blow after blow, striking bone and breaking bodies.

None of it matters. My focus narrows to a single, burning point. I already killed him once. *So I thought.* I will finish it. No one will stand between me and that grave. At the courtyard doors, I slam both palms against the wood. The hinges shriek in protest.

If it is war he wants, then I will give him ruin, and I will personally drag him to his demise.

Chapter 35

Edin

The great hall doors groan and splinter at our push, and the echo of their swing reverberates like a drum of warning through the chamber. Torches flare at the sudden gust. The shadows curtain the room in flickering light, catching on polished stone and gilded banners. Guards freeze mid-step, weapons raised, but confusion overtakes training.

Verenia moves first, dagger slicing through the air, striking down the nearest threats before their instincts can respond. Nyx follows instantly, a shadow made flesh, teeth and claws cutting down the remaining guards with terrifying, fluid grace. The sound of their movements sends chills down my spine; the low rumble of Nyx, the soft metallic clash of Verenia's blade. Both fill the hall, punctuated by the sudden, unnatural silence of bodies falling.

Then my gaze finds him.

King Thayer.

He is frozen, rigid, the sword in his hands trembling despite his attempts at control. His eyes snap toward Blythe first. The expression that crosses his face is impossible to miss: disbelief, horror, betrayal. His lips part as if to speak, but no words form. He had expected a girl cowering, a powerless pawn, anything but this.

Blythe steps forward, unbound and fierce. Her chains are gone, but the heat she radiates is hotter than any forge. She holds herself with defiance so raw it threatens to crush the room itself. Verenia whistles to Blythe, then tosses her a dagger. She catches it smoothly, sliding it into the strap on her hip. I step up beside her, my boots echoing off the stone, heart hammering with anger I have kept buried for far too long. Every nerve screams, every beat of my pulse is a call to reckoning. I can feel it rising from my chest, spreading into my hands, into the tension in my shoulders.

King Thayer finally speaks, voice faltering, "I knew my time would be cut short once the Wixen showed her face here."

"Leave him to me," Blythe says, voice sharp, crisp, slicing through his stunned disbelief. She does not need to raise her voice; the authority in it is enough to still every breath in the room. Her glare locks onto him, and I can see the flicker of terror bloom behind the shock in his eyes.

I step closer, letting the weight of my presence bear down on him. "I trusted you," I growl, teeth clenched. "You will pay for every moment you thought you could manipulate, betray, or destroy without consequence." Purple mist pours from my palms, swirling around me.

The shock on his face deepens. His jaw tightens, eyes widening as he takes me in, standing beside Blythe, goddess and mortal, fury and resolve entwined. He had thought us divided, isolated, powerless. He had counted on that. He had underestimated the fire he had created, and now it stands blazing before him.

Verenia sweeps the room with trained precision, dagger poised, but even she hesitates for a heartbeat, catching the moment of Thayer's panic. His composure is gone. Every calculated façade falls away as he finally realizes exactly who has come for him. The hall seems to hold its breath. Even the torches flicker nervously. Every guard left standing, few and shaken, shifts toward the exits, falling back on instinct rather than loyalty.

Blythe's eyes flick to me for the briefest instant, just long enough for me to see her defiance mirrored in mine. Then she turns back to him, and I know, without a shadow of doubt, that he is finished.

She strikes first, an emerald mist swarming around her. The stone floor splits open with a violent crack, vines exploding upward and wrapping around King Thayer's boots, dragging him back as a chair scrapes into place behind him. They coil relentlessly, hauling him down.

Fire detonates from his palms. Flames roar outward, searing vines to ash and forcing Blythe back half a step. Heat washes across the hall, stone blackening. Thayer snarls, fire climbing his arms as he tears free, eyes wild now, desperate.

"You should have killed me when you had the chance," he spits.

Blythe's smile is razor-thin.

The earth answers her fury, and she does not hesitate. The moment is hers. The calm before the storm evaporates in a heartbeat as the stone floor shudders. The guards left standing freeze, mouths open, unable to process what is happening. The vines twist around his limbs and body, anchoring him to the chair like roots clutching at soil. His hands claw at the vines, struggling against the unyielding grip, but it is hopeless. The chair rises with him, suspending him upright, completely immobilized.

Blythe waltzes over and straddles him, and I feel my pulse spike, not fear, not regret, but awe at the raw, controlled power she wields. Her knife slides up his face, dragging along his cheek with a hissing scrape. King Thayer's eyes widen, disbelief mingling with terror, lips twitching as if to scream, but the vines at his throat choke out any sound.

The vines react to her will, thick thorns bursting from their surface, slicing into his skin and digging deep. I flinch at the sound of flesh tearing, and a low groan of pain pours from Thayer's lips as the thorns inject their poison. His mouth twists, a mottled blue spreading across it, and he coughs, clawing at the chair and the tendrils that hold him. His struggles grow frantic as Blythe's eyes lock with his. King Thayer's eyes dart toward me, begging, cursing, pleading, but I do not falter. I do not interfere. I only watch as Blythe, unflinching and terrifying, takes what is owed to her.

Finally, his struggle begins to weaken. The poison spreads, the thorns keep him pinned, and the life in his eyes dims to the same gray as the stone beneath us. The great hall becomes hushed except for the low hum of the earth and the rattling of Thayer's final breaths.

Blythe rises, letting the vines retract slowly, leaving him as a grim monument. She wipes her knife clean on the hem of her sleeve. I step closer, hand resting lightly on her shoulder, a quiet, grounding weight. I exhale slowly, letting the tension drain from my body.

Verenia steps forward. "That is quite some earth magic you have there, Fox."

Blythe curtsies, "Thank you… Deerling."

I step between them. "We have to move, ladies."

King Thayer's body lurches forward and hits the stone, but we are already moving, boots pounding through corridors that seem to recoil from what we have done. The castle blurs around us: torches whipping past, banners snapping in the sudden drafts, alarms beginning to rise, too late to be of any use. Blythe is at my side, jaw set, blood dried dark on her sleeve. Verenia takes point, while Nyx moves like a living shadow, clearing our path with low warning growls.

War is already in motion. I can feel it now, like pressure building behind my eyes, like a storm breaking bones somewhere far away. The lower quarters rush up to meet us. The veil chamber yawns open, stone ringed with sigils older than Windemere itself. I do not hesitate. I step into the circle and lift my hands, breath steady despite the hammering in my chest.

"Stand back," I say.

The veil answers me instantly. It parts like silk drawn through water, light tearing open the space between worlds, and what waits on the other side steals the air from my lungs.

Elysia is burning.

The sky is split with fire and shadow, angels and demons colliding in violent spirals of light. Wings tear the clouds apart. Magic detonates across marble spires and golden fields, heaven cracking under the weight of hell's advance. The sound hits next; metal, screams, thunder, the roar of something ancient finally unleashed, and there, at the very heart of it…Endricks.

He stands amid the chaos like the axis of the war itself, Helheim's power blazing around him, shadows bowing as angels fall. His blade moves with devastating certainty, every strike reshaping the battlefield.

This is not a prince.

This is not a commander.

This is a king at war.

My chest tightens painfully, pride and fear colliding so hard it almost brings me to my knees. I open the veil wider, anchoring it, holding the path steady even as the violence beyond it presses close.

"We're late," Blythe breathes.

"No," I say, voice hard, unyielding. "We are exactly where we are meant to be."

The second war of realms has begun, and I am not watching from the shadows anymore.

CHAPTER 36

ENDRICKS

I step out into the courtyard and into ruin. Water surges around my boots, ankle-deep and rising, rippling across once-immaculate marble, now fractured and slick with ash. The great courtyard fountains have ruptured, their sanctified basins vomiting torrents that slam into fallen statuary. Cherubim carved from white stone lie shattered and half-submerged, their broken wings smoothed by the relentless flow.

Divine structures burn along the courtyard's edges, holy flame turned feral as it claws up ivory pillars and devours silk banners. Gold leaf melts and runs like ichor down the walls. Roofs collapse inward with thunderous cracks, sending cascades of embers hissing into the flood. Steam boils upward where flame meets water, shrouding the courtyard in heat and smoke.

Above it all, the sky is war-torn. Winged Hellions clash with Elysian soldiers in violent spirals of steel and flame, their battles tearing through the burning gold of the sunset. Blades lock midair, sparks scattering like falling stars as bodies collide and break apart. Shadows streak across the courtyard as bodies fall. Angelic wings snap and burn, feathers drifting down in scorched, bloodied spirals, while demons wheel and dive. A halo shatters against a Hellion's gauntlet. A demon plummets, wings torn, vanishing into smoke and fire below.

On the ground, angelic soldiers wade desperately through the flood, armor heavy, wings soaked and dragging. Some rally, forming glowing ranks that push back against the tide, until Hellions crash into them like living weapons, cutting lines apart with ruthless efficiency. Prayer turns to screams, and order dissolves into survival.

I stand unmoved at the center of it all. Water curls around me without daring to rise higher, fire bending away as if the flames themselves recognize power when it walks among them. The chaos parts instinctively, leaving a hollow ring of devastation in my wake as my forces claim the courtyard piece by piece.

This was once a place of worship.

Now it is a battlefield.

The doors explode open. Sacred oak and gilded steel splinter as Osiris bursts through the far end of the courtyard, rage incarnate, sword already in motion. The blade blazes with Elysian light, a burning white-gold that cleaves through smoke and shadow alike. Power rolls off him in violent waves, forcing water back in hissing arcs as his boots strike the flooded stone.

Anger has stripped him of restraint. His wings flare wide, vast, radiant, feathers blazing as if lit from within. Angelic soldiers rally at the sight of him, their broken lines snapping taut with renewed desperation.

"Endricks!" His voice tears through the chaos, raw and thunderous, carrying across fire and water. "You have defiled sacred ground."

I turn to face him at last.

Around us, the battle slows, not because it ends, but because every soul present feels the shift. Control has found its counterpoint. Hellions hold their ground, blades dripping, wings beating slow and steady as they sense what approaches.

Osiris stalks forward through the flood, sword leveled at my chest, light bleeding down the edge like molten sun. His eyes burn with fury and something deeper, humiliation, perhaps, or the fear he refuses to name.

"You dare bring Helheim into Elysia," he snarls, lifting the blade higher. "You dare threaten the heavens for a half-born queen."

The corner of my mouth lifts. I step forward, water parting cleanly around me, flames bowing as I pass. "Careful," I say calmly. "Every word you speak is another sin you will have to answer for."

His grip tightens. "You will fall here," Osiris vows. "I will carve you out of my realm and cast you back into the abyss."

I meet his blazing stare without flinching, my power coiling, patient and vast. "No," I reply softly. "You will kneel."

The courtyard holds its breath.

"I am the king of realms! I kneel to no one," he snarls.

Osiris does not charge, he does not even flinch, but he smiles, and then the world *tilts*. For a heartbeat, the courtyard is gone, replaced by blinding white, endless, and hollow. The roar of battle fades to a distant echo, and I stand alone on unmarred stone, water gone, fire gone, sky empty. Peace, offered like a lie.

Chaos magic.

I snarl and drive my sword point-first into the ground. Ice detonates outward from the impact, crawling across the marble in a violent ring. Cold bites up my arm, anchoring me. The illusion fractures, white splintering into smoke and flame as reality slams back into place.

Osiris is already moving, and our blades meet with a shriek of metal, sparks bursting where holy light collides with hellish steel. He is fast, faster than before, chaos threading through his strikes, bending angles, making distance unreliable. One moment, he is in front of me, the next at my flank, wings beating hard enough to scatter embers and spray water into the sky.

Time seems to stutter around me, halting for half a second. *Valker.* He bolts in faster than light itself, landing a direct hit to Osiris, hurling him back through steam and smoke. The pressure rattles the courtyard, banners tearing loose as Valker lands at my side, eyes sharp, hands already moving, slowing the chaos around us.

"You seeing him clearly?" Valker snaps.

"For now."

Osiris laughs as he regains his footing, boots skidding across ice-slick stone. "Two against one. Let us even those odds."

He lifts his hand, and the courtyard multiplies. Two of him, then three. Each one is solid and breathing. Chaos crawls at the edges of my thoughts, whispering false openings, bending sight and sound alike.

Valker reacts instantly. The sound of a clock tolls out as he sweeps his arms outward, pressure pounding in a wide arc. Time shifts the illusion from reality, shredding a false Osiris into nothing. I follow with fire, brutal flames rolling outward to burn away what chaos tries to leave behind. Ice answers next, jagged spears erupting from the flood to pin another false body before it disintegrates.

The real Osiris comes from above. He crashes between us like a meteor, sword flashing. I catch the blow, but chaos twists the follow-through, and my vision stutters.

Chains.

Blood.

Edin is on her knees before him.

I roar and counter with water, a crushing wave slams Osiris sideways as Valker drives in, blade striking true. Osiris staggers, wings flaring unevenly.

Then Osiris smiles again, and chaos snaps tight. The world lurches just enough for me to miss it, just enough for Valker to see something that is not there.

Osiris pivots.

His sword punches forward, holy light screaming as it drives clean through Valker's torso. Air explodes outward in a violent shockwave as Valker gasps, the wind around him collapsing in a sudden, deafening vacuum.

"Valker!"

CHAPTER 37

EDIN

The veil spits us out into chaos. Heat slams into me first, then the burning marble, scorched air, and the metallic tang of blood. We hit the steps hard, boots skidding as we rush downward into the heart of Elysia. The sky above is split open, light and shadow tearing at each other, wings crashing, magic screaming. The roar of war drowns out Nyx's growl, but he stays tight at our heels as a living shield.

Then I see it, clocking it seconds before anyone else. It slams into me before I can even brace myself. Osiris stands at the entrance of the courtyard, as calm as a god at prayer. His sword slides free of Valker's chest with a wet grating sound. Valker crumples, armor ringing against stone, blood spreading fast and impossibly red against Elysian white. Osiris does not even look at the body as it falls; he turns into a dead sprint towards Endricks.

"Blythe," I say under my breath, "get Verenia out of–"

Verenia's scream tears through the air.

It is not a word at first. It is a sound dragged from the marrow of her bones, raw and animalistic, the kind of noise that does not belong in a body meant to survive it.

"No!"

She launches forward, not as a soldier, but as a sister, as a *twin*. She surges forward, fury obliterating discipline, white hair flying, blade half-drawn as if she might cut down a god with her grief alone. There is not a drop of strategy in her movements, no discipline. Just a sibling who has watched half her soul collapse onto the stone.

"Verenia!" I shout.

She does not hear me; she cannot, her world is crashing down before her eyes. She drops beside Valker, sliding in his blood, hands already on him, frantic, trembling, trying to lift him, shake him, hold him together.

"Valker. Valker, look at me," she demands through gritted teeth. "Look at me!"

His head lolls.

Her hands press against the wound as if she can hold the life inside him. Blood pours between her fingers. She chokes on a sob that turns into a vicious growl.

"No. No! Stay," she stutters. "Stay with me. Don't you dare leave me."

Her forehead crashes against his, erratically shaking. I have seen Verenia deal death blows without flinching, but I have never seen her *break*.

"Breathe," she whispers to him, as if she can command it. "You breathe when I tell you to." Her voice cracks on the last word.

Osiris is halfway across the courtyard now. Elysia will not survive this if I do not move, but Verenia… she curls over Valker's body. She looks like a feral animal, shielding him, snarling when the ground trembles beneath us. Her grief sharpens into rage in an instant. She reaches for her blade again, wild-eyed, ready to charge after the being who did this.

I move before she can. "Blythe!" My voice is harsher than I intend. "Get them out. Now."

Blythe nods, already moving, a green mist blooming around her. Vines wrap around Verenia's waist just as she lunges forward again.

"Let me go!" Verenia screams, thrashing violently. Blythe reaches her side and restrains her just as Verenia slices through her vines. "He is not dead. He is not… I can fix this, Blythe. I can fix this!"

"Edin!" Blythe yells. "Edin can fix this, but we have to move," she grinds the last few words out through bared teeth.

Nyx barrels in beside them, teeth bared, snapping at anything that dares to come close. The ground answers to Blythe, and vines explode through marble, cracking sacred stone, wrapping around Valker's body in a desperate, protective cocoon. Even like this, Verenia claws at the vines as Blythe drags her backward, step by brutal step. She is sobbing and snarling all at once, grief turning her voice ragged and unrecognizable.

"Let me go!" she wails. "That's my brother! That is *my* brother!"

The words sweep across the space, twisting my heartstrings and restricting my breath.

Blythe tightens her grip. Verenia's hands stretch toward the cocoon as she is pulled away, fingers trembling, reaching. The earthly casket trails behind them, vines crawling up the walls, weaving a pathway, ushering his body to safety. Nyx follows behind them, giving me one last glance, a look of reassurance, before he disappears.

"Valker!" I hear Verenia cry out as the last bit of leaves slip up the spiral staircase to the veil tower, but her screams do not stop. They echo, through marble corridors, through the open sky, through to me. Even as I turn back to the fight, even as steel clashes somewhere beyond the courtyard, I can still hear her. It is the sound of something cherished and *unbreakable*, splitting in two, and it follows me all the way into war.

I wait till Blythe gives me the signal from the tower that they are safe, and then I drop. My knees hit the shattered marble hard enough to bruise. I do not feel it, I refuse to feel anything in this moment. I slam my palms to the ground, fingers splayed, breath tearing out of my lungs as I reach downward not to Heaven, not to Hell, but to the space *between*.

Purgatory answers.

The world goes still.

Then the ground screams.

Cracks rip outward from my hands in violent rings, light draining from the stone as cold floods up through the fractures. Hands burst free first, skeletal, clawing, desperate, followed by bodies, rusted armor, torn wings, faces half-remembered by death. The fallen rise in waves, dragging themselves from beneath

Elysia's perfect floor, eyes igniting with hollow, spectral light.

Osiris finally pauses across the courtyard, jerking his gaze back towards me. For the first time, something sharp flickers across his face, not fear, not surprise, but recognition. I rise slowly, power roaring through my veins, the dead assembling behind me in silent ranks. Broken angels. Slain demons. Warriors forgotten by both sides, now bound to me alone.

"You wanted war," I say, my voice carrying unnaturally across the battlefield. "You wanted judgment."

I lift my head, eyes locked on him, unblinking.

"Now face the goddess who rules what comes after."

Chapter 38

Blythe

This is wrong. Every step of this is wrong. Somewhere between strategy and survival, the plan died. This was not supposed to happen.

"She will fix this," I whisper, pushing off the railing of the veil tower balcony. "Edin will fix this." I reach for Verenia, and she jerks away like my touch burns. She paces instead, frantic, with uneven steps that could carve a path into the stone floor. Her breaths come sharp and shallow, each one scraping out of her like glass. Nyx curls around the side of the vine-woven cradle, and a lump forms in my throat at the sight.

"She's the Goddess of Purgatory," I push, forcing steadiness into my voice. "She will save him." My voice cracks on *him*, betraying me. Verenia doesn't answer. I don't think she even hears me. She drops back to her knees beside

Valker, hands wrapping around his as if she can anchor him here through sheer force. As if she can command his soul not to wander too far. Storm clouds gather behind her eyes. I see it, the pressure building, dark and violent. The first tremor of thunder in the tightening of her jaw. Then the drizzle. Tears slip free, silent at first, tracking down her cheeks before falling to the floor beside the cocoon.

My vines hold Valker, thick and unyielding, wound tight around his body in a living shroud. They pulse faintly with my magic, green and gold veins of light threading through the bark. Protection, a death shroud disguised as hope.

"Verenia," I whisper.

She bows over him, forehead nearly touching the woven cradle of branches. Her shoulders shake once, a suppressed tremor, then again.

"He said…" she says hoarsely. "He said he would never leave me."

Her voice breaks completely this time. The storm inside her finally splits open. She presses her face to his hand and sobs, not the restrained, dignified grief of a warrior, but something raw and feral. The kind of sound torn from the center of the soul.

I move closer, slower now, kneeling beside her. "I've got him," I murmur, even though the words feel small, useless. "We've got him." My stomach tightens as I look at the cocoon, at the stillness inside it, and doubt coils tight in my chest. All I can think is that if Edin doesn't come soon, the storm behind Verenia's eyes won't be the only thing that breaks. Nyx jerks his head up, and a low growl crawls out between his barred teeth.

"You're mine, bitch."

The words slice through the waiting stillness. I whirl around before the echo fades, power already surging through my veins. Vines explode from the marble floor, violently, weaving themselves over Valker's cocoon in an instant, bark and thorns layering into living armor. Osiris's *whore* stands framed in the doorway. Fallon. Vengeance burns in her eyes, sword already drawn, blade catching the pale light from the tower's balcony.

"I would just *love* a pretty set of antlers and fox ears to hang over our mantle," the words drip with venom as they leave Fallon's lips. They curve upward into a sickening smile as she laughs.

"Verenia, stay with Valker," I call over my shoulder, but I know it's unnecessary. She would die before letting anything touch him. I need her to hear it, though, that I've got this. I step forward and curl my fingers toward Fallon, beckoning. "Come on," I murmur, a slow smirk pulling at my mouth. "Let's see what tricks Osiris's *pet* can do."

She charges. She must think I'm defenseless without steel in my hand, an easy kill. *Idiot.* With a flick of my wrists, the marble beneath her feet fractures. Vines spear upward in a thick wall of thorns. She slams into it shoulder-first, the impact cracking through the tower. She recovers fast. Her blade hacks through my growth in brutal arcs, splinters flying.

Good. While she cuts, I plant something else. Ivy creeps across the floor behind her, thin, patient, and deliberate. Green ropes snake toward her ankles. She barrels toward me again, sword leading her charge. I pivot sideways, almost perfectly. Almost. The blade kisses my shoulder. Heat explodes through me as blood wells and runs down my arm. She stumbles past, regaining balance and finally notices the ivy tightening at her heels. She slashes downward, shredding leaves and vines alike. Her eyes shift past me, to Verenia… and to Valker.

"Don't you dare," I growl.

She lunges toward them, bringing her sword down against the vines suspending his body. Verenia intercepts, their blades lock inches from Valker.

"Over my dead body," Verenia hisses.

Fallon knees her in the ribs. Verenia grunts but doesn't drop. She twists, trapping Fallon's sword arm and driving her own blade toward Fallon's throat. Fallon barely tears herself free in time. The tip slices across her collarbone, and blood splatters the marble.

Pain screams down my arm as I lift both hands and reach deeper, past the tower, past the stone, into the soil beneath Elysia itself. I pour everything into it. The marble columns explode inward. Stone rains down around us, slicing my cheek and stinging my skin. Wind roars through the chamber as tree limbs burst through the shattered arches like an ancient beast answering a primordial call.

Nyx lunges forward, clamping down on Fallon's leg, and my branches slam into her, knocking the sword from her grip. It clatters uselessly across the marble. The limbs pluck her from the floor by her waist, and Nyx bares down, slowly letting his teeth drag down her shin as she's ripped upward. She frantically claws at the branches with her nails, but the wood is relentless, splintering and reforming, thick as a battering ram. She screams, kicking against the air. Her olive skin turns red as the trees squeeze her tighter. A crunch echoes out, and Fallon screams as her ribcage flattens a bit. Then a final snap rings through the room, and her body falls limp. It hangs broken in the limbs of the tree as it backs out of the hole in the wall, taking her with it. As the rustling of the trees fade, silence crashes down, just as loud as the clash of steel.

"Fuck," I pant, turning my gaze back to Verenia. She's already curled over Valker again, shielding him, shaking. Desperation has carved new lines into her face, lines that didn't exist this morning. She looks like someone standing on the edge of an abyss, ready to bargain with anything, or anyone, that will throw her a rope. I summon fresh vines, softer this time, thicker, cushioning Valker, cradling his body carefully. Her eyes flick to mine as I slide down the wall next to her. I grab my still bleeding shoulder with a grunt.

"You are hurt," she says, quickly ripping the edge of her shirt. She moves in front of me, applying pressure and attempting to tie off the makeshift bandage.

"Here," I hiss through the pain, placing my hand over hers.

Her eyes lock on mine, holding the briefest moment, and something different flickers across her face. Then she slowly slips her fingers free and ties off the knot.

"Edin will fix this… all of this. We just have to stay hidden…and *alive,*" I breathe out as my eyes dart to Valker. I lean my head back, resting it on the stone wall. Verenia moves from in front of me and slides down the wall beside me. She places a hand on the cocoon and lays her head on my shoulder. I tilt my head, resting it on hers. "She will fix this," I whisper, trying to convince even myself.

CHAPTER 39

EDIN

***

The courtyard opens before me in a wash of fire and ruin. Behind me, the dead pour forward in a near-silent tide, armor clattering, wings dragging, hollow eyes burning with borrowed light. They fan out across the courtyard, ranks forming without command, the weight of them bending the air itself.

For a single, stolen heartbeat, my gaze finds Endricks. He stands at the center of the carnage, blade slick with blood, shadows coiled around him like a second skin. When his eyes meet mine, something soft cuts through the fury in my chest, sharp and tender all at once. A fierce, instinctive need to shield him from what comes next. It lasts no longer than a breath, then I look past him.

Osiris waits across the courtyard, heaven's fire licking along his sword, his expression dark with something far too close to satisfaction. The sight of him churns something vicious inside me. Every memory slams forward, *imprisonment, Blythe, Valker's body hitting the stone*. They crash together in a surge of rage.

The air around me hums, the undead reacting to my fury, claws flexing, jaws parting in soundless anticipation. My gaze locks onto Osiris, unwavering. Whatever softness lived in me a moment ago burns away.

I lift my chin, power coiling tight and merciless in my chest, and the army behind me shifts as one, waiting. Endricks moves before I can blink. He cuts through the chaos and comes to my side, shadows snapping into place around him. The moment his shoulder brushes mine, something locks, power aligning, intent sharpening. We do not utter a word; it is not necessary. We have never fought *alone*, not really, and Osiris has just made the mistake of reminding us why.

His gaze flicks between us, fire flaring higher along his blade. "How *touching*," he says, voice smooth and poisonous. "A bastard and his tramp."

Endricks's mouth curves into a humorless smile. "You should have finished me when you had the nerve, Osiris."

The ground hums beneath our feet. I feel it then, his strength sliding effortlessly alongside mine, Helheim's shadows threading through Purgatory's cold, the living and the dead answering at once.

Across the courtyard, Osiris tilts his head and smiles. "Dispel," he growls, and a grey mist filters across the ground.

Chaos blooms, not as flame or force, but as *distortion*. The world *slips*. The courtyard bends at the edges, stone rippling like water, pillars leaning where they should not. Sound stretches, war cries warping into whispers that crawl under my skin. For a moment, the undead behind me hesitate, their forms blurring as Osiris's magic claws at thought itself. Then he looks at me. Pain is not what he sends… only memories.

I am back in Purgatory. Chains hang around my wrist. His body slams into mine, and tears stream down my face. I scratch at my skin, disgust and unworthiness seeping deep into my bones. For half a breath, it presses in, suffocating, and I grit my teeth. "No!" I scream, fury snapping me back into myself. I feel Endricks then, a fire at my back, steady and real, and the intrusion shatters.

"I am here," Endricks mutters, grabbing my wrist. "We are here."

I steady myself, and Osiris strikes, swinging his blade as the world continues to shift around us. Endricks steps through the distortion, fire roaring outward, forcing Osiris to shield his face. Water surges immediately after, slamming into Osiris, knocking him back as the stone beneath him turns slick at Endricks's command.

Osiris laughs, even as he stumbles, and chaos swirls through again. The air fills with murmurs of Endricks's fears and doubts of my own. The whispers are flung like weapons meant to turn us inward.

You will lose her.

You are not
enough.

She will die here...

You can save no one.

...just like your mother.

I take a deep breath, pushing out the voices, and answer with will. The dead surge at my command, anchored by my voice. They rise around Osiris, closing ranks, limiting the space his magic needs to unravel us.

Endricks moves with brutal speed, and fire cuts off Osiris's step. Water crashes in from his side, freezing his footing, stealing momentum. He adapts quickly, but not fast enough to regain control. Osiris's smile finally cracks, turning into a snarl. His magic still claws at the edges of my thoughts, still warps the stone and air, but now it has resistance. Now it has *order* to push against, and we advance together, step by synchronized step, forcing Osiris backward through his own unraveling illusion.

Osiris stops, and his face twists into a wicked grin again. "You see what I allow you to see," he says, and the courtyard *multiplies*.

Four of him circle us now. No… seven. No mist, no telling signs. Each one breathes, moves, and *radiates* power. We fight back-to-back, my hand brushing Endricks's arm, a silent promise passing between us. Heat rolls off around me in a sudden, brutal wave, flames spiraling outward in a controlled inferno that incinerates an illusion on contact. A single Osiris vanishes, screaming into smoke. I glance over my shoulder at Endricks as he slings his palms out. He meets my eye with a wink, then ice follows, shards erupting from the flood, locking one more false body in a frozen snarl before it shatters.

I slam my hands down, summoning the dead from the ground beneath Osiris's feet. Skeletal hands claw up, grasping, slowing him for half a second, just long enough. Endricks drives forward, ice binding Osiris's sword arm. I send my magic out in the opposite direction, power ripping, cold and absolute. Then I see it out of the corner of my eye. *I truly see it.*

All the illusions flicker, *except one*, and he stands neatly tucked in Endricks's blind spot. Osiris lifts his blade once more, and for the first time since this war began, his eyes gleam with something dangerous. I do not hesitate, swinging around Endricks's back, ripping my dagger from my thigh, and meeting Osiris head-on.

My dagger sinks into his chest with a sickening resistance. Flesh and then bone. I feel it give, the impact of it shuddering up my arm and rattling my teeth. Heat splashes across my knuckles, the copper tang of blood sharp in the air. For a second, everything narrows to that single point of contact, my hand, the hilt, his chest, and a brutal, feral satisfaction coils in my gut. The tension in my chest gives way by a fraction as relief washes over me.

It is over.

Then a voice curls around my ear.

"Finally."

No.

Osiris's form ripples, edges blurring like smoke caught in a sudden wind. Confusion fractures through me just as agony explodes across my back. Cold metal punches between my ribs, stealing the air from my lungs in a sharp, helpless gasp. I look down in disbelief as a blade bursts through my chest, slick and crimson, its tip trembling with the force of the strike.

Osiris is suddenly behind me, real, solid, his breath warm against my neck as he leans close, driving the sword deeper, and the illusion collapses into grey mist. I jerk my neck back, and his eyes meet mine, too calm, too knowing. A smile ghosts over his mouth, slow and deliberate, as if I have done exactly what he wanted. Pain consumes everything. My knees buckle, strength bleeding out of me with every heartbeat, and the world tilts violently as I realize, too late, that I never struck him at all.

The chaos around me slows, my undead army halting. Osiris plants his boot in the small of my back and shoves. His sword rips free of me with a wet, tearing pull, and the world fractures. I am flung forward, momentum stealing the air from my lungs as I stumble. Pain shoots through my back, white-hot and blinding, radiating outward until I can not tell where it ends and I begin.

I catch myself just long enough to look up. Endricks is already turning. Our shoulders brush as he spins, too late, the motion sharp and panicked. We are close enough that I can see it all play out across his face in a single flash. Shock hits first. Then outrage, raw and incandescent. Then something far worse, something that caves his chest in from the inside out, *breaking* him.

I stare at him, blood already filling my mouth.

"I am sorry," I choke. The words come out broken, drowned in red.

Blood sputters down my chin as my knees buckle completely. I crash to the ground at his feet, the impact knocking the breath from what is left of my lungs. Endricks drops to his knees, landing beside me. Frantically, he grabs at me, rolling me over. I slump into his arms, too weak to move. I cough, and more blood spills from my mouth, dripping down my cheek, smearing across my throat. Each breath gurgles, shallow and useless, the pain in my back blooming into something so vast it blurs the edges of the world.

"No!" He screams. "No, Edin, please," he begs, his voice cracking from the strain. "Please!"

Endricks presses against the gaping hole, desperately attempting to apply pressure. I feel the blood slowly drain from my face. Pin pricks crawl across my skin. The ground around me begins to feel warm with what I can only assume to be my own blood. Endricks screams my name. He is right there. I know he is. I can hear him, feel him, smell his sweet, smoky scent, but reality begins to stretch, warp, and fade as everything else bleeds together. My heart fractures into a million pieces. The sound of his pleas hurt far worse than any wound Osiris could ever hope to land.

"Edin," he cries, lifting my head and brushing my cheek.

His hand is burning against my cold skin. All I can do is stare up at him, too weak to meet his touch, too weak to even choke out a word. I meet his gaze, praying to the gods that he understands my attention. Time seems to move in slow motion, but I know it has only been mere seconds by the sound of my army, still dropping their weapons where they stand.

Above us, the sky over Elysia is tearing itself apart. Angels and demons collide midair, their wings shredding, as light and darkness clash in violent bursts. The war rages on, uncaring and relentless. I lie there on the blood-slick stone, the chaos of heaven and hell burning overhead, breath slipping away, and wonder, distantly, if this is the last thing I will ever see.

The edges of my vision begin to darken, completely stealing my view of Endricks's gorgeous face, a luxury I have taken for granted. The pain that has consumed me begins to fade away. My body begins to still, no longer shivering. The darkness creeps in, and I finally feel warm. I can no longer hear the chaos, the warped screams, the clang of metal on metal, and worst of all, Endricks's voice.

Silence settles in, heavy and suffocating. I feel myself sinking into the abyss, slowly descending as darkness closes in around me. I fight the paralysis, the silence, the void, but every struggle is useless. My lungs burn, then fail, and I finally give in, slipping over the edge.

Just as I accept my fate, the void splits open, and a flash of white cleaves through the black. The light grows brighter, almost impossible to look at, as if I am witnessing the birth of a sun. Voices whisper at the edge of my awareness, unintelligible, a chorus layered atop itself, ancient and endless, threading through my bones.

The Liminal? The resting site of the gods.

Through the brilliance, I glimpse something vast, large enough to blot out the stars, silhouettes carved from radiance itself, descending not as saviors, but as witnesses. The light tightens, focusing, pressing into my chest, my spine, *my soul.* Something answers it inside me, something that has been waiting far longer than I ever knew. The darkness fractures around me with a sound like breaking glass, and I realize, with sudden, terrible clarity, that whatever has found me in this moment did not come to let me die.

It has come to *claim* me.

Chapter 40

Endricks

Pain explodes across my chest like a blade driven straight through bone. I gasp, staggering as the fated-mate tie snaps taut, yanking so hard it nearly sends me sprawling forward onto Edin. It is not physical, not entirely, but it hurts worse than any wound I have ever taken. Panic claws up my throat as the pull tightens, sharp and screaming, and then Edin goes limp in my arms.

"No," I breathe.

The world spins. Sound dulls, muffled beneath the roar of blood in my ears. I sink with her, pulling her weight against my chest, my hands shaking as I gather her closer. Her head lolls against my arm, too still, too heavy. The rage comes later. First is the hollowing out, the sudden, devastating quiet where her presence should be.

Despair presses in, thick and suffocating.

I brush blood-matted hair back from her forehead with careful fingers, gentle as if I am afraid she will shatter. My thumb traces up the curve of one of her short black horns, solid, familiar, *hers*. I lean down and press a kiss to her brow, lingering there like I can anchor her to this world if I just do not let go.

Vanilla and clove mixed with the coppery scent of blood fill my lungs. Her scent, warm, alive, tainted with what Osiris has done to her. I draw in one last breath of it and let it burn into me.

"Enough with your games, Osiris," I mutter, my voice low and wrecked.

I ease Edin down onto the stone, laying her flat with reverence, like a promise. Then I stand. The courtyard comes back into focus in brutal clarity. Her undead army lies scattered and still, magic extinguished, bodies crumpled across the blood-soaked ground. Smoke coils upward, mixing with ash and screams and the distant clash of steel. I take it all in with dead eyes. Then I turn. Osiris stands amid the wreckage, watching, chaos magic curling lazily around him like smoke, smug and unbothered.

"This ends," I say, my voice carrying across the courtyard, cold and absolute.

I lift my hand.

"Now."

My fingers snap.

Fire erupts across the battlefield in an instant, wild, unforgiving, and inescapable. Every Elysian soldier ignites where they stand, flames racing over armor and wings alike, screams ripping free as divine fire consumes them from the inside out. The heat roars skyward, reflected in my eyes as Helheim answers my call.

This war has taken my queen, and I will burn heavens down to answer for it.

The wind surges, as if it is matching the inner turmoil that swirls inside me. It slams into the courtyard with sudden, vicious force, ripping through smoke and flame alike. Banners tear free from their poles. Ash spirals violently into the air, stinging my eyes as the ground trembles beneath my boots. The heat from the burning soldiers bends and is dragged sideways by the gale as if the world itself has lost its balance.

Above us, the sky darkens. The clouds churn and collapse in on themselves, rolling thick and black, swallowing what little light remains. Thunder cracks so close it feels like the sound splits my skull, the echo vibrating through my bones.

Lightning spears down. It strikes the stone with blinding fury, shattering marble, carving glowing scars into the courtyard floor.

Another bolt tears through the sky, then another, each one closer, angrier, drawn not to Osiris, not to the armies, but to the place where Edin lies motionless on the ground.

The air hums, charged and unstable. Power coils tight, crawling over my skin, raising every hair on my body. Even the chaos magic around Osiris falters, flickering as the storm builds beyond anything any mortal or divine should be able to command.

This is no ordinary storm.

This is a reckoning.

CHAPTER 41

OSIRIS

The wind spins, violent and ecstatic, as if the world itself approves of what I have done. A ring of fire detonates outward in a violent inferno, swallowing my soldiers whole. Their screams fill the air as armor binds to skin and skin melts into bone. The courtyard becomes a furnace in a single breath. Flame tears through them in a sweeping wave. Armor glows red, then white, and flesh blackens. The scent of burning soldiers rolls thick and suffocating across the stone. I do not move, I wait, allowing him to rage.

Desperate bastard. Get over it and stop throwing a tantrum.

Endricks stands at the center of it, fire spiraling around him like armor forged in rage. He lifts his head, and the fire obeys him like a living thing. It coils around his arms, crawls up his spine, and crowns him in gold and ruin. Grief has stripped him raw. His chest heaves. His hands tremble, not from weakness, no, from restraint long since abandoned.

"Well," I call over the roar of flames, adjusting my grip on my blade, her blood still warm along the steel. "Are you finished with the dramatics?"

His eyes find mine. There is nothing human left in them. The sky splits with thunder. He moves, and the air fractures as he hurtles toward me, faster than sound, faster than any sense. I barely lift my blade in time. Metal collides with a shockwave that cracks the courtyard in two. The force drives me back a step, but only *one*, of course.

He disappears in a burst of heat. The air warps before he materializes in front of me again, blade wreathed in white flame. I twist aside, but his fire kisses my shoulder. It burns, even through my magic's shields.

I smile, and chaos answers me. The world bends. Gravity shifts sideways. The ground liquefies beneath his feet. The sky fractures into a spiral of darkness overhead. Reality itself peels like torn parchment as I reshape the battlefield.

He stumbles for half a heartbeat, and that is all I need. I flick my wrist. The flames around him choke out as I unravel the oxygen in the air, thinning it to nothing. *Fire needs breath.*

He rips it back. The inferno surges again with a violent inhale, his power overriding mine through sheer force of will. He launches forward, fist colliding with my jaw, and my bones crack.

Delightful.

I let the impact carry me backward, then manipulate the momentum, reversing it. He is the one who flies this time, hurled through a column that explodes into marble debris. He rises instantly. Liquid fire pours from his wounds now, sealing flesh shut in molten seams. His magic is no longer a controlled flame; it is wildfire, spreading and devouring.

"Is that all?" I sneer. "She died too easily for you to disappoint me now."

A roar tears from him, raw, broken, and the flames consuming my soldiers surge higher in answer. Ash rains down like black snow. The courtyard becomes an inferno so bright the stone glows orange beneath our feet. Heat slams into me in waves. He lifts both hands, and the fire condenses into a spear of white-hot plasma, which he hurls towards me.

I open my palm, chaos fracturing in midair. The spear splits into a thousand burning shards that rain down indiscriminately around the courtyard. He walks through it, skin blistering, healing, and then burning again.

I step forward and let my magic seep deeper, not into the world this time, but into *him.* I twist the space around his perception, multiplying my form. Ten of me circle him, then twenty, all smirking. He swings, hitting nothing.

"Edin cried out for you," I murmur from everywhere at once, "as I sank my cock deep into her."

He shuts his eyes.

"You do not get to speak her name," he growls.

He does not need sight, only rage. The flames shift. They pulse outward in a controlled ring, incinerating my illusion. My copies distort and collapse under the heat. He finds me by the disruption in his fire and barrels into me, tackling me through the courtyard wall. We crash into the outer grounds, rolling through ash and ruin.

His hands lock around my throat, and fire floods into my lungs. I laugh through the smoke. Chaos seeps from my skin and into his veins where we touch. I manipulate the impulses in his nerves, slowing his reaction time by a fraction, and his grip falters. I drive my knee into his ribs, shoving him off. He lands hard, chest heaving, flames flickering erratically now.

I rise smoothly, brushing stone dust from my shoulder as if this is nothing more than an inconvenience.

"You loved her," I say, tilting my head. "That was your first mistake."

Lightning cracks overhead, striking so close the nearest marble column explodes into shards. He launches at me again, and this time, there is no technique left, only devastation fuels his movements. Our blades collide, sparks and lightning tangling together in blinding flashes.

He fights like he wants to die if it means taking me with him.

Desperation makes him reckless.

Recklessness makes him predictable.

I twist inside his guard, slam my elbow into his sternum, and drive my blade toward his abdomen. He catches my wrist, stopping it. The air between us trembles. His grip tightens, shaking.

“You took her,” he says, voice splintered beyond repair.

“I ended her,” I correct calmly.

I watch as the desperation in his eyes evolves into something worse… Resolve. He raises his other hand, and the flames collapse inward, compressed. Every burning soldier. Every stray ember. Every flicker of heat in the courtyard tears toward him, drawn into a single blinding core in his palm. The temperature drops instantly around us. All the destruction is pulled into the one point centered in his hand.

Interesting.

He looks at me through the glow. "If I burn," he says hoarsely, "you are burning with me."

Ah. Mutual annihilation... How romantic.

I stretch my fingers, feeling the threads of reality around us. Time. Space. Matter. All pliable. All breakable.

"Then so be it," I say, as a smile creeps across my face.

The condensed sun leaves his hand, and it screams as it moves, like something alive and furious. I reach for it, threads of chaos lashing outward, burrowing into its structure, unraveling bonds, bending force inward.

It detonates anyway.

Light consumes everything and sound ceases. For one suspended instant, there is nothing but white. Then the world returns in pieces. Stone liquefies beneath us. The palace walls disintegrate into molten spray. The shockwave splits the courtyard beside us into a spiderweb of fractures that race outward into the city. The blast drives me back ten paces.

Ten... Impressive.

Smoke rolls across the ground in violent waves. Endricks stands at the epicenter, chest heaving, skin cracked with glowing fissures. He is burning from the inside out now and still glaring at me. Then the air shifts, subtly at first. The flames flicker sideways. The wind dies. Then the sky begins to change. The last streaks of gold drain as if siphoned away by an unseen hand. Pinks and oranges pale to iron gray. The sun dims, not clouded, not eclipsed, but veiled, as though something vast has stepped between it and us.

The temperature drops again. Awareness prickles along my spine. Above us, the heavens ripple, like a surface disturbed from beneath. The clouds spiral inward, forming a massive vortex that churns in absolute silence. There is no thunder, no lightning. Just pressure, immense, *divine* pressure.

I feel them, sleeping titans stirring in their celestial graves. The ones who swore never to interfere. The ground hums with their waking. Endricks feels it, too. His fire stutters as he looks upward, confusion slicing through his rage.

The gray deepens, swallowing the horizon. The sun becomes a pale, suffocated disc behind a shroud of moving shadow. The air grows heavy, thick enough to taste. Something has shifted in the balance, something ancient.

Then a flicker of purple explodes out of the corner of my eyes. I jerk my head toward it.

Edin's body.

Mist curls around her form. A luminous violet vapor that coils like silk in water. It rises from her skin in delicate spirals, lifting strands of her hair as though gravity has loosened its claim. Her body lifts inches above the fractured stone. Arms slack at her sides. Head tilted back. Hair spilling downward in a dark cascade. The vortex in the sky tightens in response.

"Osiris of Elysia."

The voice comes from everywhere and nowhere all at once. It reverberates through the stone beneath my boots, through the marrow in my bones. My breath catches in my throat, and a lump forms, too large to swallow back down. Chills prickle my skin, my hair stands on end, and my stomach twists. Then I sense him.

Shit.

I sense him only a breath before impact, the displacement of air, the scream of steel cutting through the honey-thick atmosphere. Endricks moves through the ash like a phantom, grief honed into something lethal. His sword drives forward, straight for my heart.

Chapter 42

Endricks

The voice from above sends a shiver down my spine as our swords crash together with an ear-piercing clang, the impact jolting straight through my arms. Sparks burst between the blades as I lean in, boots biting into shattered stone, forcing my weight and rage into the push. Osiris snarls, his heels skidding back as chaos magic coils around him, writhing, clawing at the air like it wants to tear reality apart just to save his pathetic life.

I bare my teeth and drive harder. Fire roars down my arm, heat flooding the steel, and water answers in the same breath, steam hissing between us as the elements collide. His blade trembles, and for the first time, I see it: the flicker of strain, the crack in his calm.

"Accept your fate, Osiris," I growl. "You will die here."

"Never," he grinds out.

The wind is no longer wind; it is a vortex. It howls around us in violent spirals, dragging embers and ash into the sky as if the storm itself is trying to rip the world apart. I brace my stance, muscles screaming as the air fights me, pressing in from all sides with crushing force.

The water turns on me. It rears and rages along the courtyard edges, slick and treacherous, surging in unnatural waves at *someone else's* command. *Not mine*. I feel it slip from my grasp, pulled away like a stolen weapon. The ground floods, then recedes, then floods again, as if the earth can not decide whether to drown or burn.

Trees split the courtyard open, roots bursting through marble, branches twisting and snapping as they coil around towers and battlements. The castle groans under the weight of it all, stone cracking, walls bowing as nature claims what it was never meant to hold.

Then the mist grows into a thicker midnight purple, dense and suffocating. It rolls in low at first, curling around my boots, my knees, my chest, until it is everywhere. It clings to my skin, burns in my lungs, and blurs the world into fractured shapes and shadows.

"Osiris of Elysia," the voice bellows out again, louder.

We both lower our swords, confusion running through us. I blink hard, and my stomach sinks, unsure if what I am witnessing is reality or illusion.

She rises through the mist.

Slowly.

Unnaturally.

Edin lifts into the air, her body caught in the current like a rag doll, head hung forward, limbs swaying as if the wind is the only thing holding her upright. Her wet hair twists wildly around her face, snapping and coiling in the vortex, obscuring her eyes. Blood drips from her feet in dark, steady drops, vanishing into the chaos below.

My heart fractures, splintering all at once, and goosebumps ripple violently across my skin as helpless horror locks my lungs. The storm bends around her, mist spiraling tighter, lightning arcing toward her suspended form like it recognizes its master. Our fated bond screams, raw, panicked, and reaching, yet underneath it thrums something vast and terrible, something else answering her ascent. Her head snaps back violently, the motion sharp and wrong, like a puppet yanked on invisible strings.

My breath leaves me in a rush.

Her eyes fly open, and the sight of them stuns me into stillness. The gold is gone. No warmth, no familiar fire. In its place burns something otherworldly, something *unnatural*, solid, milky white, glowing from within as if her skull can barely contain it. Light spills from them in thin, blinding threads, cutting through the purple mist as the storm recoils around her. The air hums, shrill and strained, like reality itself is protesting.

Fear curls cold and tight in my chest.

Not of her… but *for* her.

"Edin…" I say again hoarsely, my voice useless against the roaring wind.

Her mouth jerks open. No sound comes out at first, but it is a sharp, unnatural motion that makes my stomach twist. It stretches wider than it should, wider than any human jaw can manage, like something inside her is forcing its way out. Tendons stand out along her throat, her neck straining as if she is fighting, or yielding to whatever has taken hold. Then the voice echoes out of her, clear and commanding.

"Osiris of Elysia, you have used your magic selfishly, committing treason, forsaking your own kind, and now you have committed the ultimate offense of striking down a goddess. For your acts there will be no mercy, no forgiveness, only eternal damnation."

I feel the blood drain from my face, cold and sudden, leaving my skin tight and numb. A hard lump swells in my throat, thick enough that I have to swallow twice just to breathe. I force myself to stay upright, teeth grinding, jaw clenching on instinct as reality slams into me.

We have awakened the previous God of Purgatory, Cato.

Chapter 43

Endricks

***

Edin's hand lifts. The motion is both smooth and wrong at the same time. The air *snaps,* and Osiris is ripped from the ground so violently that it looks as if something tears him free from the earth itself. Stone explodes where his feet had been, shards spinning uselessly as he is dragged upward, spine arching as his body convulses as if seized by an invisible hook.

Edin's milky eyes lock onto him unblinking and merciless, and Cato's voice booms out again. "You have lived a life of gluttony, vanity, and greed, bringing shame to the realms."

Osiris does not even have time to steady himself. Edin's eyes shut, and her fingers curl, jerking him forward with brutal force. He slams to a dead stop inches from her face, the sudden halt wrenching a strangled cry from his throat, rattling his teeth, and stealing what little breath he had left.

Her eyes slowly open. The milky white light drains away like fog burning off at dawn, pulling inward until what remains is achingly familiar. My breath catches hard in my chest. *Gold.* Warm, molten gold, threaded with pain and exhaustion and *her*. The storm hesitates, wind stuttering as if the world itself is unsure what to do with the change.

She leans in close, close enough that their noses brush. “Now, Osiris,” she smiles, sickeningly sweet, but *familiar*, “now you must pay.”

Her small hand closes around his throat with terrifying ease and grace. Her fingers dig in, crushing, compressing, sinking until the tendons in his neck stand out like cords about to snap. I hear it, the wet, horrific sound of cartilage straining under her grip. Osiris's mouth opens wide in a silent scream as his airway collapses beneath her palm.

Chaos magic flares wildly around him, spasming instead of obeying, lashing out in useless bursts that shred the air and die before they reach her. His hands claw at her wrist, fingernails scraping, tearing at her skin, but she does not flinch.

Veins bulge dark and grotesque across Osiris's face, his skin flushing red, then purple. His eyes begin to bleed at the corners, tiny crimson tears tracking back into his hair as the pressure builds. His body jerks violently, legs kicking, muscles locking and unlocking in panicked spasms as he fights for air that no longer exists.

The storm stills around them. Lightning freezes mid-arc. The wind holds its breath. I can not move, can not even speak. I can only watch as the woman I love hangs my greatest enemy in the sky like a verdict. All at once, I understand with bone-deep clarity that this is not vengeance.

It is judgment, and she has already decided his sentence.

CHAPTER 44

EDIN

I lift Osiris higher. Just enough to make it clear how little he means to me now. His body jerks uselessly in my grip, boots kicking at empty air, the strength bleeding out of him with every strangled attempt at a breath. He is nothing but weight, bone, and *fear* in my hand.

For the first time since this war began, he understands what it feels like to be small.

I squeeze. Hard. A sharp, ugly yelp rips out of him before his voice cuts off entirely, the sound strangled into nothing beneath my palm. I feel it, the give of flesh, the panic flooding his body as his lungs betray him. For one perfect heartbeat, I hold him there, suspended, helpless.

Then I release him.

He does not fall.

Osiris hangs in midair, choking, gagging on stolen breath, his body shaking as he claws uselessly at his own throat. I watch him flail, savoring the way terror strips him bare. Then, with a lazy flick of my wrist, I withdraw my magic, and gravity remembers him.

First comes the *thud*, bone and body slamming into unforgiving stone, then the scream. Raw. Agonized. Desperate. The sound echoes through the courtyard, sharp and broken, and it sends a thrill of dark, undeniable joy through me.

Let him feel it.

Let him understand exactly what he has made of me.

I float there for a moment, suspended in the storm, and let myself *feel* it. His pain. His terror. The way his screams scrape raw against the air as he tries and fails to pull himself together. It hums through me like a living thing, dark and intoxicating, and I do not stop it. I do not temper it. I revel in it. I earned this moment.

Then I snap my fingers, and the ground beneath him convulses. Stone splits with a grinding shriek as hands burst through the earth, gray, rotted, and clawed. One after another, the undead drag themselves free, jaws hanging loose and eyes glowing. They seize him before he can drag himself away, before he can scream again.

Hands clamp around his arms, his legs, his shoulders. They force him flat against the ground, pinning him there as he thrashes, chaos magic sputtering uselessly beneath their grip. Dirt and blood smear into his skin as he fights, but the dead do not tire. They do not hesitate. They simply *obey*.

I lower myself to the ground, boots touching stone as the storm comes to a halt around us. The purple mist thickens at my back, dark and rolling, shadows folding in on themselves like something alive. Then the shadows *move*. Nyx steps out of the mist at my side, silent and enormous, his form resolving from darkness as if he were always part of it. His eyes burn bright, fixed on Osiris with a focus so sharp it makes my pulse steady. He does not look at me for permission. He does not need it.

Nyx lunges.

He jumps on Osiris with bone-rattling force, knocking the air from his lungs. The undead tighten their grip, holding him down as Nyx snaps and tears, fury unleashed in brutal, relentless strikes. Osiris screams, the sound raw and panicked, thrashing beneath the weight, teeth, and claws bearing down on him. Nyx growls low in his chest, vicious and protective, as if every bite is a promise kept. I stand over them, unmoving, watching as Osiris is finally made small and broken, as he is forced to understand what it means to be hunted.

Some debts are paid in blood and fear, and this one has been a long time coming.

Endricks steps forward, drawn by instinct, by the bond pulling him toward me like gravity. Our eyes meet through the blood and the screams. For a heartbeat, I let myself soften. I look at him with everything I can not say in this moment: love, relief, the quiet certainty that he is still here and so am I. It flickers between us, fragile and fierce.

Then my expression changes. Not cold. Not cruel. Just *absolute*. I shift my gaze, just slightly, a silent command carried in the space between breaths.

Stay back.

He stills. I see the struggle in his eyes, the need to protect, to stand beside me, but he understands. Endricks inclines his head in a single, sharp nod, trust settling where fear might have lived, and he steps back.

I turn my gaze back to Osiris. *What is left of him*. He trembles beneath the undead, restrained and bloodied, chest heaving in broken, uneven pulls. The chaos magic around him has thinned to a pathetic flicker, smoke without fire. When he looks at me now, there is no defiance left, only the dawning horror of understanding.

I lift my hand slightly. "Nyx," I command, my voice calm and final.

Nyx freezes mid-snarl, teeth still bared inches from Osiris's ruined face. For a moment, he hesitates, hackles raised, every instinct screaming to finish it. Then he pulls back with a low, displeased growl, stepping away from Osiris's body and returning to my side. He presses against my leg, massive and solid, a silent promise that he is not done, only waiting.

Osiris coughs, dragging in air, shaking as the undead tighten their grip.

Good. I want him to be conscious for this.

I turn my hand upward and call out, not with my voice, but with the truth of what I am. The name of the place that made *me*. The place that still answers. *Purgatory.* The word sinks into the world like a blade into flesh.

The air above my palm splits with a low, resonant crack, reality peeling back as cold pours through. Not wind, only *absence.* The smell of ash and old parchment bleeds into the courtyard, heavy and unmistakable. From the tear in the air, something begins to descend. It falls slowly, reverently, bound in blackened leather that looks less crafted, and more so grown from the depths of Purgatory. Thin chains wrap around it like veins, etched with sigils that burn faintly as they move. The pages whisper to each other, turning on their own, ink shifting like it is alive, names forming, erasing, and rewriting themselves.

Death's Grimoire settles into my waiting hand.

The moment my fingers close around it, power slams into me, cold and ancient. The undead still. Even Nyx pauses, teeth bared, sensing the weight of what I now hold. Osiris feels it. His thrashing turns even more frantic, terror stripping the last of his arrogance as his eyes lock onto the book. He knows what it is. He has always known.

I look down at him, Grimoire humming softly in my grip, and for the first time since this began, I truly smile. "This," I say quietly, opening the cover as the pages flutter to life, "is where gods learn they are not eternal."

I step closer. The undead shift, tightening their hold as I kneel and place Death's Grimoire on the stone beside Osiris's head. It lands with a dull, final sound, chains clinking softly as if the book itself is breathing. He flinches at the noise, eyes flicking to it and then back to me, terror streaking his face.

I do not rush. I sink to the ground slowly and crawl forward, not with hunger, not with grace, but with resolve. My hands press into the stone on either side of him as I move up his body, the undead holding him immobile beneath me. He bucks weakly, muscles trembling, but it is useless. They keep him pinned, forcing him to feel every inch of my approach.

I stop with my weight centered over his chest, close enough that he has to look at me. Close enough that he can see the gold in my eyes, steady and unyielding. Blood streaks his face, his breath comes in ragged pulls, and panic rolls off him in waves. I lean down, just enough to make him understand how completely trapped he is.

"You took so much," I say calmly. No shouting. No rage. "Lives. Worlds. *Choices*."

My hand settles flat against his sternum, not to hurt, *not yet*, just to remind him I am real. That this is happening. I meet his gaze and hold it, letting the weight of inevitability sink in. I fully drop down and straddle his hips, locking him in place beneath me. He gasps, the sound sharp and broken, eyes blown wide as purple electricity crawls up my arms. It bites at my skin, stinging, power threading through bones and blood until my hands tremble with it.

I brush his hair back from his face, slow and deliberate. He flinches at the touch. My thumb drags across his torn lip, smearing his own blood along his mouth. I feel him shudder beneath me. Then I grab his face. My fingers dig in, nails sinking into his skin as I force his head back. I make him look at me, really look. Panic floods his eyes as I lean closer.

"Is this *not* what you wanted?" I ask quietly, my voice unwavering. "You can be *my* pet, now."

I release his face only to drag a finger down the center of his chest, leaving a line of blood and electricity in its wake. His body jerks against the undead's restraint, a helpless, broken motion.

I lift my hand. Power coils up my arm, violent and bright, electricity snapping and hissing as it gathers. The air condenses in my palm, light hardening into shape until a dagger forms, solid, gleaming, humming with death and judgment. I hold it there above him, letting him see it, letting the truth settle.

My fingers tighten around the hilt, and the world fractures. Flashbacks slam into me in violent succession. *Faces twisted in fear, screams swallowed by chaos, blood on stone that never washed away. Chains biting into my wrists.*

Power stolen, warped, and used. Every moment Osiris laughed. Every life he shattered because he thought he owned them.

I snarl and drive the dagger down. It punches into his chest with a brutal *thud*, stealing the rest of his breath in a strangled, broken cry. He arches beneath me, a raw scream tearing free as the blade sinks deep. I do not stop, I can not. I drag it downward, slow and merciless, carving judgment into flesh as he chokes on every breath he cannot quite pull in.

The undead hold him steady while he thrashes, screams breaking into wet, panicked gasps. His voice cracks. His body shakes. The sound is ugly and desperate and entirely *earned.* Purple electricity surges along the blade, flaring brighter with every inch I pull it free, every memory burning through me like fuel. I lean over him, unflinching, my face hard as stone as his cries echo into the storm.

"This," I hiss, dragging the blade lower, "is for every world you thought was yours to break."

Death's Grimoire flies open beside his head. The pages begin to flip, not fast, but *hungrily*. One after another, parchment whispers as chains rattle softly with each turn. The symbols along the margins flare, then dim, as if something unseen is reading along.

I tear the dagger free from his flesh at last and let it fall from my hand. It clatters across the stone and skids out of sight, forgotten.

Osiris is barely breathing now, chest heaving in broken, uneven pulls. I give him no mercy. I draw my arm back and drive my fist forward into the wound I have already carved, power surging through me in a violent rush. Purple electricity snaps and coils, flooding the space, filling him with something far worse than pain.

"Osiris of Elysia," I proclaim, wrapping my fingers around his heart. "I damn you to Purgatory."

He screams.

The sound tears out of him, raw, shattered, stripped of all divinity, as his body locks beneath me, chaos magic imploding instead of obeying. The undead loosen their hold as his strength finally gives, his struggles dissolving into helpless spasms.

The Grimoire's pages stop turning. Ink burns into the parchment.

A single name is written.

I lean close, voice low, unwavering, and final.

"Where I will haunt you for all eternity."

My teeth grind against one another, and with a savage wrench, I rip his heart free, wet and still beating, dragging his life out of him in one brutal pull. For a single, suspended moment, everything goes quiet. The screams of war themselves seem to hold their breath. I feel the frantic, failing thud against my palm, the last, ugly proof that he was ever alive.

His body convulses beneath me. The chaos magic gutters out in a choking gasp, snuffed like a dying flame. Osiris's mouth opens, but no sound comes this time, only a shudder that runs through him and stops. Whatever he was, a tyrant, a nightmare, a *'god',* empties out of him all at once. I stare down at what remains, my hand still clenched, my pulse finally slowing as the weight of it settles into something like peace.

I slide off his body and sink to the ground beside him, knees hitting stone, breath shuddering out of me. My hand opens, allowing his heart to fall to the ground. What is left of him is no longer my concern. My gaze drifts to

Death's Grimoire. I trace the open page with my finger, slow and reverent, feeling the finality of it settle into my bones. A long breath leaves me, shaky but relieved, like I have been holding it for a lifetime.

NAME: OSIRIS ENGELSTON **LIFE:** TRAITOR OF THE REALMS **DEATH:** EXECUTION **JUDGMENT:** PURGATORY

A darker purple mist coils around me, thicker, *deeper than mine*, heavy with something old and watchful. It curls at my feet, climbs my spine, and presses close enough that my skin prickles. Then a hand lands on my shoulder. The contact snaps my attention sharply, instincts flaring as I twist toward it, power rising on reflex.

I freeze.

Standing behind me, half-formed from the mist itself, is Cato. He looks exactly as I remember and nothing like he should. His presence bends the air, edges blurring as if reality struggles to keep him whole. His eyes burn the same deep, endless violet as the realm he once ruled, ancient and unreadable, carrying the weight of countless endings.

I blink, searching for words vast enough to hold the gratitude swelling in my chest, knowing that whatever I come up with will never be enough. My throat tightens anyway.

"Thank you," I manage, the words breaking as they leave me. "I am forever in your debt."

A small, knowing smile tugs at his mouth as he nods, his grip on my shoulder firm, grounding. Then his gaze slides past me to Osiris's lifeless body.

"May I?" he asks, his eyebrow lifting as something mischievous dances in his eyes.

I nod.

The Grimoire snaps open with a violent rush of air. Chains explode from its pages, barbed and shrieking, coiling tight around Osiris's throat. His eyes snap open in horrified awareness. A strangled breath leaves him as his body shudders.

Color drains from his flesh, skin turning ashen, then translucent. The ground shows through him. The blood, the wounds, the weight of him all fall away, leaving something hollow. His mouth opens in a silent scream as the last of his corporeal form dissolves, and Osiris remains, pale, ghostlike, bound and flickering between worlds.

Cato snaps the chains upward, ripping Osiris off the ground and hauling him close, so close that their faces nearly touch. The links bite into Osiris's spectral throat, forcing his head back as his form flickers violently.

Cato's voice is calm, cold, and absolute.

"You wanted to play god?" he says. His grip tightens, the chains glowing as Osiris convulses. "I will show you what it means to be a god."

Osiris trembles, panic finally cracking through as his spectral form shudders in Cato's grip. With a slow flick of his wrist, the chains snap taut, and the ground answers. Skeletal hands burst from the earth, clawing around Osiris's legs, his torso, his throat, dragging him down inch by inch. He thrashes, screaming as the undead pull him toward the darkness, the soil swallowing his cries until only the chains remain, rattling once before sinking beneath the ground with him.

I stare off as the last echoes of battle fade, relief finally washing through me now that it is truly over.

"Edin."

Endricks's voice cuts through the quiet. I spin toward him just as he reaches out, his hand brushing my cheek, loving and gentle. I lean into his palm, grounding myself in his warmth, in the steady truth that *we* made it. I lay my hand over his, my fingers curling into his touch, and look up into his blue eyes. A small, exhausted smile tugs at my lips.

"You cannot get rid of me so easily."

He pulls me into his arms without another word, like his fears finally caught up to him now that there is nothing left to fight. His grip is tight, almost desperate, as if he is afraid I will slip through his fingers if he loosens it even a little.

"I thought..." his breath shudders against my hair. He does not finish. He does not have to.

He buries his face in the crook of my neck and breathes me in, slow and deep, like he is proving to himself that I am real. That I am warm and alive. His arms lock around me, broad, shielding me from a battle that is already over. I feel his chest rise and fall beneath my cheek, uneven at first, then gradually steadying as he holds me there.

"I felt it," he murmurs, voice rough. "The bond, going silent. I thought I had lost you."

My heart aches at the raw honesty in his words. I curl closer, wrapping my arms around his waist, pressing myself into him until there is no space left for doubt. I thread my fingers into his shirt, anchoring us both, because I alone know he *did* lose me.

"I am here," I whisper. "I am not going anywhere."

He exhales again, long and shaky, his chin resting against the top of my head. He does not let go, not for a second. He just holds me, breathing me in like oxygen, like something he can not survive without, like he is memorizing this moment in case the world ever tries to take it from him again.

I tilt my head up, drawn to him without thinking, and his mouth meets mine like it has been waiting there all along. The kiss is soft but desperate, all the fear and relief pouring into it, and his hand slides to the back of my head. For a heartbeat, the world disappears, no war, no gods, no blood. *Just us.*

Then a pointed cough cuts through the moment.

Chapter 45

Blythe

"Sorry to break up the moment," I half smirk, kicking at the rubble. Edin pulls back from Endricks, breathless and radiant, and when she sees me, her entire face transforms.

"Blythe!"

She's in my arms a heartbeat later.

The force of her nearly knocks me back, and I laugh, an unsteady, disbelieving sound as I wrap her tight. She's warm. Solid. *Real.* I press my cheek to her temple and close my eyes for half a second.

She's alive.

For a moment, it's just us, two women who have crawled through hell and come out breathing. Unfortunately, the courtyard is still thick with smoke, with blood, and with the weight of what it cost.

I step back first. My gaze shifts past her to where Verenia stands, leaning over the rails of the tower, spine straight despite the ruin around us. Grief sits on her shoulders like a crown she never asked to wear.

I give her a small nod, and Edin follows my line of sight. The joy on her face softens into something resolute. She turns toward Verenia fully, and their eyes lock.

"Bring Valker to me," Edin says. The words are quiet, yet still carry across the courtyard.

Above us, the broken tower cuts into the sky, its crown split and jagged. High within its remains, wrapped in the cocoon I made, Valker's body waits. I feel it before I move. The vines I wove around him pulse faintly in my bones, my magic recognizing its own.

I inhale slowly and press my palm to the blood-streaked ground.

The earth answers.

The stone beneath my fingers trembles. Cracks spider outward in thin, emerald, glowing seams as roots push through mortar and shattered rock. Vines unfurl from the tower's fractured spine, thick and strong, green against ruin.

They do not rip, only cradle, and the cocoon shifts. Slowly, deliberately, the vines unwind, revealing glimpses of dark cloth, pale skin, the stillness of a body that once carried too much ambition and too much rage.

A murmur ripples through the gathered soldiers.

I rise to my feet and lift my hand. The tower groans as the vines extend outward, forming a living bridge of twisting branches. Leaves unfurl in a sudden rush of green, softening the brutality of broken stone. Then, gently, *impossibly gently*, the cocoon descends.

The air smells of crushed ivy and fresh soil mixed with blood and ash as the structure bends slowly toward the courtyard floor. When Valker reaches us, the vines thicken beneath him, shaping into a bier of living wood. I guide him down the final inches myself. The roots spread across the ground, weaving into a wide, circular bloom beneath his body, petals of bark and leaf unfurling like an earthbound flower.

When he settles, the courtyard falls silent. Then armor clinks. One soldier drops to a knee. Then another, and another. Steel meets stone in a rolling wave that spreads outward until the entire courtyard kneels. Hellion heads bow before their fallen brother.

The wind stirs the leaves once. Then stills. I let my hand fall to my side. The vines remain, steady and unmoving, guarding him even in death. Power hums beneath my skin, no longer wild, nor raging, but *rooted.*

The courtyard is still kneeling when something in the tower shifts. I feel it before I see it, a tremor along the vines wrapped around broken stone. A flicker of movement at the crown, and heads tilt upward. She steps into view like she's stepping onto a stage.

Verenia.

Wind tears at her icy white hair, but she does not reach to tame it. Blood streaks her sleeve. Her posture is immaculate. She pauses, standing at the edge of the fractured tower, looking down at the sea of bowed heads below her. Then she grabs one of my vines and steps off.

Gasps slice through the silence.

She descends in a controlled slide, boots skimming stone, fingers wrapped tight around the living rope. My magic hums at the contact, aware of her weight, her balance, the precision in her movements. I thicken the vines instinctively beneath her grip.

She moves like a blade drawn clean from its sheath. Halfway down, she releases, twisting in the air, and lands in a low crouch beside the open cocoon. Not a stumble. Not a single misstep. Just lethal precision.

She rises slowly. The cocoon already unfurled. Vines cradle Valker's body in a woven bier of bark and leaf. His face is pale beneath the grime of battle, his expression finally emptied of rage.

Verenia drops to her knees beside him. The sound of fabric against stone is soft, but it carries. She reaches for his hand and her fingers close around his. For a moment, she does nothing else. The courtyard is utterly silent. Even the wind stills. She bows her head over their joined hands, shoulders straight despite the tremor that runs through her once, *just once*, before she restrains it.

"I told you," she whispers, so quietly I almost don't hear it. "I would not let them take you from me."

Her thumb brushes over his knuckles, smearing dirt and dried blood. This is not the strategist, nor the assassin. This is a sister, grieving in front of an army that dares not look away. Around us, soldiers lower further, some pressing fists to their chests, others resting their blades flat against the stone in silent honor. I feel my vines respond to her grief, tightening subtly around the bier, protective. Guarding him even now.

Verenia inhales slowly. When she lifts her head again, her eyes are no longer shining. They are sharpened, forged. She does not release his hand, but she straightens her spine, kneeling beside him like a sentinel. Then her daggering gaze meets Edin, and they nod in unison, a silent discussion.

CHAPTER 46

EDIN

I lower myself beside Valker. The vines cradle him in a blanket of living green, the courtyard silent around us, but all I can hear is the pounding of my own heart. Verenia kneels at his other side, her hand wrapped around his. I do not dare touch him, not yet. Instead, I look to her for permission. Her eyes meet mine. They shine, not weak, but glass-bright with something she refuses to let fall. For a long moment, she studies my face, searching for something I cannot name. Then she gives me a single, final nod.

I place my hands flat against Valker's chest. His body is cool beneath my palms. I inhale slowly, then breathe out, and the world falls away. Sound collapses inward. The courtyard dissolves into silence so complete it hums. My eyes close, and I let myself slip, not downward, not upward, but somewhere *between*.

The Liminal takes me gently this time. When I open my eyes, there is only white. Mist stretches endlessly in every direction, soft and soundless, swallowing horizon and sky alike. The air here is neither warm nor cold. It simply is.

I step forward. My boots make no sound.

"Valker?" My voice drifts into the fog and disappears.

Nothing answers. Then voices come in a chorus of screams that sound all so familiar. It is as if I am reliving their final moments on the battlefield. Every one of them. Screams of terror and agony rip through the mist from Hellions and Elysians alike. They beg for peace, for mercy, for salvation.

I close my eyes again, not to leave, but to focus, to *feel*. Souls have weight, *texture*. A pull in the chest that does not belong to the body. I reach outward, letting my awareness stretch beyond myself, searching for anything that feels sharp, restless, and burning. Anything that feels like him.

For a moment, there is only mist. Then, laughter. Small, bright, and boyish. My eyes snap open. It echoes faintly through the white, distant but clear enough to follow.

"This way!" the voice is high, delighted.

A second voice answers, breathless with laughter.

I turn toward the sound and begin walking. The mist thins with each step, unraveling like gauze drawn back. Shapes begin to form ahead of me, color bleeding softly into the white.

An alleyway.

Stone walls warm with late afternoon glow.

Then two boys.

They cannot be more than eight. One has black hair falling into striking blue eyes, too vivid to belong to any ordinary child. Small black horns curve outward, sharp and unmistakable. The other boy stands with his back to me, pointing excitedly down the narrow alley. Long white hair spills over his shoulders, bright against his dark tunic. Short antlers curve gently from his head.

"This way, Endricks!" the white-haired boy laughs.

The name hits me like a blow.

Valker grins, wide and unguarded, before taking off, and the alley flickers. Valker's laughter echoes once more, then the scene fractures. Sunlight bleeds into white. Stone dissolves into mist. The boys blur, stretching thin like reflections on water, and vanish.

I stand alone again in the Liminal. The silence here is deeper now. I steady myself and step forward. The mist parts reluctantly, curling around my legs like it wishes to hold me in place. Each step feels heavier than the last, like I am walking against an unseen current.

"Valker," I call softly, not to the boy, but to the soul.

At first, there is nothing. Then, a faint glow. Silver. Far ahead, barely visible through the endless white. It pulses once, slowly, like a heartbeat on the verge of stopping. My own breath catches.

There.

I move toward it, faster now. The mist thickens as if resisting me, but I push through, eyes locked on that fragile light. The closer I get, the brighter it becomes. When I reach it, I stop. Suspended in the mist before me is a cord of silver light. Thick. Heavy. Coiled in slow, drifting arcs. It hums with restrained power, threads of memory flickering through it, flashes of silver, sharpened steel, a heart too heavy for any one soul.

Valker.

His tether, the tie that binds him to the living world; it is fraying, thin in places, and dim along its edges. He is closer to slipping free than anyone knows. I reach out carefully. The moment my fingers brush the cord, pain lances up my arms, not physical, not entirely. It is grief, rage, and regret. Every violent breath he ever took surges into me like a storm. I grit my teeth and tighten my grip.

The cord resists. It pulls back, straining toward the deeper white, toward whatever waits beyond the Liminal. I plant my feet and wrap both hands around the silver tether. The mist howls. The cord grows impossibly heavy, like dragging an anchor across the ocean floor. My shoulders burn and my palms feel as though they are splitting open.

The Liminal does not like being emptied.

"You do not get to leave yet," I breathe, straining. "Not like this."

I pull again. The silver light flares violently, searing bright enough to blind. The cord tightens, trembling in my grip as if deciding between surrender and severing.

"Your sister *needs* you!" I grind out.

For one terrifying second, it thins, almost snapping.

"No," I gasp, digging in deeper, wrapping the tether around my forearm, bracing with everything I am.

I draw on the bond, on Verenia, on Endricks, and on the living world that still beats beyond this veil. The cord answers. It shifts, and then it moves an inch, then another. The weight does not lessen, but it follows. Slowly, painfully, I begin dragging Valker's tether back the way I came, carving a path through the white that closes behind me as if I was never here. Each step feels stolen. Each breath feels borrowed. The silver glow pulses brighter with every inch we gain. The mist screams around us, and still, I pull.

Chapter 47

Blythe

The courtyard does not move. It barely breathes. I lower myself beside Verenia, close enough that our shoulders almost touch, but not quite. Close enough to feel the tremor she refuses to show. From a distance, she looks carved from stone. Up close, I can see it. The tightness in her jaw. The way her fingers clutch Valker's hand like if she loosens her grip, he'll slip away entirely. *The fear*. The kind that doesn't scream, just claws you apart from the inside out.

I want to say something, something steady and reassuring, but there are no words big enough for losing your brother. So I sit. I let the silence stretch, and when it becomes unbearable, I reach for her. Gently, my fingers brush hers first, *a question*. She stiffens for half a heartbeat. Then her hand turns, and her fingers curl into mine, tight. She holds on like she's anchoring herself to the earth, and I squeeze back, waiting.

Edin kneels on Valker's other side, hands pressed flat against his chest, eyes closed, breath gone still. The air around her feels thinner somehow, *stretched.* The vines beneath him hum faintly, responding to something I cannot see. Seconds pass, far too many. Verenia's grip tightens painfully around my hand. Her lips part, but no sound comes out. I feel it before it happens, a shift in the air, like the world inhaling.

Valker's chest jerks.

A sharp, ragged breath tears into him. He coughs violently, body arching as air slams into lungs that have been empty for hours. Gasps erupt from the courtyard.

Edin's eyes fly open.

She sucks in a desperate breath of her own, raw, unsteady, and then she topples backward off him, landing hard on the stone with a choked gasp.

Verenia doesn't look at Edin. She surges forward. Both hands grab Valker's face, fingers digging into his cheeks, forcing his unfocused gaze onto hers.

"You will never," she says, voice shaking despite her effort to lace steel through it, "do something so arrogantly stupid again."

He coughs again, blinking, disoriented, and *alive.* Her composure shatters. She pulls him into her, wrapping her arms around his shoulders and dragging him upright against her chest. Her forehead presses hard against his temple. For a moment, she says nothing. She just holds him, and this time, she doesn't stop the tears, which fall silently into his hair.

Around us, the soldiers remain kneeling, but the silence has changed. It isn't tinged in mourning anymore, it's encumbered with awe. Across the stone, Edin lies on her back, staring up at the sky like she just wrestled death itself and won by an inch. Endricks crouches beside her, lifting her carefully.

"I am okay. Go," she murmurs, sitting up and steadying herself. "Go check on him."

Endricks turns and kneels beside Valker, helping him shift upright, one hand steady on his back.

"As I said before," he says lightly, patting him. "You *might* want to stay on Edin's good side with *your* life choices."

Valker coughs, blinking, body still trembling from the pull between life and death, but he manages a small, shaky grin.

My attention shifts. *Verenia.*

Her tears are flowing freely now, unchecked, trailing down her cheeks, wet against her skin. She moves toward me in a rush I didn't expect, all tension and raw, desperate relief. Her arms curl tightly around me, pulling me close, almost crushing me in her grip. I freeze for a heartbeat, stunned by the weight of her need, before I relax into it, letting her lean in. She inhales, a ragged breath full of gratitude and exhaustion. When she leans back, she keeps her fingers entwined with mine, locking her eyes onto mine.

"Thank you," she says.

Then she turns her gaze to Edin, voice carrying across the courtyard.

"Thank you," she repeats, just as earnest, just as raw.

Her eyes return to mine. This time, her voice drops, softer, almost reverent.

"Thank you," she whispers again, the words trembling, clouding her gaze with something *new*, something tender.

Her face tilts closer. I can feel the heat from her cheeks, the sharp inhale before her lips meet mine. The kiss is gentle, but full of all the unsaid words, all the fear, the relief, the gratitude, folding together into one quiet, perfect moment. I respond instinctively, leaning in, letting the press of lips speak into existence what words cannot.

Chapter 48

Edin

Blythe stands there, hands fisted in Verenia's clothes like she is afraid she will vanish if she lets go. Verenia's usual steel has melted away, her white hair falling forward as she leans further into Blythe. My chest tightens so hard it almost hurts.

Blythe. My best friend. After dungeons, chains, war, and almost losing her, she is still herself... and she is kissing a woman who fought through hell to stand here with us.

A laugh threatens to break free, tangled with tears, and a smile spreads across my face before I can stop it. *Of course, it is Verenia. Of course it is.* A familiar warmth sweeps across my back, pulling me gently from the moment. Endricks steps in behind me, close, careful, as if I might still break if he moves too fast. His arms wrap around my waist, solid and sure, and I melt into him, resting my weight against his chest. He presses a kiss to the crown of my head, lingering there, breathing me in like he still needs to convince himself that I am real.

The clouds begin to crawl back across the sky, thick and heavy, swallowing the sun in a slow, deliberate hush. Endricks's hold tightens just a fraction, protective. Shadows stretch over the courtyard as the wind rises, sharp and restless, tugging at my hair and snapping against the ruined banners like warning bells.

The air *shifts*.

Familiar.

A voice coils through the wind, everywhere and nowhere at once, sliding along my spine, brushing my ear without breath or body. It is not a shout; *he* does not need it to be. It carries on the storm itself, threaded with power that makes my magic stir uneasily beneath my skin.

"Edin, Goddess of Purgatory."

Cato's voice cuts cleanly through the wind as his form begins to pull itself from the mist, first the suggestion of a silhouette, then something of substance, and then the full weight of him standing before us like he never truly left. Power hums around him, daunting and immense, settling into the ground beneath our feet.

"Cato," I say softly, bowing my head in respect.

Behind me, I feel it rather than see it, the shift, the scrape of boots and armor as everyone follows my lead, lowering themselves in unison. For the first time since the war began, the world feels… still. As if even the storm knows who stands before us now.

"It seems the gods have been a touch too generous with their power in the mortal realms," Cato says, his gaze sweeping over the shattered courtyard, the scorched stone, the bodies that have not yet faded. There is no accusation in his tone, only weary truth, edged with something sharp and ancient.

His eyes settle on me at last. I straighten instinctively, meeting his stare without flinching, the weight of everything I have done still humming beneath my skin. The wind curls tighter around us, as if listening.

"You, though, Edin," Cato continues, his voice steady and carrying through the hush of the courtyard, "have shown an insurmountable perseverance. You have stayed true to your judgments, even when you thought it meant casting out your own mate for the sake of your people."

I squeeze Endricks's hand, feeling the warmth of him beneath my fingers, rubbing it with my thumb. The simple contact grounds me, reminds me that what I have endured and what I have chosen has meaning beyond this battlefield. I step forward, releasing Endricks, and Cato's hand lands on my shoulder.

Cato's violet eyes sweep over us, sharp and penetrating. "With that in mind," he intones, "the council of the gods has chosen you to watch over the three *living* realms. No rulers. Only a guardian who will ensure balance and justice across Helheim, Elysia, and Windemere alike. Purgatory will continue to be your domain, as well."

The wind calms, as if waiting for me to speak, to accept what has been given. I lift my gaze, meeting the faces around me, friends, allies, survivors, and feel the weight of this new mantle settle over my shoulders like a storm with one purpose.

"Do you accept, Edin?" he says, voice low and echoing, like it comes from a thousand graves at once. His hand remains on my shoulder, heavy with weight of his offer. "With great power comes great responsibility."

I swallow hard, my lips trembling as I finally nod in acceptance, unable to say the damning words: *I will.*

A sudden, searing heat races across my chest, crawling over my skin like fire laced with ice. Pain explodes along my ribs and down my arms, forcing a gasp from me. My knees buckle beneath me, and the world tilts as if gravity itself has betrayed me.

Endricks's arms wrap around me instantly, strong and steady, holding me upright even as I tremble. His warmth cuts through the burning haze, anchoring me.

"Only divine judgment shall govern," Cato's voice carries, swirling through the wind that dances around us, "in hopes that this will deter the chaos that has ensued today."

I grit my teeth against the ache, pressing my hand to my chest, fighting to stand through the trial of his decree. Then, as suddenly as he appeared, Cato dissipates, leaving nothing but the echo of his words in the air and a faint curl of violet mist that slowly fades into the sky.

I lean against Endricks and feel the weight of what has been entrusted to me settle over my soul. This is no longer just *my* survival, but *humanity's* as well. I take a deep, shuddering breath, letting the air fill my lungs and steady the storm of fire and ice still crawling through me. My fingers brush lightly over my chest, tracing the familiar curve of my goddess mark.

The edges glow now, opalescent, shifting in color like it is covered in liquid light, radiating power I have only just begun to understand. It hums beneath my skin, warm and alive, pulsing in time with my heartbeat. I watch it shimmer, feeling the weight of the realms it binds me to, the responsibility now etched into every fiber of my being.

The mark no longer feels like a brand. It feels like my *purpose*.

I turn slowly, letting my gaze sweep over everyone assembled. Soldiers, allies, friends, *even Endricks,* kneel instinctively, heads bowed, and for a moment the world feels impossibly heavy. Then, one by one, they rise, voices lifting into a chorus of cheers that shatters the tension of the day, filling the courtyard with vibrant life once again.

Before I can even process the roar of the crowd, Blythe is at my side, throwing herself into me. Her arms wrap around me tightly, breath hot against my shoulder, shaking with a mixture of joy and relief. I hold her just as fiercely, because at last we are safe. She pulls back slightly, hands cupping my face, eyes glistening with tears.

"I knew you could do it," she whispers, voice raw.

I smile, letting the weight of everything melt, before pulling her back into a hug that is just as tight, just as desperate as hers. For a moment, the war, the blood, the chaos, they all fall away. It is just us, together, back in Windemere, an unstoppable friendship, and it feels impossibly good.

I slowly glance up across the courtyard, still holding Blythe. Verenia stands a few paces away, her white hair catching the sunlight now that the storm has passed. She gives me a sharp, respectful nod, the kind that says *well done* without needing to speak aloud. I can not help but smile, a small, genuine curve that carries all the relief, pride, and unspoken joy of the day. I release Blythe, spinning her gently around toward Verenia. Her eyes widen, a mixture of surprise and happiness, and she mirrors the smile creeping across my face.

"Go on," I murmur, voice soft, almost teasing. "Find your happiness."

Blythe beams, cheeks flushed, fox ears angled straight ahead, before stepping forward into Verenia's open arms. I turn back, and there he is: Endricks, still kneeling, his face streaked with cuts, bruises blooming purple and red across his jaw and cheekbones. Dirt clings to his clothes, smudging the leather of his once-pristine armor, and a faint sheen of blood mixed with sweat coats his skin. His blue eyes catch mine, sharp and teasing despite the grime and pain, and a smirk quirks at the corner of his mouth.

"Your highness," he says, voice low and playful, the hint of exhaustion threaded through it. "Shall we go home?"

I can not help the laugh that escapes me, soft but full, and I extend my hand toward him. Relief, pride, and something far sweeter settles over me in a tide I have almost forgotten existed. Valker steps up beside him as Endricks rises and silently clasps his shoulder. The gesture is small, an acknowledgment of everything he has endured, everything we have all endured. Endricks lets out a short, ragged laugh, shaking his head as if to say: *How did we survive this?*

Verenia steps in beside Valker, her shoulder brushing his as she leans into him, a quiet, unconscious claim. The sharp edge of fear has finally drained from her eyes, leaving only relief and something tender beneath it. She reaches for Blythe without hesitation, squeezing her hand as if to reassure herself that this moment is real. Blythe returns the grip, warm and steady despite everything, their fingers threading together.

My gaze drifts over them one by one: *Blythe, Verenia, Valker, and Endricks*, alive, together. The simple act of it feels fragile, almost sacred. It is such a small gesture between them, yet it steadies us, a quiet promise carried from one heartbeat to the next. My chest loosens, the air a little bit lighter now, as if we have all remembered how to breathe again.

"Home," I echo, intertwining my fingers with Endricks. Together, we step forward, battered and bruised but still standing, to leave the chaos behind at last.

CHAPTER 49
ONE YEAR LATER
EDIN

***

I walk the main road of Purgatory at a leisurely pace, boots tapping softly against stone worn smooth by time. The village hums with a quiet kind of life, lanterns swaying between beautifully rebuilt homes, warm light spilling from open windows, laughter drifting from doorways where there used to be only fear.

Nyx pads close at my side, his massive frame somehow gentle as ever. He dips his head as we pass, allowing souls to brush their fingers against his shadowy, smooth skin. A few smile at him. A few bow to me. Most simply look… tranquil.

I tilt my head, gaze lifting to the hill overlooking the village.

The chains still hang there.

Thick, ancient links sway faintly in the breeze. Two bodies dangle from them, gaunt, broken, and *unmistakable.* Fallen angels, one with wings that look to be nothing more than torn remnants now. Malnourished. Hollow-eyed. Alive just enough to understand exactly where they are and why.

A smile curves my lips.

I turn away just as their voices rise, shrill and venomous, echoing down the hill.

"Edin, you bitch!"

"You will rot for this!"

I do not break my stride.

A villager beside the road hesitates, then leans toward me, lowering his voice with something like eager politeness. "Would you like me to muzzle them, Miss Edin?"

I glance back, watching the chains creak as they thrash uselessly against them. Their screams tangling together, rage, despair, and *possibly* regret, all blending into one endless punishment.

I shrug, light and careless.

"Let Osiris and Fallon listen to each other scream."

Nyx lets out a low, pleased rumble, tail swaying.

"Come on, Nyx," I say, continuing down the road as the village disappears behind us. Their screams fade into the distance, swallowed by the wind, exactly where they belong.

Ahead lies Gehenna Castle, quiet, balanced, and finally at peace. I pause on the rise, taking in the view. Even from here, its spires pierce the sky with blackened stone that has been softened by the slow bloom of life creeping back into this desolate wasteland. Smoke no longer curls from the battlements; vines climb over walls once scarred by war. It is impossible not to feel the weight of how far this place has come, from chaos and bloodshed to something *almost* alive again.

I let my eyes linger a moment longer, memories flickering with every scar and shadow, until a shrill, excited voice cuts through my reverie.

"Edin!"

I squint toward the castle balcony and see her, a small Nephilim, bright-eyed and grinning, waving her arms wildly. Her energy is infectious, almost jarring against the quiet that has settled over the land. I lift a hand and wave back, smiling despite myself. "I will be right there, Della!"

Nyx chuffs softly beside me, tail swishing in amusement. I start down the path toward the castle, the wind carrying both the scent of growth and the promise of a new way of life, a new form of judgment.

I reach the castle doors, the familiar weight of the wards falls over me, grounding me after the open air. The doors swing open, and there Endricks is, waiting. His blue eyes catch mine the moment I step inside. He closes the space between us in mere seconds, pressing his lips to mine in a soft, lingering kiss that carries away every memory, every battle, and every fear we have survived. My arms find their way around his neck as I melt into him, letting the warmth and safety of him seep in.

He pulls back just enough to look into my eyes, and a small, teasing smirk marks his lips. "Belladonna," he welcomes me, voice low, the word rolling off his tongue like it was always meant to belong to him.

I can not help the smile that breaks across my face, tugging him back for another kiss, letting the quiet joy of the moment settle over us like the first rays of sunlight after a storm.

The noise of the castle suddenly erupts back into focus with laughter and voices, warm and bright, bouncing off the stone and echoing down the halls. My heart skips as I recognize the familiar tones, my family, alive, whole, and finally here.

Della comes barreling through first, a blur of energy and joy, and I catch her just in time. She scrambles into my grasp, her arms wrapped tight around my neck, squealing with excitement.

"Dinner's ready!" she shouts, grinning from pointed ear to pointed ear, her face pressed against mine.

I laugh, hugging her close, letting the happiness of this moment wash over me. Endricks steps closer, running a hand down my back as he watches with a smile. I set Della down gently, brushing a stray lock of raven hair from her face. She does not let go, wrapping her small hands around three of my fingers.

"Let's go, Lady," Endricks winks, resting his hand at the small of my back.

Della tugs me toward the dining hall like she has been planning this moment for years. The room is warm, bright, and filled with the comforting scent of *home*. My mother, father, and six other siblings are already taking their seats at the long table, laughter and chatter filling the space with a life I thought I might never hear again.

Blythe and Verenia step in through the corridor, fingers intertwined, smiles soft and quiet, full of unspoken happiness. Valker follows behind them, steady and calm, carrying the kind of presence that always makes a room feel safer.

Sera appears last, balancing the final tray with a large roast that dominates the center of the table as she sets it down. She chirps in her usual exuberant voice, “Sit, sit!” before lowering herself into her own chair, eyes bright with excitement.

Della finds her seat among our siblings, chattering happily about the day’s adventures, while I take a slow, deep breath. Endricks joins me at the head of the table, sliding his hand into mine, grounding me, letting me feel his steady warmth.

I sit, surveying the room, the people I love, the laughter, the voices, and the peace. My chest swells until it feels like it might burst. Joy bubbles up from somewhere deep inside me, uncontainable, unstoppable, and I let myself smile, taking in this moment.

I lift my glass, the polished crystal catching the soft glow of the candles lining the walls. The joy in the room presses in around me, but the laughter and chatter pause as every eye finds mine.

"To us," I say, voice trembling just enough to betray the swell of emotion in my chest. My eyes sting, shimmering with unshed tears, but the smile I wear is pure and full. The others raise their glasses in unison, all of us bound together by blood, friendship, love, and the scars of what we have survived.

"For enduring a realm that lies between," I look to Endricks, "and to the joy of what lies beyond."

Honorable Mentions

We would once again like to show our appreciation to our editor, Marla Vincent. She so viciously reemed our asses, each and every time we ***still*** did not know how to use a comma, and we enjoyed every single second of it. Thank you, Marla, for helping us bring our fantasy to life.

Thank you to all of our wonderful ARC/Beta readers for reading through our chaos.

Thank you to all our friends and family who supported us through every crash out along the way.

And most of all, thank you to ***you***, our readers, we would not be here today without each and every one of you.

Wanna stay up to date on our book journey?

Follow us!

TikTok/Instagram: RottingandReading

Facebook: CN Pettit and TD Findley - Authors

What Lies Beyond

www.ingramcontent.com/pod-product-compliance
Lightning Source LLC
LaVergne TN
LVHW100500110826
845146LV00002B/461
* 9 7 9 8 2 3 4 0 1 2 3 2 6 *